truth

a rock star romance

S.J. Sylvis

DEDICATION

To those needing to face the truth.

ACKNOWLEDGMENTS

This is the part where I thank basically everyone who has ever had an impact on my life, or heck, even just glanced at my book and said "huh, that's pretty cool!" LOL! But really, whether you're a family member, a friend, a bookstagrammer, a blogger, a reader, or WHOEVER you are, THANK YOU!! Thank you for picking up my book and reading it. I wouldn't be publishing today if it weren't for you. I'd love to name every single person who has ever left me a decent review, who has bought my book, who has given me words of encouragement, posted on their social media, or told someone about me, etc. but the list would be endless and plus, I'd never forgive myself if I accidentally left someone out (hah!) so you know who you are.

Thank you so much.

I love you more than I could ever express.

Regardless if this book does well in sales, or reviews, etc., I'm going to continue to write and publish books because of YOU. Because of your encouragement and support.

Thank you, again!

Xo,

S.J.

PROLOUGE

REID

The blood rushed to my head as a chill traveled down my spine. My heart all but flat-lined as my hand rested on the shiny, golden doorknob. I twisted it slightly, swallowing my fear, and when I opened the door, I could feel the unhinged cages on my heart closing and locking with each breath that escaped my mouth.

Several months ago, I brushed off her disappearance as one of her stupid games—those games she liked to play and then later say, "I just wanted you to know what it was like to miss me as much as I miss you when you're on the road." After that first month had passed, I was pissed. I was pissed, and the only thought in my head was, *This isn't worth it*. So, I did what any other man would do—I ended it. I called her voicemail, hearing her flirty voice on the other end, and told her I was done. It was a freeing feeling, although it stung a bit, too. I mean, we were together for a little while—longer than I'd been with anyone else—but I just couldn't deal with the bullshit anymore. She finally ended up calling me and begging me to take her back. She apologized and gave me every excuse under the sun, rambling on about someone named Lori whom she was with the entire time, but I was too busy focusing on my music and the upcoming tour to truly let her words affect me. Distraction at its finest.

The phone calls were endless there for a couple of weeks. I usually brushed them off, ignored them, irritated that she was acting so hung up on me when just a few months ago she acted as if I were some annoying fly swarming over her untouched food.

It was always a cat-and-mouse game with Angelina. When I'd catch her, I'd feel like I could truly see myself with her—maybe even love her—but then, when she'd slip out of my grasp, I'd have to take a step back and ask myself if she was even worth the chase.

The second month after our breakup, I hadn't heard from her. The tabloids had died down a bit; they stopped speculating about what had happened between Reid King and his up-and-coming model girlfriend. Things seemed to even out. But I couldn't help the unusual feeling that slithered through my veins when I'd think about how she basically dropped off the face of the earth. I didn't hear a single peep from her. The late-night voicemails had stopped, the abundance of text messages faded, and I'd be lying if I didn't feel a little lighter without her constantly trying to get back with me, but it was strange for her to just stop.

And then her parents called me.

I'd actually never met her parents. Angelina and I weren't a traditional couple in the slightest. I'd met her a year prior, through some friends who I'd consider "up-and-coming," just like Angelina with her modeling career. She and I never did much of anything in the beginning, except have sex, but then she started accompanying me to red carpet events, hanging off my arm like a bronzed beauty with her dazzling smile—she lived for those things. The woman I met a year prior was replaced by someone who had stars in her eyes as she gazed at flashing cameras and famous people.

When her parents had called, I realized that they had come to me as a last resort, looking for their daughter who apparently had also stopped talking to them. No one had heard from her since our breakup, and that didn't sit well with me.

At first, I chalked it up to typical Angelina behavior, but something inside of me began to fester. The irritation and annoyance of her behavior was replaced with worry and fear.

I realized that I might have cared for her a little more than I thought, because I truly was fearful that something had happened. It wasn't often that I grew close with someone, and that was simply because I'd been burned so badly in the past. Anyone that I'd ever loved in my life had disappeared within a flash, which is why I'd kept her at arm's length at all times.

Angelina had been in my life for several months—close to a year—and now I was standing here looking down at her as she began to disappear, too.

Right in front of my very eyes.

A strangled noise sounded from my mouth, and those hinged-up cages around my heart weren't only locking, but the key was being thrown into the Pacific Ocean, floating down to the sandy bottom, salt water eroding the metal. Every wall that I had unknowingly let down rebuilt itself as fast as the blood was pooling out of her stomach.

I rushed over to Angelina's lifeless body and held back my vomit. Sweat coated my forehead, my dark hair sticking to the skin. My head bodyguard came flying into the hotel bathroom after finally catching up to me, and his eyes grew wide as he watched my hand press firmly on the open wound in Angelina's torso. It was sliced open, bright red blood seeping through my fingers.

Frank grabbed his phone, his jaw locked and loaded, and called for help. My teeth clenched as I applied pressure to her tiny stomach, my mind reeling with questions. I kept thinking back to when she'd called twenty minutes ago.

She *finally* called as I was about to step my foot onto the stage, the crowd roaring so loud that I could hear them all the way into my dressing room. I instantly began to reprimand her. I kept my voice at a neutral level, but with every word that came out of my mouth, a bitterness was clipped onto it.

"Your parents are worried sick about you! Where have you been? These disappearing acts have to stop, Angelina."

Then, she started to sob, and the words that came out of her mouth were enough to make me run in the other direction to the hotel I was just occupying hours before.

"Reid!" Frank yelled, pulling me from my panicked trance. I quickly took my eyes off the slowing blood and stared at his worried face. He hurried over and kicked the knife out of Angelina's unmoving hand. "Move."

I shook my head gruffly.

"The paramedics are here. You've gotta move."

I couldn't. I couldn't move my hand. I was too afraid to see what was underneath it.

Frank growled and rushed over to me with his broad shoulders and unusually large hands and pulled me backwards at the same time the paramedics came barreling in with black bags strapped to their backs and a gurney in tow.

"Holy fuck," one of them said, their eyes on me being held back by an annoyingly strong Frank. "Are you Rei—"

"It'd be best if you kept your fucking mouth shut and do your job, or you'll regret it," Frank urged, his grip on me tightening.

The young paramedic's face turned a bright red as he dove down to Angelina's body, feeling for a pulse. The pair quickly got to work and placed her body onto the gurney, her black hair flinging upward as they pulled her up and onto it.

My body relaxed a smidge due to the relief that washed over me knowing she still had a pulse. Frank let go of my body, and I rushed over to the one paramedic as the other talked rapidly into his walkie-talkie. "Do you know what happened?" he asked, his face now a normal shade of peach. They began to roll the gurney through the doors and down the hallway.

I could barely get the words out. It felt like my throat was being crushed between two jack stands. My nostrils flared as the words left my mouth. "She said…" I clenched my eyes, bringing my hand up to the bridge of my nose. "She said she was cutting our baby out and that Lori told her to do it."

The men paused their rushing for a split second out of shock. "Who is Lori?"

I shook my head. "I—I don't know."

They each gave a curt nod before climbing into the elevator with a few of my other bodyguards and Rod, my tour manager. *When the hell did they show up?* I heard Rod yelling to anyone in sight to keep this situation out of the media, as if that truly mattered at a time like this.

Me, on the other hand? I stayed in the same spot on that red-and-gold swirled carpet, staring after her lifeless body, even after the elevator doors shut. A wicked vine of both guilt and fear wrapped its thorny fingers around my entire body and all but strangled me.

A heavy hand came and rested on my shoulder. "Did you know she was pregnant?" Frank asked, his voice softer than I'd ever heard before.

My jaw was as hard as it could possibly get. "No." I shook my head, my eyes still trained on the closed elevator doors. "I didn't know."

CHAPTER ONE

BROOKLYN

My desk was piled high with music sheets and papers I desperately needed to grade. The picture that a student drew for me in their art class had a coffee stain on it from my morning cup, and a strange-looking, coiled mess of pottery that had every color of the rainbow sat perched in the corner, holding my stack of permanent markers. I knew very well that I should have been grading those papers, or creating a lesson plan for the last week of school, or hell, maybe even cleaning off my desk and dumping out my five-hour-old coffee. But instead, YouTube was pulled up on my computer, and I sat back to admire all the amazing up-and-coming artists—the ones that didn't hold back. The ones that put their entire soul on the line, the ones that took their mind and heart and interweaved them together and formed something so beautiful.

I almost envied them. Especially as I sat at my desk, sitting in a fifty-year-old swivel chair that had most of its springs missing, in the middle of a sweltering classroom (because why would the school pay for air conditioning?).

Of course, the introverted side of me knew that I would rather chop my arm off than record myself on my phone, singing one of the songs I'd written, and upload it to some social media outlet to get "likes." Because you know what the problem with likes is? You also get dislikes. Likes and dislikes went together like peanut butter and jelly, especially on the internet. What was it with people gaining so much confidence on the internet? Like the screen of their smart phone or Macbook hid their face, so all of a sudden, it didn't matter that they were throwing the Golden Rule behind their shoulder and completely demolishing someone's work.

To be honest, I was more afraid of getting a dislike from someone out in the real world (and by that, I mean on the internet) regarding my music than if there happened to be another lice outbreak in my classroom. (Like, seriously. Bugs in hair or someone saying my songwriting sucked? I choose the former.) If I were an extrovert, someone who didn't care what people thought, someone who had the confidence of say... Beyoncé, I'd gladly put myself out there. I mean, look at all those brand-new pop artists who were scoring Grammys left and right. They started at the bottom. They put their video up on social media, and BOOM, they were famous.

Okay, fine. I knew it didn't really work like that. But it usually started with said person somehow gaining followers or a second look online, and then they were climbing the rails to the top.

I'll admit, I was a little resentful.

Instead of uploading a video of myself with my thrift shop guitar in my shabby, poorly lit apartment, cooing the words of some heartwrenching song that I'd written—one that I'd fully formed from my own head—I was making a mediocre income as an elementary school music teacher.

I mean, I was fine with it. Sure, the loose spring in my chair was digging into my butt so hard it was beginning to ache, and my classroom smelled like rotting cheese due to my last set of students coming straight from gym class, but

I was being paid to teach music all day to little smiling faces, and I got to wear cute dresses with pockets. *What could be better than wearing a dress with pockets?*

Sympathy washed over me as I took my gaze away from my computer and slid it over to the photo collage I had on my desk. I *loved* my students, along with dresses with pockets, and I had a pretty good life, but writing songs was something that fed my soul. It always had, even from a young age. A ghost of a smile covered my face as my eyes roamed the photo of me when I was a child, a guitar in one hand and a crumpled-up piece of paper in the other, a pencil tucked behind my ear with my auburn hair a curly mess. Freckles dotted my chubby cheeks as a toothless smile took up over half of my face. I shook my head and put my eyes back on the computer.

Songwriting was a childhood dream, one that I never sought out to reach. Now, writing songs was an outlet for me. It was profoundly personal, and I had basically kept it locked inside all my life. Once I went to high school and realized that burying my head in a notebook while tapping my foot obnoxiously to a tune that only I knew wasn't considered cool and was kind of... *odd*, I'd stopped being transparent with it.

I knew it was too late for me to be discovered. My dreams burned up in flames the second Jacob Keller, my first real crush, told me I was a *weird* freshman for always singing songs and scribbling jumbled words down on a piece of paper. He snatched my notebook out of my hand one day and read the muddled mess, embarrassing me to no end. Honestly, I wanted to melt into the lockers I was cowering against.

The memory still made me sweat. Heat blasted my cheeks any time I thought of his taunting laugh.

I couldn't blame it all on Jacob, though. It was me, too. The doubts, the embarrassment, the shyness that I could never really get over. I wasn't destined to put myself on the line like that, to put my heart on the line. So instead, I lived vicariously through all the rock stars and pop artists that Jane, my best friend, wrote articles on, all while eating Ramen noodles in my holey sleep shirt, listening to my upstairs neighbor have kinky sex every Thursday.

"Watching YouTube again?"

My head snapped up as I quickly clicked the red square in the top right-hand corner of my computer screen.

"What?! No! Who? Stop."

Jane smashed her pink matte lips together. "You're doing that thing again where you get caught doing something you're not supposed to be doing and you start stringing words together that make zero sense." She laughed. "I love how awkward you are, Brooklyn. It's why I keep you around."

I rolled my eyes, leaning back in my chair, a squeaky noise filling the room. "You keep me around because I'm your best friend, the comic relief is just a bonus."

She shrugged. "So true. My life would be so mundane without you."

I raised an eyebrow. "Lie." I placed my hand over my chest. "*My* life is mundane. Boring with a big ol' capital B. Your life? You get to interview famous people, you learn all the gossip, and plus… shall we bring up last weekend?" I wiggled my eyebrows as her face turned pink. "Big. *Shlong.* Those are the two words that stick out to me the most about your endeavors. I have the text right here; let me get it."

My best friend, Jane, was the definition of cool. We couldn't have been more opposite if we tried—which is probably why we were the best of friends; we evened each other out. Jane climbed the ladder after graduating college with her journalism degree and now worked for one of the most popular tabloids in the celebrity world. And there I was, graduating with a "safe" degree and working an 8-3 job, teaching rugrats. Total opposites.

"Don't you dare!" she hissed, pointing her finger at me. "What if there is a student hiding in here somewhere?"

I laughed. "Why would a student hide in my classroom?

And where?"

She rolled her eyes as she crossed her arms. "I don't know. I don't know anything about these booger-heads you hang out with all day."

I gave her a pointed look. "What are you even doing here? I was just about to head home for the day." My eyes wandered over to the papers I needed to grade. *Eh. They can wait another day.*

"I came because…" Jane walked over and sat her butt on the edge of my desk. "You and I are going to Seven tonight for dinner."

I shook my head. "Sorry, no can do. I told Cara I'd come over and watch the *Bachelorette* finale with her."

Jane pouted as she crossed her arms. "Do it afterwards. I need to talk to you tonight. Cara can wait. I mean, she kinda owes you."

I laughed while rolling my eyes. "You're as bad as she is about that. She doesn't owe me anything."

She rebutted. "Cara will understand if you come over an hour later."

Jane was right. My sister would understand. You know that cliché where big sisters are snobby and hate their little sister? That was never Cara. She never acted that way toward me. Cara was an amazing big sister and an all-around *good* person. She was the type of person who wanted to impress everyone, and she often did. She was a go-getter—that girl in high school that was good at everything. And what made it worse was that she was completely stunning. She'd do anything for anyone with a beautiful, glowing smile on her face—even for me, her annoying little sister who followed her around everywhere until she left for college.

She never once complained that I was always tagging along, or that I had silly, school-girl crushes on her cool, *older* boyfriends, or that I wore her clothes even though the boob area was three sizes too big.

The thought of her made my stomach uneasy as grief floated all around me. Cara had everything: perfect career, perfect husband, beautiful baby. But then her kidneys got worse from the Hydronephrosis and everything spiraled out of control. The last few years had been a whirlwind.

My family and I continued to stay positive and thanked God on the daily that I was a match to Cara. She now walked around with that bright smile still plastered to her face and with one of my kidneys inside of her body. She still continued to laugh and have a certain lightness to her, even with the heaviness of our financial problems on her shoulders. I said *our* because, in my family, everything was one. It was not just Cara's financial problem, it was *ours*.

Even with insurance, kidney transplants were expensive.

Hospital stays were expensive.

Medication was expensive.

Everything was expensive.

And when it all added up? You were left feeling like you were drowning. I imagined that Cara and Jack felt like they were in a boat that had an awful leak, allowing small droplets of water into it with every passing second. We were all happy—and who wouldn't be after a long, *long* year of doubt and fear, worry clenching at our hearts every second of every day as we watched my sister push through all the procedures and struggles? Now that she was doing better, we were now faced with the fear of Cara losing her house, or worse, my parents losing their home—our childhood home. My parents had helped so much, and Cara had given all that she could, but it was just too much. Cara and Jack couldn't afford two car payments and her medical bills, along with a mortgage and everything needed to support a family—not to mention the medication that the insurance company would stop paying for after so many months. My parents had done what they could, as had Jack's parents. But even combined, they didn't have enough money to spread out to keep things afloat.

And me? I barely made enough to live on my own.

But Cara was healthy again. She was raising my beautiful niece, so that was one thing to be happy about. There was always a little bit of sunshine even when you were surrounded by rain. *Always*. It may not be clear at first, but it'll peak through eventually.

I finally took my hand away from my face and peered up at Jane. "Fine, I'll go, but only for a little bit."

Jane's face brightened up, her arched eyebrows shooting to her hairline as a smile spread out on her cheeks. "Yay! Okay, perfect. Now…" Jane walked over to the other side of my desk, her heels slapping against the tiled floor that was in desperate need of a polishing. "Hover that little curser"—she nodded to my hand still resting on my computer mouse—"and reopen the YouTube page that you so casually exited out of."

I raised an eyebrow but did as I was told.

"Okay, now type in Reid King."

My eyes flashed up to hers. "Why am I YouTubing Reid King? I know who he is. What I should be YouTubing is how to grade 120 papers in less than twenty-four hours."

Jane snickered. "Just watch some videos and get familiar with him. I have a proposition for you."

My stomach dipped. "A proposition dealing with Reid King?" I threw my head back and laughed. "I can already tell it's going to be a big ol' no."

"Just get to know him, but stay off any of the tabloid sites. You know most of the journalists I work with bullshit their way through an article and get their information from God knows where."

I gave her a weary look, tapping my fingers on my desk. "I don't like the sound of this."

Jane smiled naughtily. "Dinner tonight at Seven. My treat." Then she walked backwards until she got to my classroom door and turned on her heel, leaving me alone with my 120 papers that needed graded and an opened page on YouTube.

I bit my lip as my fingers clicked on the keyboard. *Reid King.*

Just seeing him on YouTube gave me butterflies. He was

amazing. His voice, even with the terrible quality of someone's cell phone video playing a snippet of him at a concert in his earlier years, was enough to send a tremor down my spine. Reid's voice was some sort of liquid sex. It was raspy in all the right spots—rough around the edges yet soft on all the rest. He sang from the soul, deep within his depth, and the words he sang so flawlessly, so effortlessly, captured my entire being and lit it up. Maybe it was because of my love for music, or maybe he was truly some type of singing siren, but his music was breathtaking, soul-crushing, and so heartbreakingly beautiful.

My heart clenched in my chest as I listened. I was lost.

I was lost in his voice.

He deserved every Grammy he'd ever won. It amazed me, too, because he was my age—twenty-six years old—yet he sung like he'd lived a hundred years before me. He wrote his own music, too, which was just another attribute that not all young artists had. He had it all: the looks (GOD did he have the looks), the voice, the charisma, the talent—everything.

After the YouTube video ended, I clicked on one that was intriguing, to say the least. The title of it was "Reid King No Longer a King?"

Perplexed, I leaned back, my chair squeaking annoyingly, and began watching a video that made me motion sick from the camera wobbling every few seconds. I sat up slowly and tried to figure out what was going on in the video.

I could make out a very blurry Reid King on a small stage. It wasn't a huge concert like he'd hold if he were on tour, but it was some kind of small concert—maybe for a charity? Maybe at some small venue that he used to perform at before he got really big? That was a thing, for sure. I knew of a lot of bigger names that would go back to smaller venues for free to bring in revenue for the owner, all because the artist tried to stay humble and give back to the community that helped form them into who they were today. *Seemed charismatic, if you asked me.*

The longer I tried to follow the video, the more I became nauseous.

Reid was on the stage, but he wasn't standing properly. Something was off. Even with the jerking of the camera, I could tell that he was smashed. He'd sway one way and then the other, his head dropping every few seconds as he tried to sing the lyrics of his song, "You." I couldn't tell if he was slurring the words of the song because he was drunk or because he was heartbroken. He looked distraught when the camera would zoom in on his face. Every glimpse I got of that chiseled jaw and high cheek bones was heartbreaking. I didn't even know the guy, yet seeing his distressed face, as if he were in pain, was enough to make me speed through the video. Finally, when I got to the end, I could see some sort of commotion onstage, so I paused, rewound it a bit, and then hit play.

The person taking the video yelled, "Oh, shit. No, he's not!"

No, he's not what?!

I zeroed in on Reid's body, which was cowering on the ground. He was resting on one knee, his head dropped low, his dark hair falling over his forehead. His shoulders were shaking, and his bandmates were slowly walking over to him, the music coming to an abrupt stop.

He was crying.

Reid King, the king of today's music, was crying. No, not just crying… *bawling.*

My heart hurt watching him. My mom always told me how much she adored that I *felt* so deeply. That when others were in pain, I felt it too. That I carried everyone's hurt and guilt because it was just who I was—from day one. She said it took a special person to truly know what someone else was feeling without feeling it for themselves.

I loathed watching sad movies because they truly made me sad. I hated when anyone I knew was hurting.

That time my sister's boyfriend broke up with her because she threw up his mom's homemade green bean casserole? It felt like it was my boyfriend. I cried with her. My heart broke too, and it was silly, really. She was sixteen, and they had been dating for a month, yet it was like both of us were mending broken hearts.

When she ended up in the hospital due to kidney failure? I was devastated.

Of course, I pretended that I wasn't. I had a great way of wearing a mask and trying to make everyone else happy by stealing away all their pain and putting it inside my own heart.

It was the worst and most exhausting trait that I had.

Watching Reid King was heartwrenching. Even as he projectile vomited on his fans below the stage, I still felt his pain. I'm sure they didn't feel bad watching him cry onstage like that, especially after getting puked on—even if it was Reid King—but *I* did.

I sat crisscross in my chair, staring at the screen, the video of Reid crying now over and an ad for kitty litter playing in the background.

I felt conflicted and confused, but most of all... intrigued.

What in the hell happened to Reid King? And why am I watching this five-minute ad for kitty litter?!

CHAPTER TWO

BROOKLYN

The bars in New York were few and far between.

Totally kidding. There were so many bars that, even after several years of being legal and being allowed in said bars, I still hadn't been to all of them. Jane always picked high-end bars, the types of pubs that wouldn't actually be caught dead being labeled as such. Even looking at the drink menu made me sneer.

Who can afford a Sidecar when it's more than an actual car?

Of course, I didn't drink much because I didn't like to test my limits having one kidney, but it was always humbling to look at the prices.

"Pick what you want, Brooklyn. It's on me." Jane slid her slim body onto a barstool, giving a flirty wave and wink to the bartender.

"I hate when you pay for me. It's like I'm a charity case." I snapped the menu shut, knowing very well that I was still going to order a fancy appetizer even if it did cost me slipping a twenty into Jane's purse later.

"I'm your best friend. You shouldn't feel like that."

"You'd feel like that if the roles were reversed."

She sighed after telling the bartender what she wanted to drink and ordering me a water, like usual. She clasped her hands together on the bar top and smiled connivingly at me.

I looked anywhere but at her face. I stared at the gleaming liquor bottles lining the far wall behind the bar. I stared at the shiny, sleek bar top—not a droplet of water in sight. Then I looked at the bartender, mixing Jane's drink, all dressed up in his black vest and bowtie.

He was cute.

But he was nothing like Reid King, whom I couldn't get out of my head. I kept replaying him on his knee onstage, his broad shoulders shaking in his tight grey t-shirt, his bandmates slowly surrounding him, getting ready to haul him backstage to upchuck some more.

Before leaving to meet Jane—still avoiding grading papers—I dug up a few articles about Reid. The recent ones. The ones surrounding his "uh oh" onstage. People were ROASTING him for being that inebriated while performing. People were so cruel behind their computer screens. Reason number 6,087 why I had never ever posted a video of me with my guitar, singing a song that I'd written.

Hell. No.

"What are you thinking about?" Jane finally asked after I successfully avoided her for maybe ten seconds.

That's all it took? Ten seconds for my mind to wander back to the famous Reid King? Nice.

I ran my hand through my reddish-brown hair. "I'm thinking of an excuse for whatever it is that you're going to ask me to do."

She laughed. "Relax. It's not like I'm going to ask you to go skinny dipping with me and Alex Richards again."

The image of Alex naked still scarred me to this day.

"The worst moment of my senior year—hands down."

Jane threw her chocolate locks back and cracked up. The bartender came by and dropped our drinks off, grinning at her sudden burst of laughter, and then walked away with his head shaking.

I sipped on my water until she was done.

"I think it was the worst moment of my senior year, too," Jane said before turning serious. "But really, I need you to hear me out."

I cringed. "Nothing good has ever come out of your mouth when you say that I need to hear you out."

She bit her lip. "And you can't get mad at me."

My shoulders dropped. *"Jane…"*

God love my best friend, but she was one of those people who lived by the old adage *"It's better to ask for forgiveness than for permission."* It should be her life motto, and I know her parents would agree wholeheartedly.

Jane downed her drink with one final swallow and set her eyes on me. "Do you remember Vinny?"

Raising an eyebrow, I asked, "Your Uncle Vinny?"

"Yeah."

"The Uncle Vinny that you and I spent spring break with three years in a row?"

"Yeah."

"The Uncle Vinny that sent us care packages all throughout college?"

"Yeah, him."

I finally looked at her like she had lost her mind. "Oh, no. Sorry. I don't remember him." Jane's hand stung my arm as she smacked me. "Obviously I remember him, Jane. Quit being weird and just spit it out."

She blew air out of her mouth and turned her attention away from me. "Well… I kind of told him about you and your writing."

My ears burned.

My heart stilled.

And just like that, my entire body went numb.

"You… what?"

She closed her eyes. "You promised you wouldn't get mad!!"

I shook my head, although she couldn't see me through

her closed, shimmery eyelids. "I did not promise I wouldn't get mad. Why did you do that?! You know that's... off limits. I don't talk about that stuff with anyone except you and Cara, and even that's rare."

"I know, I know. But just hear me out before you clam up."

I stayed silent, picking at the soggy napkin my water was sitting on. I was a little angry and maybe a little hurt. I didn't like people knowing I had this far-fetched dream buried inside of me that I continued to push away because I was a big, fat scaredy-cat. I didn't like it one bit.

"So, I was at Vinny's a few weeks ago, and he was talking about work. You do remember where he works, right?"

Only at the biggest record label in the entire music industry, which is how Jane created all these kick-ass relationships with all the famous people that I never got to meet because I wasn't about that extroverted life. Hence, why I taught tiny humans for a living. They were easy. Adults—especially *famous* ones—were not my thing.

Meeting Ed Sheeran? That would be pretty freaking cool.

Did I take her up on the opportunity to do so months ago when she had an exclusive interview with him here in town?

Negative.

Even the thought of being in the same city as him made my palms sweat.

"Yeah, I remember," I said, my voice on the verge of snapping.

"Well, he kept going on and on about how one of his clients was having a really rough time writing his new album. Like, even Vinny's bosses were breathing down his neck because they expected him to have at least given them a single by now."

"Okay. And..." I signaled for the bartender. I needed to order my food so I had something to do with my hands other than clenching them tightly together in my lap.

"And he was stressed. They were at a total loss. They had no idea what to do with him. He's one of those artists that's known for their own songs, you know? Like, that's his appeal. He writes his own shit. Everyone wants a piece of him because they think they truly know him from his music."

I nodded. It was true. Those artists that wrote their own songs were like gold in the music industry. They turned pain, happiness, love, *anything* into music that captured just about anyone.

Jane paused as I ordered the most expensive appetizer on the menu, all while sipping on her drink, before she turned back to me. She bit her lip, knowing very well that I was upset that she told Vinny about me.

If there was anyone on this earth that I didn't want to know, it would definitely be him. Next time I saw him, he'd probably ask for a sample or a demo, and then I'd have to sit there and watch as he listened or read my lines and tried to fake a "WOW! You've got talent!" like we were on *America's Got Talent* or something.

"Well, anyway… to make a long story short, they were trying to come up with a plan to bring someone in to help guide him to write new music—not necessarily take over for him and write songs on his behalf, but to guide him."

"Okay… What does this have to do with m—" I instantly snapped my mouth shut, then opened it again, only to close it one more time. *"You didn't."*

"Just listen!"

"If you told them I'd write music for some musician who is probably doped up on drugs or something, then I'm going to kill you right now."

Jane grabbed my wrist with her hand. "Let me finish."

"Fine." I huffed, grabbing onto my water glass a little harder than before.

"First off, he's not on drugs. He's not like those other artists you hear about that go to rehab every five months. That's not the case. Something is blocking him, and he just needs some guidance. I mentioned to Uncle Vinny—once his colleagues were gone—that I had an idea, which was when I mentioned you and your talent."

I opened my mouth and sighed. "It's not talent, Jane. Just a hobby."

She gave me a knowing look, so I turned my head away. Praise. Why was it so hard to accept? Even from the one person who probably knew me better than anyone.

"And what did Uncle Vinny say? That you were nuts thinking I'd be qualified for such a job? Come on! Plus, who is this artist we're talking about? The one who isn't on drugs?"

"Do you want to know what Uncle Vinny said... after I gave him some of your stuff?"

I didn't snap my head over to Jane. No. I was too stunned. Instead, I slowly...very slowly... craned my neck to her and just stared. "Please tell me you didn't."

I wanted to evaporate into thin air. I wanted to hop over the bar and ask for a job so I could cut music out of my life indefinitely. *Sorry, kiddos, your music teacher has officially said goodbye to banging triangles and playing piano.*

I was seconds from plugging my ears so I couldn't hear what Uncle Vinny thought. I wouldn't be able to write again if he said it was shit.

"Uncle Vinny wants you to work with Reid, Brooklyn."

All thoughts of myself stopped when I heard the name Reid. He was the one we were talking about here?!

Jane didn't give me a chance to say anything. "He read your songs; the ones you sent me long ago. The ones that aren't even as good as the ones I know you're hoarding somewhere in your apartment in some tattered old journal. Probably the one with pink flowers."

I smashed my lips together because she was right. It was totally the pink flower journal.

"You already know what the answer is, Jane. And we'll get back to me being pissed at you for sharing my *personal* songs later. I'm not even close to being qualified to write music for someone like Reid King. And Reid King?! Is that why you had me YouTube him earlier?"

Jane swallowed the rest of her drink before turning her entire body toward me, her heels hooking on the rimmed barstool. "They weren't that personal if you sent them to me, and come on! Don't I get any credit for believing in you and your talent so much that I shared them with him? You help younger children write songs and learn music during the summer, what's the big deal?" She shook her head. "Yes. I shared your stuff with Uncle Vinny, but it was only because I knew he'd see your talent. And guess what? He thinks you're good. Like really, fucking good. So good that he wants you to work with someone like Reid King."

I wasn't believing a single word that came out of her mouth.

Me? *Me?! Were they nuts?!* I was an elementary school music teacher. Sure, I taught some basic songwriting lessons on the side, but I wasn't some fancy music writer that was getting royalty after royalty from selling artists and record companies lyrics to hit songs.

I was a nobody, hiding in the shadows—just where I liked to be.

"You know very well that the answer is no. The majority of me doesn't even believe you right now."

Jane rested her hand on mine and squeezed. "Before you say no, you need to hear the rest of the details."

I rolled my eyes and laughed. "The rest of the details? All you had to say was Reid King and you should have known that I'd say no. Could you even imagine me in the same room as him?! I cannot help him write a song. My God, Jane, I probably wouldn't be able to form words or even breathe!" I shook my head. "Jane, I'm not like you! I couldn't even handle being on homecoming court in high school because people were staring at me! How do you expect me to act when Reid King even glimpses at me?"

Jane interrupted my stress-induced rant. "Vinny will contract you and pay you seventy-five thousand dollars for even attempting. That's two months of being in the same room with Reid for two years of your salary. TWO YEARS. Then, if Reid and you collaborate well, and he writes a killer single or album, they'll pay you one hundred… thousand… dollars."

She was right.

I didn't need the rest of the details.

Reid King, the King of Music? That didn't scare me one freaking bit.

They could ask me to allow Reid King to puke on me just like he did to his fans a few weeks ago. And for that much money? I'd gladly allow it.

That money would change everything for my family.

No more stress for my parents.

No more tears from Cara while she tried so hard to be strong.

No more talk of them moving in with Jack's parents because they couldn't afford their mortgage and the medical bills.

No more talk of my parents selling our childhood home to save Cara's.

I reached out for my water, the cool liquid traveling down my throat. Ha. I could afford to buy this entire bar after summer—given that I could help Reid, of course.

I looked over at Jane with her wide eyes and pink lips. "Sold."

———

"Are you sure that Uncle Vinny isn't just giving me this opportunity because he knows about my family's financial issues?" I asked Jane as we sat out in front of Vinny's New York home—*cough* *castle* *cough*.

Green eyes stared at me from the driver's side of the car. "I didn't even tell him until after he said how much he'd pay the person. I mumbled something like, 'Oh my God, this would solve all her family's problems,' and then he made me spill. But truly, he didn't know until afterward."

I swallowed and looked out the window. Bright light was casting down through the fluffy, pillow-like clouds, creating almost a kaleidoscope of golden yellow hues on the ground. I'd always loved coming to Uncle Vinny's. It was a nice break from the hectic streets of the city. I was raised in the outskirts of New York but now resided in the city in one of those apartments that everyone thought were amazing because they had that HGTV exposed brick and super tall windows that overlooked the busy streets of New York. But I can tell you right now that my apartment was everything short of amazing. The coolest thing about my tiny, closet-like home was the old, recycled bicycle planter I'd secured to the wall. I told myself it was a statement piece, but really it was there to draw your eyes onto it instead of the crappy, scratched floors and old windows that allowed the freezing cold winter air to filter through every January.

"Are you still mad at me?"

I turned, taking my eyes off the cottony clouds, and stared at Jane. Her bottom lip was pulled between her teeth, and I could tell, even through her I'm-a-boss-lady, hard-as-stone exterior, that she truly felt bad about telling Uncle Vinny about my hidden talent (her words, not mine). How could I be mad at her, though? She had enough faith in me that she took a leap and got me this amazing opportunity.

I was scared to death, honestly. Working with someone like Reid King? Even working with someone half as famous as Reid King—no, one-fourth was more like it—was stressful and intimidating. It was why I worked with children. They didn't scare me in the slightest. But someone like Reid King, who knew his shit? It was almost like a nightmare, yet it was exciting, too. It was exhilarating. Getting paid all that money to write songs? To do what I loved to do?

Sure, I wasn't writing the songs for him, but I'd be with Reid King, talking to him about music! And once again, for all that money? That was really the most important thing of all. It wasn't just an amazing opportunity; it was something that I desperately needed. Something my family needed.

I wasn't going to let my fears get in the way of it. I wasn't going to let anything get in the way of it.

My dream of becoming a songwriter went on the back burner a long time ago. That was the funny thing about dreams. What was once a dream ten years ago was now replaced with a new dream. People evolve, as do their hopes and ambitions. My new dream was to help my family. To get the happy, laughing, stress-free family back that I so desperately missed.

I grabbed onto my coffee that Jane snagged for me, no doubt intended as an "I'm sorry" gift, and smiled. "I don't think I'm even justified in being upset with you, Jane."

She instantly relaxed into her leather seat. "It was the coffee that did it, huh? I knew you couldn't be mad if I brought you caffeine."

I laid my head on the headrest and laughed. "Oh yes, it definitely wasn't the fact that you had enough faith in my writing that you somehow scored me this terrifying yet exciting job opportunity which might pull my family out of their financial burden... it was the coffee that sealed the deal. A woman after my own heart."

Jane laughed again and then turned her car off. Before exiting, she looked over at me one last time. "Did you tell them?"

I bit the inside of my cheek and gazed at the gates surrounding Uncle Vinny's. "No, and I won't." I turned, taking my eyes off the pretty blue bird perched on top of the steel pillar. "For one, it'd open up an entirely new can of worms over the fact that I was still writing songs in my spare time, which would then lead to an hour-long conversation about how I can still do such a thing for a living, even though we all know that's not true. And for two, they're not going to like this. Not at all."

I thought about telling my parents, or maybe even just telling Cara—she'd probably flip out if she knew I was going on a tour bus with the King of Music. But the second I said anything about the money, or about how I was giving it to them to pay for past medical bills and the anti-rejection kidney medicine, they'd refuse. My plan was to do the job that needed to be done, get paid, and drop a shit ton of money on their heads like I was the richest person alive. I'd probably brush my shoulder off, too, afterward.

They wouldn't be able to talk me out of it or reject it at that point. They'd feel too grateful.

"So…what are you telling them, then? You have to tell them something since you'll be missing all the Sunday dinners."

"I'm just going to have to come up with a plan. Teacher's retreat?"

Jane raised an eyebrow as her lip tugged upward. "Perf." Then she opened the door, allowing the balmy suburb air to filter through the car. "You ready to go sign your life away… for the summer, at least?"

Nerves clenched at my throat, making it hard to swallow my caramel latte. "He's… he's not in there, right? I need time to prepare."

"Who, Reid?"

My throat clenched even tighter, along with my legs— really, every muscle in my body grew taut. "Yeah," I choked out.

Jane laughed, climbing out of the car in her red, pressed dress. She leaned down and peered at me. "He's not here, and I'm glad because we're going to have to work on that face-reddening-just-by-the-sound-of-his-name thing."

I rolled my eyes and climbed out of the car, too, cursing myself for my stupid heat-blasted face.

I wonder how odd it'd be if I showed up to meet Reid with a brown paper bag over my head?

Part of me didn't care. I was there to do a job and that was it.

It was just Reid King—not intimidating at all.

CHAPTER THREE

REID

My fist was aching from the sudden impact of a nearby wall. My entire body was shaking from the abrupt burst of anger that was coursing through my veins after hearing the words come out of Rod's mouth.

A partner? Was that what he was really going to call it? He was trying to sell the idea to me. I could tell by the way his words were strung together like he was a fast-talking auctioneer. He had been walking on eggshells around me, afraid I'd flip my shit and do something stupid—much like punching a wall. And it was stupid. I fucking knew it was stupid. I played guitar for a living. My hands were more than just hands. They were tools for success—them, and my voice, of course.

"Sit the fuck down, King."

I growled as I swung my body around, staring down my agent like a bull glaring at a red flag.

"And wipe that look off your face."

I continued to stare, my chest expanding with every breath I gasped at. "What look?"

"That look you get when you really want to fire me but know you'd drown without me."

"I don't need a fucking 'partner.' I don't need someone to help me write songs. I fucking know how to do it. I have several albums that say so. This is complete fucking bullshit and you know it!" I was shouting now, spit flying from my mouth.

The pain I'd carried around for months and months often morphed into anger. Pure, raging anger. And I was losing my battle with trying to keep my sanity. There weren't enough outlets in the world for all the shit I carried.

It was catching up to me, all of it was, which was why I was having this conversation with Rod.

You know, all my life, I was particularly good at keeping my emotions in check. I'd always been that one to put a face on, to push away the insecurities, the pain, the worry, the doubt, all of it. But now it was like I was broken or something. I was crawling underneath my skin, like I was seconds from exploding at any given second. Music was my outlet. I took every ounce of agony, grief, happiness, *whatever*, and channeled it into making music. My songs were real. They were raw and authentic, and they were truly my own emotions. Every song had a piece of me. Every set of lyrics had a piece of my soul. And now I was empty.

That was my problem.

I was empty, and now I couldn't channel all the shit that caved in on me on the daily. Some artists turned to drugs— a temporary fix nonetheless—but I'd never done that shit. Ever. I wouldn't. Music was my fix, and it wasn't a temporary high… until now.

It was fleeting away from me so fast I couldn't hold on.

But if the record label and Rod thought some hotshot professional music writer was going to help pull me out of the fucking abyss that I was in and get me over this stupid fucking mental block, they were poorly mistaken.

Jesus Christ. I couldn't even believe I was hearing the words come out of his mouth.

"No. The answer is no, Rod."

Rod scratched his chin, his finger resting right on the dimple below his mouth. "Reid…" He walked toward me before catching my narrowed eyes and stopping in his tracks. "This isn't really a negotiation, and it's not even up to me. It's the record label—the big guys, the ones who pay us both. They were ready to drop your ass after the last show. Do you know how hard it was for me to convince them to give you space, to let you work through whatever it is that you're fucking dealing with? I even had your bandmates write a statement on your behalf." He sighed, and I continued to stare at him with a pissed-off expression on my face that was most definitely not there by accident. "It's either you take their help or you'll be a washed-up rock star whose only connection to the word 'king' is the fact that it's on your birth certificate. Is that what you want? Do you want to be that guy the other night who vomited all over his fans because he was too drunk to sing? I still can't wrap my mind around it."

Oh yes. You heard him right.

I did that. I, Reid King, the King of Music, who always had his head screwed on right, the guy who never got in trouble, the one who said no to drugs—no, seriously, my picture might as well have been on D.A.R.E billboards all around the world—got piss drunk and upchucked all over his fans at a charity concert. I watched the video on YouTube before Rod, and my main manager, Carissa, along with our social media crew, got it offline. It didn't matter, though. Every magazine from here to New York had some type of drama-filled article over the infamous Reid King losing his shit.

I didn't bother reading them.

I didn't bother looking them up on the internet.

I knew what a mistake it was to do that, but her words stung me that day. Like a thousand yellow-jackets attacking my skin, their sting staying with me for so long that I had to do something. I fucked up.

It seemed I'd been doing that a lot lately.

"I don't need some hotshot musical genius to come in and fuck with everything, Rod. I just don't. I know I'm struggling. I don't need you, or anyone else, breathing down my goddamn neck every second of every day. I'll figure it out."

"You'll figure what out, Reid? How to pull yourself together? You're falling apart and you know it."

I cracked my neck to the right and heard a loud pop. I focused on the sound instead of ramming my fist into the wall again. Maybe I should just write a song about punching Rod in the face.

Yeah, that would be a best-seller. A number one hit.

I chuckled out loud, the laugh sounding dry and downright sarcastic. I mumbled under my breath, resting my head along the wall with my hands caging me in. "This is fucking bullshit."

"Glad to have you on board, King. Now let's go introduce you two, shall we?"

I pushed off the wall, glancing at myself in the mirror. I looked as defeated as I felt, my cheeks drawn downward, dark bags under my eyes, a scowl on my face that would hopefully scare the pants right off my new fucking teacher. I grimaced even harder at Rod's cropped haircut as I followed behind him.

"When am I even going to work with this dipshit? On the tour bus for the next couple of weeks? Please tell me that he's not coming with us."

Rod glanced behind his back, hitting the button on the elevator. "Who said it's a he?"

My normal 98.7 degree body temperature rose so fast that my blood was likely boiling under my skin. "Are you fucking kidding me? It's a *woman?* What is she, some sixty-year-old Betty that likes cats? Fucking shit," I mumbled again.

I was picturing the new addition to the tour group the entire time Rod and I were in the elevator traveling to the hotel suite below us. I'm sure the woman was old. The record company probably wanted someone that wasn't the least bit attractive or young. You know, because she was going to be on a tour bus with not only me but also two other bandmates who had a hard time keeping their dicks in their pants.

The only benefit of the teacher being a she instead of a he was that I was likely to scare her quicker. I wouldn't cooperate, the old woman would quit, and then I could be on my own again—just the way I preferred it.

No woman was going to put up with my shit—nor my bandmates'. Hell, she wouldn't be able to keep up with us; she probably liked to be in bed by eight every night.

When Rod and I stopped in front of the suite door, I prepared myself for the worst. I inhaled through my nose as my teeth clenched together. I narrowed my eyes, prepared to stare down my new enemy so hard that it caused them to look away nervously. But what I saw was so much worse than I expected.

I took one look at my new teacher and gave a big ol' "Fuck no" before storming out of there, swiping my guitar out of my room, and retreating to the hotel roof.

To do what? Who the hell knew, because it seemed I couldn't write a fucking song to save my life, and that was exactly what I needed to do. I needed to save myself before I was nothing but an empty vessel.

CHAPTER FOUR

BROOKLYN

I was shocked. Instantly. Almost as if Carissa, my new-ish boss, had pulled a taser out of her Louis Vuitton bag and stunned me. I was left standing in a hotel suite that put my apartment to shame—like seriously, the bathroom was bigger than my ENTIRE living space—staring at a pair of very amused men who were trying their hardest to hold in their laughter as their "king" stormed out of the room like a pouting five-year-old.

Was he serious?

What? Was I not good enough for him? I didn't understand. Those deep, honey-colored eyes poured into me and then sucked out any ounce of confidence that I'd had, which was next to none. I dropped my head down to my Converse, wondering if that was what did him in. Did I look too much like a child for him? Not professional? Maybe I should have borrowed one of Jane's fancy pantsuits. Maybe I should have gone with a Hillary Clinton vibe instead of my usual casual-but-still-professional vibe. I wore a nice dress (with pockets, of course), but I paired it with a pair of white Chucks to make me seem approachable. I didn't want to come off as some business woman.

I mentally berated myself. *Stop it right now, Brooklyn! Do not let him make you feel like you're not good enough. Remember what Vinny said.* I breathed in and out of my nose, calming my nerves, replaying what Uncle Vinny had told me when I'd signed the contract last Friday.

Before I scribbled my signature down onto the piece of paper with my shaky hand, I peered up at him and asked, "But why me?"

Vinny cocked his head, his deep-brown eyes squinting as he tried to understand my question. I clarified, pen still in hand. "Why me? You could hire any of the thousands of successful songwriters in the business, Vin. Someone that knows what they're doing. Someone that could truly help Reid. Why me?"

Vinny smiled softly at me. "Here's the thing about Reid, Brooklyn. He knows how to write music. He knows all there is to know about it—he has albums to back that up, Grammys to back that up. He doesn't need to *learn* how to write again. He doesn't need some stiff music teacher or songwriter to tell him the difference between a chorus and a verse. He knows what rhythm is; he knows what key is. What he needs is someone like you reminding him how to put his heart back into his music. The love. I've read your songs. The difference between the songs you write and the songs that all the other candidates I had lined up for the job write is that you put heart into your work. *Soul.* Your songs weren't perfect, but they were real. Raw. The imperfections in your songs were downright perfect. You know what it's like to write from the heart, and so does Reid. He's just... a little lost. I think you'll be a good fit for him."

My eyes welled up as Vinny spoke, and they were doing it again as I stood in a hotel suite with a bunch of famous people that I didn't know. I wiggled my toes in my shoes, trying to remind myself that I was good enough. I didn't have all that fancy stuff that every other songwriter had—

like experience, per se—but I had heart, and that was good enough.

It had to be.

It *really* had to be, because I needed the money, and there was nothing else to it.

I had to succeed.

Suddenly, the door to the room opened back up, and my head snapped over. I locked onto Reid again but quickly looked away.

Great start, Brooklyn. You can't even look at him without getting all sweaty. I was certain that even the skin between my toes was sweating.

Reid King was nothing less than completely and utterly intimidating.

My God.

Seeing him on a computer screen (because, let's face it, I deserved an A+ in online stalking) versus being in the same space as him, breathing the same air as him, was completely different. He was so... real. He had flaws that were unseen to the naked eye while scrolling on Instagram or YouTube. But being in person, seeing his flaws, his blemishes, I almost felt bad for those that *couldn't* see them.

His dark, unruly, curly hair that resembled a mop on top of his head caused him to appear messy and wild. The angled jaw just below his scowl made him look not only sexy, but resilient, too. He had a slight scar on his cheek. From what? I had no idea, but it somehow fit his persona. And his eyes? I couldn't look into them in fear that he'd somehow wipe away my memory like swiping at a fogged-up mirror. His eyes were like endless pools of amber crystals, dark around the edges and lighter in the middle. His eyes seemed soft against his hard exterior, but I had a feeling that if I were to truly stare into them, they'd be unbreakable, too. He looked indestructible, strong, unyielding.

It perplexed me that he was struggling with writing.

He looked anything but weak.

"This won't work," Reid grumbled, crossing his arms

over his black t-shirt. The muscles in his arms were twitching back and forth, and I couldn't stop staring, my eyes switching between the two forearms. The muscles were so defined, probably from years of strumming strings on a guitar.

Carissa stepped up beside me. "And why is that, Mr. King?"

I heard one of the bandmates snicker under his breath, soon followed by another.

Reid gave them a death glare, and I was right: those soft, honey-colored eyes were anything but forgiving. It didn't seem to faze them, though. One of them stepped forward— the one with red hair whose name I already forgot, a smile etched onto his face.

"Reid, come on. You're not going to win this battle and we all fucking know it. Carissa means business, bro."

Reid's face contorted as he wafted his hand out toward me. "She's like fucking eighteen!"

I clenched my teeth, making my shoulders stay upright.

"Well, at least that means she's legal," the other bandmate said after a seductive wink.

Cue my face turning bright red.

I coughed, pushing my brownish red hair behind my ear. "I'm the same age as you." I directed my words toward Reid. Nerves were attacking every inch of my skin. I was likely to have hives in approximately three minutes.

Reid started out with a huff, but Carissa swooped in and saved the day. "Surely, you're not about to say that she isn't good at what she does because of her age, Mr. King. She's the same age as you, so that would make you quite the hypocrite, wouldn't it?"

He opened his mouth again, but Carissa put her hand up, showing off her diamond ring that probably cost more than Cara's entire kidney transplant plus more. "This isn't up for negotiation. A copy of the contract that Brooklyn signed has already been placed in your room, and really, Reid, there is nothing respectable that can come out of your mouth right now, so just close it." My eyes shifted to him, and his lips formed a pouty scowl before Carissa continued. "I'm your manager, and you know what I say goes, whether you like it or not. This is me trying to save your ass with the help of Rod. The record company wants this, and they expected me to make it happen. Don't make me look like an idiot."

He growled through his irritated mouth. "I don't fucking need any help."

Carissa smashed her lips together, and my nervousness kicked up to an entirely different level. "Reid, it takes a strong person to ask for help, and I know you better than you think. You're strong. You're not weak. So get your shit together and accept the help we're trying to give you."

"You expect this girl to help me?"

Girl? This girl?!

"Dude, come on!" the ginger-haired bandmate droned. "If anything, you can use her as your muse."

I wanted to stomp my foot and protest. Who the hell said anything about "using" me? Reid's face turned to stone. The small wrinkle in between his eyebrows disappeared, his jaw clenched, and somehow his eyes turned dark. "I'll never use another woman as a muse ever again."

And then he stormed out of the room, slamming the door behind him. I jumped in my skin, my heart traveling up to my throat.

My mind instantly started going a million miles a second. A muse? Who was his last muse? Then the lightbulb clicked.

It had to be Angelina. The ghost of Reid's past. One second, Angelina was tied to Reid's arm like a ball and chain, her beautiful black hair always glossy and somehow perfectly straight, even in the most humid of places, her smile bright and inviting, Reid's eyes constantly on her and no place else. Then, it was like she disappeared after their breakup—if it even was a breakup. It was hard to trust all the tabloid jargon. But I do remember reading actual article titles spewing things like, "Angelina Khan. A ghost after the split. Where did she go?" She had somehow vanished. No one knew anything about her. Trust me, the tabloids tried to find every bit of info on her that they could, but it was all speculation.

As soon as Angelina quit showing up hand in hand with Reid, that was when the panty-dropping smiles of the King of Music stopped. It seemed that was when everything for Reid King stopped.

I shook my head, dissolving the thoughts as Carissa and Rod talked to the two other bandmates about me being on the tour bus with them for the remainder of the tour, and I listened intently as they gave them each a set of rules to try and make this situation go as smoothly as possible.

Things like "Go easy on Reid" and "Be there for him and help him through this" were being spouted out of both Rod and Carissa's mouth. I couldn't help but wonder what the hell happened to Reid. The YouTube video of him crying onstage assaulted my brain once again, but I shut all those thoughts down.

Instead, I pictured myself wearing those bright green, sparkly dollar sign sunglasses—you know, the ones you can get at any Dollar Store—while saying, "I'm rich, mutha-fuckaaass," in a Ken Jeong voice as I paid off all my family's debt.

A little tiff between me and the famous Reid King wasn't going to get in my way of helping my family.

I was just going to have to figure out a way to deal with his temper tantrums and prove to him that he still had what it took to make a platinum album—regardless of what happened to him in the past.

Newsflash, Reid King: I was here to stay.

———

The day passed without a peep from Reid King. Like nothing, not even an occasional grunt as we all poured onto the tour bus. The bus that was *also* bigger than my apartment. I'd texted Jane and filled her in on Reid's little burst of excitement earlier, and she replied with, "That's why I don't sleep with famous people." Which I then wrote out a long list of famous people that she had indeed slept with.

For some reason, she didn't text back, but I kept hoping she would. At least it would give me something to do other than sitting on the tiny benchseat/couch with my phone clutched in my sweaty palm, staring at the two other bandmates. I kept messing with my yellow sunflower dress, counting down the seconds until we were in the pleasant L.A. sun. That's where the next show was—none other than Los Angeles, California.

"Soooo…" Jackson stood up from the other couch and came to sit beside me. "Tell us a little about yourself, Brook."

"It's Brooklyn," I corrected with a small smile on my face.

I'd finally learned everyone's names: you had Reid—aka, the brooding alpha, King of Music; Jackson, the redheaded guitar player; and then Finn, who played the drums. Jackson and Finn were both nice, and I could tell they were trying to make me feel comfortable but also hysterically amused at the fact that Reid was pissed beyond belief that I was sent here to help him.

Jackson scooted a little closer to me on the couch. "Okay, Brooklyn. Tell us about yourself."

The thought of telling them anything about myself made me want to puke. What was I going to say? *Oh hi, I'm Brooklyn. I'm from New York, and I'm an elementary school music teacher. My apartment is smaller than this tour bus, I have never sold a written song to anyone, yet here I am, ready to help one of the most successful artists there is. Oh, and I have one kidney because I donated the other to my very deserving sister, but now my entire family is in debt, which, by the way, is why I'm here. I need the money. I'm poor. The end.*

Should I have added in the part where I listen to my

neighbor have kinky sex on Thursdays? Because that was really as exciting as my life got.

Instead of saying all of that, I went with, "There's nothing really special about me."

Then my eyes shot over to Reid because he snickered. Like a child.

My heart started pounding in my chest. The nervous jitters in my stomach were quickly fleeing and being replaced with pure, rampant foot-stomping anger.

Just then, Rod's head popped out from the front of the bus. "We're here, boys. Get out and get some food, stretch your legs, and be back on the bus by eleven. We're driving through the night, and then tomorrow you can rest before sound check and the show." Then, he turned his attention to me. "Brooklyn, you're welcome to go out as well. There are plenty of food places around here, but if you need anything, just holler. Okay?"

I nodded and he disappeared yet again. I had never felt so awkward and out of place in my entire life, and there have been plenty of moments in my life that I have been awkward. It was as if I were in a different universe. One second, I was standing in my classroom door, waving to all my students as they departed the school for summer, and now, I was on a tour bus with famous people! Reid King! I was on a tour bus with Reid King! What?! I felt like I was being thrown to the wolves. I was the lone sheep who was trying to tread lightly and blend in because I had no clue what direction I needed to go. I didn't even know what to say.

Finn jerked me out of my panic when he yelled, "Yippee! Party time!" and bolted off the bus, smiling like a psycho. A small laugh escaped me. Then, Jackson peered down at me. "Wanna come with us? We can probably get to know each other better outside of this bus, considering someone is sucking all the energy out of it." Then, he looked over at Reid and very dramatically—although, I believe he was trying to be somewhat discreet—pointed to him while rolling his eyes.

"Umm…" I started.

"Come onnn, come hang with us," Jackson begged. "I promise, you'll feel less out of place once you get to know us." *Ha, out of place is putting it lightly.*

I wanted to go with Jackson, because from the looks of it, Reid was staying put, which meant that if I stayed put and ate the old crumbly granola bar that was resting nicely at the bottom of my bag, I'd be staying in here with him. It would be awkward, and my nerves were already fried from my first run-in with him. I was supposed to be creating music with him, writing songs, and he hasn't even spoken directly toward me yet. Plus, Jackson and Finn combined were the lesser of two evils. Reid King was brooding and intimidating, and I could feel the hold on my nerves slipping with each second that I was around him.

Give it time, Brooklyn. You're gonna have to jump over the heap of awkwardness eventually.

"I think I'll stay in for tonight, but I promise next time I'll go out with you guys and have some food."

Jackson's shoulders dropped as he gave me a puppy dog look. "Okkkayyy." Then he walked over to the door slowly, his head still drooping. I laughed and he turned around and winked at me. Then he looked to Reid and intoned, "Don't be a dick," before walking out the door.

Awkward wouldn't even touch this tour bus with a ten-foot pole.

CHAPTER FIVE

REID

I was a fucking asshole. I knew it, my bandmates knew it, everyone knew it. I was certain that Brooklyn, my new pet, knew it as well. I wasn't always like this, though. In fact, this was new behavior from yours truly, which was probably why the record label was losing their shit and sending someone like *her* to "help" me write music.

I was still pissed off about it. I'd been sitting here at this tiny table on the bus with a notepad and pencil in front of me, agitated that she was still in here. Anger was clawing at my throat, clouding my senses. There was no fucking way I could write with her in here, staring after the tour bus door like her best friend just abandoned her at a bar with a sketchy guy.

My mouth was opening before my brain could react. And sure enough, what came out of my mouth probably proved any doubt she had that I was, in fact, an asshole. "You know he's just trying to get into your pants, right?"

Brooklyn, with her silky auburn hair, snapped her head over to me. I wished I could have read her mind. *What was going on through her head?* Was she a curser? Or was she a goody-two-shoes who never cussed a day in her life? Was she mentally berating me and plotting my death, or was she cowering and contemplating calling Carissa to dip out of this bogus arrangement? My guess was the latter. She was wearing a stupid, girly, yellow dress dotted with sunflowers. Her cheeks were painted pink, and her wide, forest eyes looked as if she were full of an innocence that I'd only ever seen in children.

You know, reading minds would probably solve all my problems. If I could read minds—one in particular—I wouldn't be in this position. I wouldn't be stuck in this strange place of not knowing what was the truth and what was a lie. But was it really a lie if someone honestly believed what came out of their own mouth? I wasn't sure.

Brooklyn looked down and played with a loose thread at the hem of her dress as she mumbled, "Nice icebreaker."

I shrugged and wrote down the words "mind reader" on my blank piece of paper. As if those two words were actually going to somehow give me inspiration to write a full verse.

"It's true," I mumbled. "He's just trying to get in your pants. Why do you think he was trying to get you to go out with them?"

Brooklyn cleared her throat, but I kept my eyes trained on the blurring blue and white lines below my pencil. "Is that how it works? Jackson invites me to dinner, and boom, he's in my pants?"

I slowly raised my head to meet her stare. I purposefully trailed my eyes down her somewhat wavy hair, the curve of her chest covered by a cottony fabric, all the way to her ridiculous shoes. "By the looks of you, yes."

I was lying right through my teeth. She didn't look like some groupie that somehow always ended up in Jackson's arms. She had yet to flirt with my bandmates, or even bat an eyelash my way…which was unusual. Her clothes screamed virtue. She seemed pure and soft in all the right places—docile even. But I wanted to get under her skin, drive her away so I could focus on this task at hand—*alone*.

Brooklyn pulled her shoulders back, and her gaze never wavered from mine. I had to give it to her—she wasn't fazed by me in the least. She almost appeared as nonchalant as I did. My good looks did *nothing* to affect her. There was no squirming in her seat, no batting of her eyelashes, no stupid girly giggle. "Well, think again, Reid. I'm here to help you, not them. Shall we get started?"

I threw my head back and let out a loud, sarcastic laugh. "Get lost, Teach. You and I both know that this isn't going to work."

Brooklyn let me laugh for a few before straightening her shoulders even more. "It's not going to work with that attitude. I can tell you that much."

The grip I had on my pencil grew hard, the wood almost splintering in my bare hand. *Damn, she was hard to crack.* Irritation was setting in. "Let me ask you something, Brooklyn."

She raised an eyebrow. "Okay…"

"How many songs have you actually sold? How many songs have you written? Do you even have experience? I'm having a hard time understanding why the company chose you. Please enlighten me."

She tilted her head just slightly, her eyes straying from mine. *Good, I hit a soft spot. Now let me push on that soft spot over and over again until she's packing her bags.*

Brooklyn's mouth opened but then slammed shut again. She pulled her bottom lip in her teeth, teetering it back and forth before looking at me once more. I found myself locking onto her big, almond-shaped green eyes and seeing something behind them that seemed unreachable. I rolled my eyes. "Cat got your tongue?" A spark of life flared within her, but she still kept her mouth clamped. I shook my head, throwing my pencil down as I crossed my arms. "Okay, how about this? What would you do right now if I asked you to write me a song? How would you show me your worth?"

A loud sigh escaped her mouth, but she took the bait.

"Well, this isn't really about me, but okay, fine." Brooklyn reached down and untied her shoes and plopped her legs up on the couch, leaning back to make herself comfortable. "I usually like to start with something that is provoking me to feel whatever it is that I'm feeling in the moment."

I scoffed. "Oh, *great*. So…you think you're the next Taylor Swift."

"First off, no. Taylor is on her own level of greatness. Like honestly, I don't know of many people that could top her. Not even you."

My face stayed even because I agreed with her.

Brooklyn tucked a piece of hair behind her ear and looked away as the next words fell from her lips. "If I were to start writing right now, I'd start by writing down everything I was feeling in the moment." I said nothing and that must have provoked her, because she raised her eyes to mine. More silence. I watched as her big eyes turned into little slits. "So right now, I'd write words like… agitated…annoyed…worried, etc."

I snorted under my breath and shook my head.

"So, go ahead, Reid. Your turn. What am I making you feel? And don't hold back." She shook her head. "Not that you'd spare my feelings anyway. Apparently, to you I'm a teenaged, crappy, no-experience songwriter that has no business helping someone like you."

I clenched my jaw tight. *So she may have heard my earlier conversation with Carissa when I'd called again, bitching about this entire ordeal, but whatever. I gave zero shits.*

I leveled her with a stare, unfazed by her statement. "I said it earlier, and I'll say it again. I don't use women as muses, Brooklyn. And I couldn't care less that you heard what I said to Carissa."

She nodded. "Oh, trust me, Reid. I know you don't care. That's your problem."

"What?" I asked, my voice almost a growl.

"You don't care. That's exactly why you can't write shit."

My blood ran cold. "Excuse me?" *Who the fuck does she*

think she is?

Brooklyn stood up and placed her shoes back on her feet, purposefully slow. She walked over to the small kitchen area and pulled open three drawers before she found what she wanted. *Was she really going to make food right now?* Suddenly, she turned around after grabbing a spoon and walked over to me sitting at the table. I hitched an eyebrow.

"Let's get one thing straight, Reid King." She bent down to my level, and I had to do everything in my power to stay still. Her scent wafted around me, and I swore it smelled like the sunflowers on her dress were real. "You and your rude, snarky remarks won't drive me away. I'm not here to sugarcoat things for you. If you write shitty music, I'll tell you, and do you want to know why?"

I didn't answer her. Instead, I was focusing on not losing my ever-loving shit.

"It's because you and your king-of-music reputation doesn't affect me. I'm not here to impress you; I'm here to help you—whether you feel you need it or not, because you do. I know very well that you can write incredible music. *You* know you can write incredible music. I'm just here to help you get back to that."

My mouth flew open, but before I could get a word out, Brooklyn slammed the spoon down on the table beside my notebook, the metal sound ricocheting throughout the tour bus. I was too confused to even speak. *Why is there a fucking spoon sitting beside my hand right now?*

"I need this shit to work, okay?" I drug my eyes up to hers. The green hue might as well have been red, because they were blazing with a fierceness I didn't see before. "You need this shit to work, too. Now…look at this spoon and write down what it makes you feel. I'm going to get food. Consider this my icebreaker, because as soon as you're done tomorrow night and you get some rest, we're getting to work. I'd rather us come out of this little ordeal on top, wouldn't you?"

Then she turned on her heel, her dark hair swaying

behind her sunshine yellow dress, and she walked off the tour bus.

I stared at the door then gazed down at the spoon.

Sighing, I pulled it in front of me.

Kudos to Carissa for finding the one person on this Earth that isn't intimidated by my shit.

Fuck!

CHAPTER SIX

BROOKLYN

Shutting the door to the small bathroom that I was now sharing with five men, I pulled my phone out in front of me and smiled as I pushed *Accept*.

"Hey! I've been trying to reach you since yesterday. I wanted to see how it was traveling to Cali? How is the retreat?"

I smiled at my sister's shining face through my screen. "The retreat is great so far," I lied, feeling a tad bit guilty.

Cara nodded. She looked good today. It was still surreal to see her looking healthy and radiant, even if I knew the stress was eating her alive. "That's great! What are you even doing there? What does a teacher's retreat even entail? And how long will you be gone?"

I swallowed, trying to remember what I'd made up when I told my family I was going to be gone for a while on this bogus teacher's retreat. "Um... a few months. I'll be back in time for school to start. We do all sorts of stuff... learn new ways to teach." I started to get clammy with all the lies that were beginning to pile up. "Hey, is Katie asleep? I wanna see her cute little face." *Distraction at its finest.*

Cara smiled, carrying the phone over to where Katie was. "Here she is." Cara started to move the camera down to Katie who was coloring like the perfect little three-year-old genius that she was but quickly pulled the camera back up to her own face. "Wait… where are you? Why is there a weird wooden door behind your head? Surely, you're staying in a nice hotel, right? Didn't the school send you on this retreat? Did they set you up in some roach-infested hotel?"

Ha. Ha. Ha. *Nice* hotel—aka, tour bus with the King of Music and his bandmates who were like a bunch of children. No, seriously. They got back last night after going to dinner and woke me up from all their hooting and hollering. I was asleep on the couch, curled in a little ball, too annoyed with Reid—who was nowhere to be seen when I'd gotten back from walking to a nearby food truck—to ask where I was supposed to sleep. So instead, I just slept on the couch. It made for a wonderful night of sleep.

Apparently, Reid got the big bed in the back of the bus, and then there were bunks in the small hallway by the bathroom. I opted to stay on the couch because I could hear the guys snoring within seconds of their heads hitting their pillows. I was already counting down the days until we got to stay at a hotel for the night—usually after a show. It just depended on the schedule, according to Carissa, but I was hoping it was soon or else I'd have to get used to this new… lifestyle. I was already having a hard time dealing with Reid's brooding scowl. He was the complete opposite of Jackson and Finn. It was like getting whiplash being around the three of them.

"Oh…" I started to mumble at my sister's curious face. "I'm in a broom closet near the conference room of a hotel." I quickly did the time-difference math in my head. "We're just getting back from lunch, about to start some more training."

LIE. LIE. LIE. But it was a good one, right?

"Jesus, let her go, Cara," Jack yelled from somewhere in

the background. "Your sister is hiding out in a closet to talk to you."

Cara laughed at Jack and then rolled her eyes. "Fine, just text me later, okay?"

I smiled and nodded. "Okay, *kiss kiss love you sis.*"

She grinned. "Kiss kiss love you sis." Then she hung up the phone.

I blew air out of my mouth as I checked my phone really quick before gathering my wits since I was about to watch my first ever, live show of *the* Reid King soon.

Gah. Just thinking about him and our conversation yesterday made goosebumps rise on my arms. I was proud of myself, though. I didn't let his sultry looks and soul-catching eyes rub off on me. I held my own. To be honest, I was kind of a badass to a man that made the majority of women fall over like fainting goats on the daily. I didn't know what came over me, but something did. My nerves disappeared the second he started being snarky. And in their place came anger and that sassiness my father said I developed at age three.

Mr. I-Don't-Need-Your-Help, my ass. And to think he was gone by the time I got back to the tour bus.

The spoon and notebook were gone, too, though. So that was something, right?

Just as I heard the guys come back onto the tour bus, my phone vibrated in my hand with a text from Jane.

Jane: How is it going? Have you dropped your panties yet?

Me: No panty-dropping here. Reid King is a complete asshole, and I'm almost certain this is a waste of time.

She texted back instantly as I leaned my back against the bathroom door.

Jane: Nothing is a waste of time for the amount of

49

money you're getting.

Agreed.

Jane: Have you gotten that whole face-reddening thing under control? I haven't met Reid, but I know how famous people are. *eye roll emoji*

Another text.

Jane: I have faith in you. You're the truest, kindest person I know. If anyone can show someone how to put their heart into something... it's you.

I smiled as I typed.

Me: I love you.

Jane: I love you, too. Now go get to work. I need my bestie back. Laters. Xo.

I shut down my phone and took a few even breaths before putting on my game face and exiting the tour bus. A few more hours until the show started. A few more hours until I saw Reid King in action.

I didn't want to be excited, but I was.

I wanted to hold on to my annoyance for him and his attitude. But after breathing the same air as him, even if it was full of awkwardness and rude comments, I knew his show would be unbelievable. I knew *he'd* be unbelievable. He was the mysterious Reid King, one of the most popular musicians right now. He was full of soul, and I couldn't wait to watch him come alive on stage, asshole or not.

———

Someone with an earpiece and a small microphone

pointed at me and barked, "Go to Reid's room and get him now! We go on in a few minutes!"

I stood on the concrete floor like an idiot, the crowd chanting so loud it was making even me nervous and I was behind the damn curtain of the stage. I was in the shadows, unknown to the outside world. Yet I felt like I was being thrown into a pit of fire. So much chaos.

"Wh... what?!"

"Go get Reid!!" Then, the woman with the earpiece rolled her eyes like I was incompetent.

I wanted to tell her that I wasn't part of their crew. I mean, didn't she see that I wasn't wearing all black and that I didn't have a matching earpiece like her? Plus, there were like five hundred of these minions running around the arena. Why on earth was I getting barked at? I suddenly wished I was in the stands, looking out onto the stage like a normal fan, but I wasn't a normal fan of Reid King. I was his *collaborator*, which meant that I got to be behind the scenes. It was a culture shock, even without some lady barking at me.

I spotted Jackson and Finn standing near the entrance to the stage just behind the curtain, each of them looking as if they downed five Red Bulls in a row. Finn was hopping up and down, swinging his drumsticks around and around, and Jackson was cracking his neck every few seconds, holding his guitar tightly in his grip.

Although I barely knew the pair, I still walked over to them and smiled. "Good luck out there!"

Jackson's cheeks rose as he pushed his long, red hair behind his ears. "Thanks, but have you seen—"

"Hey! I told you to go get Reid!" The small, feisty woman with her headset was back.

I finally turned around and placed my hands on my hips. "I don't even work here, lady!"

Finn tried to hold back a laugh but fell short in the end. The woman's face turned red as she looked at the group of guys standing behind me, but I huffed and shook my head.

"You know what? Fine. I'll go get him."

"Good luck again, guys," I muttered before turning and storming down the long hallway to Reid's dressing room. *So much for being in the shadows and trying to stay out of the way.*

I felt like I was a little Bambi walking on bony, shaky legs every second of the day. Meeting Reid King was enough excitement for an entire year, but add that to being on a tour bus with him, feigning a collectiveness around him that I truly didn't possess, and now, here I was at one of his shows acting like I was best friends with his bandmates, wishing them good luck. Insane. The entire thing made my head spin if I even gave myself time to process it all.

Honestly, I had no clue what I was doing.

I'd been to one concert my entire life, and it was when I was eight and I saw Martina McBride. Our seats were in the nosebleeds. She was like a tiny ant onstage. Yet here I was, walking down a long hallway to go find the lead singer, the guy whose name I kept hearing from fans in the arena. *Am I even going in the right direction?*

Why wasn't Rod back here gathering Reid? Why was it me? This most certainly wasn't in the contract I'd signed with Vinny.

I let out a sigh of relief when I realized that each of the doors had names on them. Reid's was the very last one, of course. With each step in the direction of his door, my blood pressure spiked a little higher.

I pushed my hair behind my ear before raising my fist to knock. But that's when I heard his voice. Even through the door and low chanting of fans, I could hear him plain as day.

"Offer them money, then! Money for an answer, that's all I want."

Whoa. What?

I took a tentative step back before allowing my nosiness to get the best of me.

I pressed my ear against the door to get a better listen.

I sooo shouldn't be doing this.

"Carissa, I really don't give two shits about what you

think. You keep asking what you can do to make things easier for me and this is it. Maybe if I fucking knew the truth, I wouldn't be the way that I am right now."

What truth?

Reid's voice was raspy, almost painful to listen to. "Yeah, well, that's the last thing she said to me and everyone just expects me to get over it. I have her telling me one thing, and then her parents withholding any kind of information possible, then everyone else in the world telling me to move on, to put my music first. Well, I put my music first last time, and now look at where I am."

Then I heard something break. My heart jerked, and every limb on my body started to tingle. I was certain my knees were shaking.

"It is my fault, Carissa. It is. I should have listened, paid more attention toward the end." Then I heard another loud crash, right beside my face, like Reid had thrown his phone right where my head was, as if he knew I was listening.

I jumped back instantly and started to walk down the long, narrow hallway because there was no fucking way I was getting caught by him after hearing that conversation. I only got a few feet away from his door before I saw Miss Headset making a beeline for me. I stopped where I stood, confused on what I was supposed to do. *Fight or flight? What do I do?*

How in the hell did I get into this situation? I kept asking myself that. I was supposed to be collaborating with Reid as he wrote music, yet somehow, I stepped into a tornado of what-the-fucks.

"Hey! I told you to get Reid! What the hell are you doing? Jesus! Who even hired you?! You're not even dressed appropriately!"

Oh…this bit—

"What the fuck is going on out here?" Reid's door opened suddenly, his naturally tanned face beet red. His entire body was simmering with heat, and his pale lips were drawn tight.

He took one look at me and scrunched his face. "What are you doing here? And *you*..." he said, looking over at the woman. "Were you just yelling at her?"

Her natural reaction to Reid was to swoon on the spot. She may even take her clothes off. "Oh, yes. I'm so sorry for the commotion, Mr. King. This... *thing* was supposed to come get you as you're now three minutes late for the show, but apparently, she can't follow directions. I'll have her fired immediately." Then she turned and gave me a dirty look. My mouth opened, but before I could say anything, Reid went into full-on protective mode.

"Talk to her like that again and you'll be fired within a second." The woman's face turned bright red, and I had to hold back my laugh. "She works for me and only me. Not you, not this arena, not the fucking soundcheck team. *For me.* So, get off your goddamn high horse and come get me yourself instead of sending someone that literally isn't even in the same paygrade as you."

I wanted to applaud as the woman scurried away without even mumbling an "Okay." I turned to give my gratitude, as I was one million percent surprised that Reid had my back, but then he turned his stormy gaze to mine, that dark unruly hair falling over his forehead.

"Taking orders from others now?" I went to shake my head, but he opened that stupid, talented mouth again. "You can stand up for yourself around me but not to someone like that?" He shook his head. "Pitiful." Then he walked away and left me standing there in a stupor.

One second, I felt bad for Reid, the next I was in awe of him, then seconds later, I was pissed beyond belief.

I was beginning to learn that being around Reid King was exhausting, and if I thought that working with him for the money to help my family's debt was going to be a breeze, I was sadly mistaken.

So, so wrong.

After watching his long, lean body and broad shoulders walk down the hallway as cool as an ice cube as I stood back like a moron, I was seconds from going back to the tour bus. The music lover inside of me didn't even want to hear him sing. God, he was so arrogant and *rude*. So, incredibly rude. I had the mere thought of dipping out of this entire agreement, but I knew I couldn't do that, just like I couldn't stop the way my feet pulled me closer to the stage after hearing the crowd kick up their volume. I couldn't help the giddiness I felt hearing Reid command an entire arena full of people.

His voice was loud and unbothered by the conversation he'd been having seconds before walking out on me and the lady who I was certain was crying in a corner somewhere.

"Hey, hey, CALI! Sorry I'm a few seconds late. I was making sure I was good to go and didn't puke on you guys like at my last show."

Cue laughter from every single person watching Reid up onstage. I rolled my eyes as a woman shouted from down below, "You can puke on me anytime!"

I watched from the side, trying my hardest to blend in like a chameleon as Reid angled his head down toward the woman. "I appreciate that." Then he winked, and by God, it made even me sweat. I gasped at my own reaction. *Don't you dare fall for his tricks! He just called you pitiful!*

I shook out my shoulders and crossed my arms, leaning against a pole, appearing unbothered at the way the spotlights above Reid's head cast an almost angelic hue around his body. I ignored the way his high cheekbones and angular jaw looked like they were cut from granite, stealing the breath right out of my body. His dark-brown locks were shining and bouncing like he was in a commercial for some high-end shampoo line that I'd never have the pleasure of using. My mouth ran dry as Reid closed his eyes and stood straight as Jackson and Finn started up the hymn for the first set. It felt like Reid was sucking my soul right out of my body as his mouth opened and the first line was sung.

A raspy, soul-crushing, feel-it-all-the-way-to-your-toes sound filtered through his lips, and right then, I was completely swept away. I was mesmerized. Unspoken for. What his voice did to my body was unspeakable. Reid King was just that. A king. He was a king onstage. He commanded everyone's attention. He sang from deep within, not only feeling his own words as he sung but also commanding everyone else to feel them, too. I felt Reid King in my core, in my entire being.

I couldn't take my eyes away, and I couldn't ignore the way his voice, paired with his steely appearance, made me burn all over.

Reid King was a cold man, but he had an unbreakable fire inside of him. He made me burn from the inside out with desire.

A desire to *feel* like him.

A desire to *love* like him.

A desire to *break* like him.

He had the curse that not many people had. He felt all too deeply, and he made others want to feel it, too.

CHAPTER SEVEN

REID

An entire week had passed, and I was still staring at this mother-fucking silver spoon that none other than Brooklyn slammed beside my hand. I couldn't even look at her without being annoyed at the thought that she gave me fucking homework.

I was refusing to do it, too.

Which was stupid, because that wasn't going to help anything. Part of me wanted to see what she had inside of her, to see if she could help pull me out of this dark hole of... *nothing*. But the other part of me wanted to refuse. I wanted to bask in my sorrow. Sometimes, I even felt like quitting. I wanted to go off the radar. To be alone and done with it all. Hell, maybe I'd even become one of those men who lived out in the wilderness with a gnarly beard and hunted for his food with his bare hands.

But then I'd think of Nana.

I'd think of the way she'd always pushed me to be a better version of myself. The way she'd pick me up and dust me off when I'd had enough of my shitty childhood. Even if she wasn't alive right now, I still couldn't let her down.

Nana was my saving grace when I was a child. Basically, from day one, she was the only one who cared for me. After my mom fucked up so many times and left me in a house alone for days on end, Nana swooped in and saved the day. She was always there to feed me, bathe me, make sure that I wasn't buried underneath the shit show that my mom's druggie life entailed. The good thing about my mom never being home when I was younger was that I was truly better off alone. I lived for the days that she'd go on a bender and leave me, because that meant Nana would come stay with me.

I always felt guilty when I thought about the day my mom passed. Shouldn't there be some moral obligation to be upset when your parents died? I didn't know my father, so that didn't count, but I did know my mom, and when she was found dead in an ally with a needle hanging out of her arm, the only thing I felt was relief. Did that make me a terrible person? Maybe. But her being gone meant that I got to live with Nana permanently.

She took care of me, built me into the person I was today. I couldn't let her down.

That was why I had one tiny little strand of me who wanted to evolve, who was trying to move past the last several months and the constant reminders of all the shit gone wrong, but sometimes, I was afraid it wasn't enough.

Brooklyn's soft laugh had me raising my head. She was quite the little ray of sunshine here lately. And to think, it only took a week for her to sweep everyone on the bus off their feet. She wasn't a joy to me—of course not—but to Jackson and Finn, and even Rod. God, she even had my bodyguards salivating at the mouth. Brooklyn continued to ignore me as much as I ignored her, except for when she'd ask if I'd done my homework yet—which only pissed me off further. But with everyone else, she was the life of the fucking party. Everyone wanted to be around her. The tour bus had never been so... *happy*. She got into a routine with my friends, my bandmates, playing card games at night, popping their damn Pop-Tarts in the morning, hysterically laughing when Finn and Jackson would joke with each other because, honestly, no one but me in the trio had seemed to mature past the age of sixteen. She still slept on the couch, a fact that I couldn't ignore when I got up in the middle of the night, unable to sleep, and saw her tiny frame curled in a ball with a blanket draped over her.

"Whatcha lookin' at?" Jackson whispered as he slid into the booth beside me. I jerked my head over to him and shrugged.

"I get it. It's hard not to look." Jackson's eyes went right to Brooklyn, who I, too, was staring at.

I tried to play it off, even internally. "What are you talking about?"

"You know exactly what I'm talking about, King." Then he leaned his head down to mine even closer. "She's not just hot, she's like… the girl next door or something." I fidgeted in my seat, swallowing thick spit. "Like, look at that hair. Can you just picture it all splayed out beneath you? And those eyes…" I finally tuned out Jackson and his annoying-as-fuck whispering self.

But I couldn't tune out her laugh. It was soft and gentle, genuine. Almost beautiful. I hated to admit it, but she was beautiful, in her own way. It was a silent beauty, something that couldn't go unnoticed but didn't smack you right in the face at first. I'd spent the last several days observing, even when I knew I shouldn't. Brooklyn never went out of her way to get attention or to look like something she wasn't. She wore simple shoes paired with girly dresses, and she never spent much time on her hair or makeup. She was carefree and sweet.

Except with me. She often gave me dirty looks and long stares full of heated anger.

Jackson swore under his breath, his eyes trained on Brooklyn. "If I could just have a small taste of he—"

I shot up out of the booth, causing the spoon to go flying

off the table, the noise causing everyone to look over at me, even Brooklyn with those bright eyes.

I pushed Jackson out of the booth, ready to retreat to the back room to hopefully get my shit together.

I heard Brooklyn before shutting the door. "I guess that means he still hasn't done his homework."

Then Finn said, "Just give him time, sweetheart. He's not the only one who needs this to work out. We need him back to the way he was before…"

And just like that, anger warped into a nasty pile of guilt, and it was pouring onto me from all angles. I was letting everyone down. Not just Nana… but *everyone*.

———

Another show down, another sleepless night in front of me. You'd think after being up on stage for God knows how many hours, singing my heart out (which took much more effort now that I was certain I didn't even have a heart), that I'd be dead to the world for at least fifteen hours. That's how it used to be. Back when I was first starting this musician gig, I'd be permanently exhausted, and after a show, I'd crash on any flat surface possible and not wake up until we were in the next city.

We'd usually drive through the night and I'd wake up in a completely different state, somewhat rested for my next show. But I couldn't sleep anymore. I couldn't do much of anything anymore, if I was being truthful.

I almost snagged a bottle of liquor on the way out of the dressing room, leaving both of my bandmates behind to "celebrate" another show, just so it'd help me sleep… but I didn't. I didn't want to fall down that rabbit hole again. The last time I drank, I ended up puking on my fans.

Partying together after a show was the norm for us back before everything in my life spiraled out of control. We'd all be on this sort of high after a show, feeling as if we were on top of the world. We'd hang out backstage in one of our dressing rooms—which were excessively large—and chill with all the "groupies" as we liked to call them. Then, I met Angelina, and I stopped doing all of that. I'd usually retreat back to the tour bus, call her, and we'd talk for a little while before I'd pass the fuck out.

How did everything get so out of order?

How did I end up here? Alone. On the tour bus. Trying to write a fucking song.

I kept staring at the spoon. The stupid spoon.

I could hear Brooklyn through the bedroom door, talking to someone quietly. This was the second show she'd been at, and neither time did she stay behind to drink and party with Finn and Jackson—no matter how many times they begged her.

Especially Jackson.

He was my best friend before we even came close to hitting the Billboards, and I loved him like a brother, just as I did with Finn, but he was driving me up a fucking wall.

He'd flirt with Brooklyn any chance he got, then he'd swing his eyes over to me to see if I was watching, like I was on Brooklyn patrol or some shit.

Guess what? I. Didn't. Give. A. Fuck.

So what if she was sent here to help me? So what if she was *my* teacher? He could have her.

She was doing a lousy job at helping me.

Giving me a motherfucking spoon as a type of "exercise."

I sighed, flopping back onto the bed, my muscles beyond sore from jumping around a stage for the last several hours. I glanced at the clock on my phone. It was just after one in the morning, which meant I wasn't going to get sleep for at least a few more hours. It seemed I could only sleep when the bus was actually moving, and we weren't going to start driving until at least three, when the guys climbed back onto the bus.

They weren't the *biggest* partiers, but they still liked to have some fun from time to time. And they should. They should celebrate the great show. You should always celebrate your lead singer not puking on the crowd.

Throw a fucking party.

I looked at the spoon again, still hearing Brooklyn's small laugh from just a couple yards away.

Finn's words echoed through my head as I slowly sat up, my feet dangling from the bed. *"Just give him time, sweetheart. He's not the only one who needs this to work out. We need him back to the way he was before..."*

I pushed the thought away and snagged my phone for my nightly ritual.

I pushed the voicemail button, and her voice filtered throughout. It always sounded so strained, so unlike her. It wasn't high-pitched like it used to be; it was dull, sad, lost.

As soon as I heard her, I cringed. "It's me again... why did you give up on me? Why, Reid?" Then some shuffling around. "I know I did the wrong thing. I know I've been dragging you around, hurting you... confusing you... but I needed you, and you weren't there."

It was like the hole in my chest grew deeper with guilt each time I listened to the voicemail, but I couldn't stop myself. I did it after every show, trying my hardest to figure out what I was supposed to do. Only... there was nothing I could do. I couldn't do a damn thing. That was what sucked about the past—you couldn't change it, no matter how hard you wanted to.

The voicemail ended, and my heart felt stiff and cold in my chest. Then the next one started up. This was the voicemail that always perplexed me the most. It was left only a few hours after the first, but it was like an entirely different person was speaking, not Angelina. Not the woman I thought I knew. But it was her, and each time I heard it, the knife in my chest was lodged in a little farther.

"I hate you, Reid! I hate you so much. I wish I never met you. I'm glad I went off with Lori, and I'm thankful I did what I did to our baby, because I know it's better off." Then click.

Those two words: *our baby*.

They were like a sting to my bare skin every single time I listened to the voicemail. *Our baby*. The baby that I had no idea existed—if it even did exist. I wished I could just sit her down and shake her until she fessed up, until she sobered herself and told the truth. I had a mile-long list of questions for her, starting with who this Lori person was that she constantly blamed things on, but that list burned to ash. I would *never* get to ask her any of those questions, because I simply had no fucking idea where she was.

Her parents loathed me now. They blamed me for her sudden disappearance and what had happened after. They blamed me, even though I was the one that got her to the hospital as she bled out in a hotel bathroom, holding the fucking bloody culprit in her hand. I hadn't spoken to Angelina since that night—the night that literally haunted my dreams. The only thing I had was two missed calls from an unknown number with her mumbling through the other end, leaving me a cryptic voicemail that I liked to torture myself with.

I didn't have the privilege of knowing Angelina's medical history, as I'm neither her spouse nor relative. Even though the words that came out of her mouth indicated that we had some mystery child together, I didn't get to know anything. Her parents refused to talk to me, now relying on lawyers to do all of our bidding.

They wanted me to fall off the face of the earth.

My lawyer wanted me to just let it go, to let *her* go.

But I couldn't let it go, because there was one small, tiny part of me that wondered if I *did* have a child out there somewhere. I thought back to that night, many months ago, when I'd found Angelina with blood pooling out of her stomach. My own stomach revulsed at the thought, but I dug through my memory, wondering if I'd missed something. Did she have the baby? I knew that what she'd said wasn't true, because it didn't make sense. You can't just cut a baby out of your stomach. But who was this Lori she was supposedly hanging out with?

Nothing made sense.

And all I wanted was the truth. The dirty, raw, heartwrenching truth.

I replayed the voicemail once more, the pit in my stomach deepening beyond belief. *"It's me again… why did you give up on me? Why, Reid?"*

Deep down, I wondered if I did give up on her. I ignored her endless phone calls and text messages because they all said the same thing: *Take me back. I'm sorry. I was with Lori, but I won't hang out with her any longer.* I finally just stopped answering. I focused on my own shit. I focused on my career and didn't want to be bogged down by someone who was so back and forth. But now, the guilt ate away at me like some flesh-eating disease. What if she was trying to call me to let me know that she was pregnant? None of her messages said so, but could she have been afraid? Maybe she wanted to tell me in person. Ninety percent of me knew she wasn't pregnant—we'd always used protection, and I hadn't seen her in months before I had formally broken up with her—but there was that ten percent that teetered over the *what ifs.*

Carissa, the only person who knew the whole truth, other than my lawyer, Finn, and Jackson, had said the same mantra since the moment I broke down and epically upchucked all over my fans—which was the same night I got those disturbing voicemails. *It's hard to fight for someone who doesn't really want fighting for, Reid. You did fight. Just because she wants you to fight now, doesn't mean that you didn't fight then.* But I didn't truly feel like I fought for her. Maybe in the beginning of our relationship, but once she started playing games, I called it quits and didn't give it a second chance.

Everyone told me to let it go, to let her family deal with the mess that she was in and take the opportunity to dip out like they so desperately wanted.

But I couldn't.

Not until I knew the whole truth. Not until I found her,

and knew that she was okay, and I got to the bottom of all the lies. Did it matter? Probably not. Because even if she was pregnant with my child, that child couldn't have survived what she did. I knew that the Angelina I thought I knew was long gone. In fact, looking back, I didn't even think I knew her to begin with. But just because the Angelina that I'd spent several nights with, her curled up beside my body, wasn't the girl I thought I knew, that didn't mean it didn't hurt any less.

Because it did.

And it was something I couldn't pull myself out of.

The not knowing, the uncertainty of it all, the guilt.

It sunk into my very bones.

Exhaling all the air in my lungs, I pulled my eyes away from my phone that I'd thrown on the bed and looked down at the stupid spoon. I started to sweat out of every pore possible, my breathing even more erratic than before. I jerked my head upward to Brooklyn crying out with sweet laughter.

I focused on it for a few minutes, trying to calm the millions of emotions swarming in my body. I tried to steady the emotional rollercoaster I was on from the voicemails and memories.

Focus on that sweet laugh. Focus on anything other than your own shit for once.

I hurriedly ripped off my shirt, needing the cotton to get off my sweat-covered skin. I felt queasy, and angry, completely out of control.

"Get your shit together, King," I snapped to myself.

Swallowing, I clenched my eyes and worked on breathing correctly and pushing Angelina from my head. When I opened my eyes once more, my gaze went directly to the spoon.

I quickly grabbed it and a piece of notebook paper and started to scribble the stupidest, almost juvenile, words down.

What does the spoon make me feel? Hopefully something other than what I feel when I think about Angelina.

Once I had enough shit written down and my heart was resuming to a normal pace, I flung the door open, stalked past the bunks, and went straight for Brooklyn who was sitting on the couch in an off-the-shoulder shirt and cotton pants. Her dark hair was pulled into a high pony, and she had the daintiest pair of black-rimmed glasses perched on her nose.

Kent, our bus driver, was sitting across the living area, laughing at something Brooklyn had said. I ignored him and walked right in front of Brooklyn, waiting for her to look up at me.

She paused for a second, staring at my naked torso before raising her pink-tinted cheeks to me. "Yes?" she asked, her voice seeming bored.

I gritted my teeth together and held out the crumpled-up piece of paper. "Here."

Brooklyn snatched the paper out of my hand and quickly scanned the contents and nodded her head. She looked up at me once more with those dark-framed glasses on her face and smiled. "Are you ready to work now?"

I rolled my eyes before nodding my head to the back room.

Was I ready to work?

No, but I needed a motherfucking distraction, and I needed it now.

CHAPTER EIGHT

BROOKLYN

Calming breaths. Calming breaths. He's just a normal person. A normal person who isn't wearing a shirt. A normal person who isn't wearing a shirt and who sings like a god. A normal person who has abs that look so hard they make my eyes hurt.

It was fine.

Reid and I were both sitting on the bed, on opposite ends, staring at each other.

I was constantly surrounded by awkward moments. I swore it.

"So, are you going to help me write some songs, or…"

Oh, right. I was there to help him write music. What was my plan again? Should I have had a lesson plan? I felt like I should have had a lesson plan.

Just wing it, Brooklyn. Fake it till you make it.

But would I make it? Would I make it out alive?

I fiddled with my thumbs, staring down at the dark-gray comforter on the bed. "Are you sure you want to work right now? Maybe you should sleep and we can work tomorrow on the bus while we drive?"

Reid shook out his dark hair, his one leg propped up with his arm resting on it. "Can't sleep."

I fiddled with my glasses because I was still being awkward. I couldn't help it. "Okay… Well then, I guess we can get to work."

He snorted. "Good… that's what you're here for, right? Or was it just to be the band's cheerleader?"

I flicked my eyes up to his and didn't even pause to catch my breath. "There's the Reid I've grown to know. The one who never holds back what he thinks. Should I start wearing a cheerleading outfit to the shows? I can, if you want."

His sculpted face stayed unmoving. Unamused. *Okay then, no joking. Got it.*

"So? What's next on the list? Do you want me to write down the things the toaster makes me feel?" Reid's voice was beyond sarcastic, and just like that, all the nervous butterflies floating around my stomach died an instant death.

I shook my head, taking my reading glasses off for a second to rub my eyes. Reid King was exhausting, but the better question was, why wasn't *he* exhausted? Even I was tired after watching him onstage. It was the second show, and although I didn't get yelled at by any stage workers this time, I still felt utterly beat.

My eyes scanned the bed before I crawled over and grabbed a pillow.

"Oh, are we taking a nap now?" he asked, annoyed.

"No," I said, clutching onto the pillow tighter. Then I pulled my arm back and decked it at his head. "I want you to do the same exercise with the pillow as you did with the spoon."

Reid ducked and then raised his hazel-colored eyes up to mine. He cocked an eyebrow, and I could have sworn I saw a small tic of a smile forming on his face, but it quickly disappeared.

"This isn't going to work."

"What isn't? You being a jerk and uncooperative when I

ask you to do something?"

"I'm not being uncooperative; you just don't know what you're doing."

I shrugged, feeling a little surge of fire in my veins. "Apparently, neither do you."

Reid's stare almost turned cold, his mouth forming a straight line. He turned his head away, and my eyes went directly to his sharp jaw. The dead butterflies came back to life and started to fly around my stomach again, but I focused on my irritation instead.

I continued to glare at Reid as he turned his attention back to me. He studied my face for maybe three seconds. But those three seconds? They were the longest three seconds of my life. I wanted to squirm under his stare. I wanted to dart my eyes away and cower, sassiness and all, but I didn't. I reminded myself of the one thing that Finn told me the other day: *Give him time, and just be patient. He's under a lot of stress.*

Well, guess what, Reid? So was I. My family's house was months away from being taken from them, Cara was so stressed I was afraid she'd somehow develop a heart condition and die, and then me? It basically felt like it was my job to save them all.

I just had to get Reid King back on track. That was it, and everything would be all fine and dandy.

I felt as if Reid King needed someone to tell him how it was. He didn't need to be coddled or babied. He needed someone to pull him up by the collar of his flannel shirt that he always rocked onstage and yell at him to pull himself out of the darkness before it was all he could see anymore.

He needed to work through whatever block he had. There was no way around it. And he definitely had some type of block—everyone noticed, although no one would tell me why. Finn and Jackson were quite the secret keepers when it came to Reid's brooding self.

"Fine," he finally huffed, abruptly sitting up. He leaned over the side of the bed and pulled the pillow up off the floor. I told myself to keep my eyes on his head, but then they traveled down, just slightly, to the muscles that were stretching on his back, moving together in an effort to reach the pillow. My entire face flamed red.

I quickly averted my gaze and glanced down at what I was wearing and wanted to cringe. I was sporting an old t-shirt that continued to fall off my shoulder and cotton pajama pants. My hair was up on the top of my head, and pair that with the glasses? I looked like a total dweeb. A homeless dweeb.

Scoffing, I took my eyes off my own attire. Reid King wasn't even giving me a second glance. He didn't care what I was wearing or how I looked. Most of the times that he had looked at me, I felt like he was looking straight through me, which was a little disappointing, if I truly thought about it.

When my eyes finally reached Reid again, I quickly slapped my hand over my face. "What are you doing?!" I squealed. My whole body felt like it had been drenched with a pot of boiling water.

"Changing?" he answered, nonchalant.

"In front of me?!"

"What? You've never seen a guy in boxers?"

OF COURSE I HAVE, BUT NONE OF THEM WERE REID KING! JESUS! He was trying to kill me. That's why he all of a sudden wanted to "work." He wasn't really trying to work; he was murdering me. And it would be a slow, painful death—I knew that for certain.

"Just tell me when you're done," I mumbled, still covering my eyes.

I felt the bed dip and then heard his sultry voice. "I'm done."

Slowly, I removed my hand and peeked one eye open. Reid was lounging back now, fully dressed, his lean body lying on the bed with the pillow and an open notebook beside him. He had a pencil in his hand, twirling it around and around with those talented fingers as he stared down at the paper.

"I can't do this with you staring at me."

I laughed, throwing my head back. "You can get up and perform in front of thousands and thousands of people, but you can't tell me what a pillow makes you feel?"

Reid grunted but didn't say anything. Instead, he just stared at the pillow.

"Okay, how about this…" I started. "Scratch the pillow idea."

"And do what? Because I can't just shit out words, Brooklyn. Otherwise, you wouldn't be here."

"Duly noted."

I had an idea. An idea that came out of nowhere. And considering I had no clue how to get Reid back to what he was before, I was blindly pulling a rabbit out of a magician's hat, hoping it would work in my favor.

"Why don't we get to know each other first, and then we can dig a little deeper? It's hard to open yourself up to people regardless, let alone someone you don't even know." Reid remained motionless on the bed, still staring down at the pillow with his face unmoving. I started to get nervous. I started to remember that he wasn't just a normal guy who just happened to be excessively attractive. I remembered that he was Reid King—someone most people aspired to be like, someone who sang like the heavens had opened up, someone who was so successful it made Steve Jobs curious. *He doesn't care to get to know you, Brooklyn. God.* "Or… okay. Maybe we shouldn't do that. I just thought—"

"That seems better than this bogus 'describe a pillow' shit."

I grumbled, "You wouldn't be describing it. It was an exercise for you to get your creativeness rolling."

Silence.

Uncomfortable, awkward silence.

"Have you ever played twenty questions?"

Reid's amber eyes drove into me, and I wished so badly that I could decipher what was going through his head. I couldn't, though. Reid was closed up tight like a clam at the bottom of the ocean floor. His well-defined Adam's apple bobbed up and down as he angled his head upward. I gulped, now sweating, and then he said, "Have you ever breathed oxygen? Of course I've played twenty questions."

I chuckled. "Well, you are Reid King. You act like most things are below you. How would I know if you had ever played such a normal game?"

"You know, I was actually a normal kid at one time. I did normal teenager stuff."

"Now that's a great start. I'll go first to piggyback off that statement. What was the most normal thing you did as a teenager?"

Reid eyed me suspiciously. "How is this going to help me write a song? How is this going to help me get my shit together?"

I cocked my head to the side. "I already told you. In order for us to collaborate together, we need to be comfortable with each other."

I had no idea if this idea would even come remotely close to working. I just figured that Reid needed to be comfortable. He needed to know that I wasn't out to get him, that I wasn't just sent here to breathe down his neck to write a song. How could you truly open up to someone if you had no idea who they really were? It was a start, right?

Maybe, maybe not. But I knew that I needed to go with my gut, and my gut was telling me to show Reid what it was like to be normal, to be comfortable, to laugh again.

Reid King had yet to smile a true smile since I'd met him over a week ago. If he was onstage, he was smiling, but it never quite reached his eyes. I could still see the drawn look that he tried so desperately to hide.

He just needed to get back to where he was before—using his emotions to create the most explicitly beautiful music I'd ever heard. He was hiding from them. He was hiding and burying things deep. I could tell. That was what my gut was saying, and my gut was never wrong. I knew it for certain.

"Why are you nodding?" Reid asked, now staring at me.

"Huh? Who? What?" My face felt hot. I was rambling, doing that nervous thing that Jane always made fun of me for and nodding my head in agreement with my thoughts. *God, I am a dweeb.*

Reid's brows scrunched as he gave me an are-you-stupid look, but his face quickly relaxed. "So you think us getting to know each other will make us more comfortable and allow me to write again?"

I bit my lip and nodded slowly.

Reid cocked an eyebrow after he scanned my crisscross applesauce position on his bed. "You look pretty comfortable to me. What are those? Pajamas?"

I sooo should have bought that matching pj set from Target.

Sighing, I rolled my eyes. "I don't mean literally comfortable. I just think that if we got to know each other, maybe we could open up a little more. Maybe it would make us less cat and dog and more like…" I thought for a moment. "Bambi and Thumper."

Reid looked at me questionably, but then he cocked his lip upward, and I was beginning to see spots in my vision. My mind traveled back to the Google search I did, and I swore that same look was on the cover of a Vogue magazine, and it caused my panties to slowly creep down my legs. I, then, hurriedly clicked out of said search. Reid was hot, and he knew it.

"Are you saying that I make you uncomfortable?" he asked, his voice barely above a whisper.

Was he making me squirm on purpose?

"No!" I shouted.

Reid let out a deep chuckle, and my eyes, which were trained on the comfortable blanket underneath my legs, widened. *How does a chuckle sound so… sexy?*

"I think I do make you uncomfortable, Brooklyn. Very, very uncomfortable," he said again, this time definitely using some over-the-top sexy voice.

He was toying with me! I almost growled aloud as I whipped my head up to his.

"You annoy me. Stop messing around and let's get to work." *There! Take that, Mr. I'm-Going-To-Do-Everything-I-Can-To-Make-This-Difficult-on-Brooklyn.* "You're not going to distract me from getting you to work up the courage to write again. Nice try."

Reid looked offended, but I was certain it was all part of his game. "I have no idea what you're talking about."

I gave him a pointed stare, and he huffed. Then he mumbled, "I hate Carissa. Giving me someone who…" Then the rest was inaudible.

"I'm here to help you, Reid."

"No, you're here to irritate me."

I grinned. "The sooner you cooperate, the sooner I'm gone."

Reid threw his head back and stared at the ceiling. After a few seconds, he swiveled his head toward me, almost appearing vulnerable with his slacked jaw and no longer steely glare. "You really think you can help me?"

I gulped and tried to sound as confident as possible. "I do, but only if you agree to participate."

I heard him sigh and watched as he rested his head on his propped-up arm. "I don't understand how this is going to help me, but whatever." Then he thought for a moment, those eyes working back and forth as he sorted something out. "The most normal thing I did as a teenager would probably be… I don't know…" He shrugged one shoulder. "Toilet papering a house."

I nodded as a smile touched my lips. "Mmm. The ol' toilet papering trick."

He let out a sound that was somewhere between a grunt and an acknowledgment.

I pulled myself up to rest on the back of the bed, far, far away from Reid and his somewhat sensual lying posture. "Okay, your turn. You get to ask me something now."

Reid sucked his bottom lip, and I had to turn my gaze

away. *So, okay. It's not just extra enhancement on all those fancy cameras that professional photographers use during shows or interviews. Google didn't lie—Reid King is really just that freaking hot.* Noted.

"Okay… Why did you really take this job?"

My stomach dropped. "Really? Diving right into the deep stuff?"

He angled his head to mine and nodded. "I just want to know your true intentions. I already know you're not here because you're some type of "super fan." I can tell the crazies from the normal people."

I chuckled. "The crazies? Please enlighten me on how you can tell which ones are the crazies."

"Not so fast, Teach. That's not how the game works. My question first, then yours."

I rolled my eyes, feeling a bit more comfortable than a few moments ago. We were actually having a conversation that didn't involve me wanting to smack him, and without him storming off like I was an annoying fly that wouldn't stop bothering him. It was a nice change of pace, even if I knew it was fleeting.

"Fine." I sighed, pulling my legs up to my chest. "There are a few reasons, but the one you want is probably the most personal, so I'm going to give it to you." I closed my eyes for a brief second before answering. "I need the money."

Please don't ask why. Please don't ask why. Please don't ask why.

I didn't give him much time to respond. "Now, tell me about the crazies. How can you tell the difference?"

I slowly turned my head to Reid and almost flew off the bed. Reid King was wearing a smile. An actual smile. It wasn't a toothy grin or anything, because let's not get crazy, but his lip was angled up a bit, his cheek pushing upward. It was a nice half-smile, too—like a smile that made you feel as high as you were after you got your first kiss as a teenager. It was almost like a rush.

The half-smile was short-lived as Reid began to speak. "One time I had a super fan show up at my house."

My brows raised. "What? How did she know where you

lived? That's not public knowledge, is it? Plus, don't you have several houses?"

"I do. This was the one in my home state."

"In Louisiana?" I internally rolled my eyes. *Great way to make yourself sound like a crazy.*

Reid gave me a wary look but didn't bother prying. "Yeah, so… she came to my house in high heels and her makeup all done. Her hair was curled like she was going to the prom or something, and she was wearing a dress that didn't leave much to the imagination."

I laughed. "So what did you do?"

"I just asked what she was doing at my house, and she acted like she didn't know who I was. She asked to come inside while she waited for a tow truck. She said her car broke down and she walked over two miles to get to my house. I knew she was lying right then, because there were several other homes that lined the road before mine. She had to have really known where I lived, because my house is completely hidden."

"Did you let her come inside?" I asked, sitting up a little taller and crossing my legs to face him.

He shook his head. "Hell no." Then he snickered. "I told her I was calling for a tow truck and I'd be right back." A teeny, tiny grin formed on his lips. "I actually called one of my old high school friends who was now a police officer, and he came by and picked her up and took her to her car, which—surprise, surprise—wasn't broken down."

"That's hilarious and a bit pathetic." I laughed. "It amazes me that people will go that far to meet a celebrity. The stories that Jane tells me are insane sometimes."

"Who's Jane?" Reid asked, adjusting himself on the bed to rest his back along the propped-up pillows.

"Oh, my best friend. She actually writes for Teen Entertainment."

He nodded his head, ready to say something, but then our attention turned to the door.

"The guys must be back," I said, hearing a lot of loud

noises, like someone was running into the sides of the tour bus.

He nodded again, staring at the door.

"Okay, it's your turn," I said. "Unless you wanted the Jane question to count."

"That was harmless. Doesn't count." Then he asked, "Why don't you drink with the guys after the show? This is the second one now, and both times, you've come back to the bus."

"I could ask you the same."

"Ah," he breathed out. "But it's my question."

I smashed my lips together. "Okay, well, for one, I'm not here to party with them. I'm here to help you get back on track, to help you write. And two, I don't drink much."

"Why?"

"Why don't I drink much?"

"Yeah." Reid's voice was becoming raspy, tired sounding, which made sense as he just sang his heart out for hours and refused to sleep.

"Is that one of your questions?"

He raised a shoulder and continued to stare at me like he was trying to figure me out.

I licked my lips and looked away, suddenly feeling nervous. "I don't drink much for medical reasons, and that's all I'm going to give you on that one."

Truly, I was allowed to drink, even with one kidney. The only thing was that it took a while to leave my system, and I didn't like to be impaired for *too* long, and half of me felt guilty for drinking and putting my body through something that already had had enough.

"Fair enough."

I brought my attention up to his and raised one of my eyebrows. "Your turn. Why don't you go out with them? Or party after a show? Isn't that what famous musicians do? I mean, haven't you read the stories about Motley Crue and Def Leppard?"

He grunted. "Those guys were on a whole other level of

partying. They were legends."

I laughed quietly. "I know, but still." I angled my head to the door. "Even if they're not even close to being crazy partiers, why don't you hang out with them afterwards?"

Reid swallowed hard, his body going a little tense. The muscles in his forearms teetered back and forth as he clenched his fists in his lap. "I used to, but I guess things just changed for me. I'm not all about that groupie sex life anymore."

My mouth gaped. "Wait... that's what they do after shows? I figured they were just hanging out and letting loose a little."

He snorted. "Oh... they're letting loose alright."

My head was spinning. *Why didn't I realize this before?* "With who, though? Like, you're being serious about groupies? I thought that was only a thing back in the day with the rock bands."

His mouth formed a straight line. "You're naïve, Brooklyn."

"I am not!" I argued, sitting up a little taller. "I just figured since they asked me to hang out with them after the shows that it was not some orgy fest."

Reid shook his head, hiding another one of those grins. "You think it's an orgy fest? That's the funniest thing I've ever heard."

"This is getting totally off topic," I said, feeling my face flush. "I'm sorry if I don't understand the rock star lifestyle. I live a pretty boring life, Reid. Nothing like the life you live. To be honest, I think I've been in shock since I stepped foot on this bus."

He huffed. "You should probably be thankful you have a boring life."

"Why is that? To be as successful as you, to have the talent that you have and express it in such a way is amazing to me. I could never do that, no matter how boring my life gets."

Reid's head snapped over to mine, his honey-colored

eyes deepening to the point that I felt stuck. Pinned to my seat. Like I was sitting in freshly poured concrete. The air around us shifted as we locked stares. His voice was quiet but coarse. "Even though this life comes with success, it comes with a whole lot more baggage than you'd think. What people see on the outside isn't what goes on on the inside. Lies, deceit, pain—that all goes hand in hand with success in the music industry. It's hard to find *real* people in this world, especially when everyone is just some type of replica of who they think they truly are."

I gulped, still keeping my eyes locked onto his. I was walking a fine line between pushing and pulling. Did I want to push him away so the agony in his eyes went back into hiding? Or did I want to pull him in closer, get him to talk about what it was that was eating him alive? "Is that why your music is so deep and real? Because it's the truth?"

"Yes," he breathed, and I swore I could feel the words skitter over my skin, even from feet away.

"That's why it's so good, Reid. Can't you see that?" I whispered, trying so desperately to get him to see that what I was saying was the genuine truth. "Your music is authentic. *You're* authentic."

"I was authentic, Brooklyn. Now I can't even write one fucking verse. Not even a word."

"Then start giving the truth, like you always have. Start writing down what you feel."

All of a sudden, Reid's posture stiffened, his eyes shifted away, and I knew right then, I'd lost him. I dug too deep. One minute, we were talking about crazy fans and his bandmates having orgies, and the next, we were going to an entirely different level of personal. *Intimate.* That's exactly what it was: intimate. Talking about your deepest feelings was emotionally draining. I could tell that he was pulling away. But if he even gave our conversation a second thought—maybe not right away, maybe not even tomorrow—but if he ever revisited the conversation and thought back to what I'd just said—which was the truth—

then maybe it would click. Maybe he'd use it and turn himself around. Maybe it was a step in the right direction.

Too much silence had passed between us. There was no noise other than our breathing in the small bedroom. I was a second away from getting up, but something made me stay.

He was the first to speak, even if it was barely above a murmur. "I feel nothing, Brooklyn. And that's my problem."

"Reid," I said, my voice almost breaking. I'll admit, I was feeling a little ballsy, maybe too ballsy, but this was completely new territory for us. Over the last week, we'd avoided one another, exchanged scowls, he'd roll his eyes dramatically and storm away when I'd ask if he did his homework, but right now, it was like he was throwing me an olive branch, and I was pulling it before I even had a firm grip.

Reid turned that distant look over to me, fear plain as day in his eyes.

I took a deep breath and asked, "What do you feel right now? Looking at me?" Reid continued to stare, his fists, once again, clenched in his lap. "Pissed? Annoyed? Irritated? Frustrated that I'm digging in your life, trying to push you?"

I braced myself for the worst. The question was a last-minute decision, one I'd probably regret later, because if there was one thing I'd learned about Reid King over the last week, it was that he didn't care about my feelings—or anyone's, for that matter.

Reid's eyes stayed glued to mine for a few more seconds before his gaze roamed over my cheeks and down past my face. I stayed still as they shifted to my bare shoulder, to my chest, and then to my crossed legs. Then he moved his gaze upward again slowly—so slowly that I started to lose track of time. When he met my eyes, his gaze was softer. His jaw was relaxed, his mouth parted ever so slightly. That angular jaw wasn't as sharp as before; his known scowl had vanished. My mouth went dry. My body did something that

I only ever felt when I was turned on, and surely, I wasn't getting turned on in this moment.

Reid King was obviously emotionally scarred, downright insulting, and struggling with something that went far beyond the normality that I was used to.

I was not getting turned on by him staring at me.

Absolutely not.

Reid's gravelly voice broke me out of my sweat-inducing panic. "You know what? I think I could probably sleep right now. For once."

I nodded my head quickly, shooting up out of the bed so fast that I tripped on the cottony blanket, clearly flustered. "Yeah, okay. Good. You need some rest. I'll... um..." I started backing my way to the door, my eyes looking anywhere other than on him. "I'll think of a few more things we can do to work out what's going on, maybe make a lesson plan or schedule, and then maybe when we get a chance, we can break out the guitar and start working on tunes and verses. Take baby steps."

Reid didn't even muster up a grunt, so I hurriedly turned around and bolted out the door. I moved so quickly I didn't even shut the thing. I paused in the dark, and took a second to gather my bearings. *What in the hell just happened?*

I breathed a few more times before using my hand to guide myself along the wall and past the bunks. As soon as my eyes adjusted to the darkness and roamed over to the couch that I took residence on, I yelped.

"What the heck?"

I looked back as Reid popped his head out of his room, the light behind him illuminating his dark hair and shadowed face. "What?"

He began to walk down the short hallway at the same time I turned on my heel to run away from the scene that I just walked in on.

Finn was lying butt-ass naked on top of an equally naked girl ON MY BED. Okay, it was the couch, but I slept there. I'd been sleeping there since the first night I'd climbed onto the bus! My skin was crawling, like a thousand bugs were skittering across it. Who knew what that girl had?! He brought a groupie back to the tour bus and had his way with her on the spot that I slept! And on top of my blanket!

Reid grunted the second my body slammed into his. He reached his hands out and gripped me by the arms, momentarily stopping the assaulting scene of a naked Finn that was on repeat in my brain. "Why are you yelling? Afraid of the dark, are we?"

I snatched my arms out of his hands and smacked his hard chest, annoyed. "There's... and it's..." I groaned. "It's on my blanket!"

"What the hell are you rambling about?"

Then, I pointed to the crime scene—*okay, yes, I was being dramatic, whatever*—and watched as Reid walked toward the darkness to see what I was yelling about. I could see his tall shadow bend down as he tried waking Finn up, but all he got was an inaudible groan as the girl below him stayed dead to the world.

Where was everyone?! Where was Rod? Kent? Was this the norm? Was this what rock stars did in their spare time after shows? God, I was in over my freaking head.

"Does this happen a lot?" I asked, my voice all high-pitched and frazzled.

Reid strode toward me. "Sometimes, but usually, the next morning when they wake up, Finn or whoever it is that thought it'd be smart to bring a groupie onto the bus hates themself, because they're stuck with the chick until we get to our next destination. Things get awkward pretty quick."

Reid and I were now standing in the unlit, small hallway so close together that I could feel the heat emerging from his body. "So, I've been sleeping on a couch that has herpes?! AND NO ONE TOLD ME?!"

I couldn't see Reid, but I had a big feeling he was doing that tipped up lip thing that made my stomach drop. "There's a fourth bunk you could have been sleeping in."

"Have you slept back here with them? They smell! They

had a farting contest two nights ago."

"Why do you think I sleep back there on the bed?"

I huffed, crossing my arms. "I don't know, because you're selfish?" Instantly, my eyes grew wide, and I slapped my hand over my mouth. "That was not supposed to come out."

And then the unthinkable happened.

Reid King laughed.

It wasn't a chuckle or a snicker. Reid King actually laughed.

I was breathtakingly surprised, just like when he'd smiled earlier. *Reid - 2, Brooklyn - 0.*

"Do you know how fucking refreshing it is to hear someone talk back to me for once? To not walk on eggshells around me?"

I began to laugh, but Reid pushed past me quickly and muttered, "I guess you can sleep back here tonight."

"What?" I followed after him, careful not to get too close, because there was no way I was touching him, not after a simple smile and laugh rendered me speechless. "Like in your room?"

Once we were back in his room, with the light on, Reid turned around and raised his eyebrows. "I wouldn't want to be selfish."

"I… well, okay," I said nervously.

Sleeping in the same room as Reid King? It was like he actually grew a heart overnight or something. *What is it with him tonight?* Is it a sort of high from the killer show he did earlier? Was he too exhausted from singing his heart out to be mean?

"You can have the bed," he said as he snagged a pillow to throw on the ground.

I pulled back instantly. "Absolutely not!"

Reid paused beside the bed and looked up at me out of the corner of his eye. "Why?"

"You need more rest than me! You just performed for hours. I don't even know how you're not a zombie." I stomped my foot. "I'm not sleeping on the bed. And don't argue with me. I'll go to the front of the bus and sleep in between Kent and Rod if I have to."

Reid shook his head and then jumped into the bed with a soft thump, his dark locks bouncing on top of his head. "Suit yourself. Make yourself comfortable on the floor, or risk waking up cuddled between Kent and Rod. Doesn't bother me any." Then he reached over and turned the lamp off beside the table and didn't say another word to me. Constant whiplash—that was what it was like to be around Reid King.

I weighed my options carefully but knew I'd rather sleep in here on the floor than out there with either the musk of sex or cuddled between two men that were old enough to be my father. I was too afraid to sleep on a bunk, knowing very well that if Finn had sex on the couch, he more than likely did that kind of stuff in the bunks, too. So, I slowly walked over to the small area between the bed and the wall and lay down with my lone pillow.

My back was aching within five minutes of being on the floor. I had never imagined a tour bus floor being comfortable, but then again, I never even knew that a room like this could exist on a bus. Shifting to my right side, I tried to fluff the pillow in an attempt to make it seem like I was on an actual bed, but—surprise—that didn't work. I huffed through my mouth as I shifted to the other side, bringing my legs up to my chest to curl into a little ball. *He could have at least spared me a blanket.*

I lay on the floor for a few more minutes, pouting while cursing Finn for spreading chlamydia on my purple blanket, and then my mind drifted to Reid. The room was quiet, and the only thing I could hear was his breathing. It was calm and steady, but it did the complete opposite to my body. Nerves were bubbling up inside of me. Every time I heard his soft intake of breath, my heart would skip a beat. *I'm in Reid King's bedroom, on his tour bus, sleeping on his floor.* How did I get in this position, and how was I not puking from the astronomical number of butterflies in my stomach? I felt like we'd danced over an invisible line tonight. I stepped one little toe over that line, and then I was shoved back so far I couldn't even see it in the distance. I didn't know what came over me. It was like I didn't see Reid King as the King of Music. I saw him as something else entirely. An old friend? I wasn't sure. But lying here on his floor as he slept above on a bed caused my heart to fly in my chest.

There was no way I was getting any freaking sleep, but I closed my eyes anyway and prayed to God that we'd be staying in a hotel soon, because these nervous jitters were for the birds.

CHAPTER NINE

REID

My nana would be so disappointed in me. I propped myself up on one arm and peered down at the girl sleeping on my floor. I was acting like the complete opposite of the gentleman Nana taught me to be. Obviously, I was no knight in shining armor. I made Brooklyn sleep on the floor. *The floor.* This girl, with her quiet beauty and bolstering laugh, was sleeping on the floor because I was an ass.

I knew exactly why I shut down toward the end of the night. Brooklyn dug into me, and I wasn't okay with that. Not for one fucking second. I let a small, tiny piece of wall crack off from my hard exterior because I became too distracted. I wouldn't lie, though; it was nice being diverted and preoccupied after listening to the voicemail. *My vice.* My favorite torturing ruse. All of the what-ifs and guilt that clouded my vision were gone last night. It was comforting shutting everything off for a second.

I continued to stare down at her unmoving body, my gaze going to the same spot it went last night: that little dip in between her collarbone and shoulder. It was flawless except for the few freckles that spotted the creamy skin. I clenched my teeth and moved my attention elsewhere. *No. Do not even think about going there.* Angelina's voice carried throughout my head with the heartbreaking words that spilled out of her mouth. I would never, ever get so deeply involved with another woman for the rest of my life. And looking down at Brooklyn, I could sense a small part of me going a little bit past the attraction that I clearly had for her. I learned that much after last night when I stared at her from across the room. It was as if I truly saw her for the first time. My anger and betrayal at the record label for giving me a "teacher" went to the back burner when it was just her and me, alone. It was a terrifying thought that being alone with her could take away such thoughts. It was almost mind-boggling that I let some of my walls down—it came out of nowhere. I glanced down at her motionless face again. How did she do it? How did Brooklyn have the power to make me forget? How did being alone with her make me forget about reality?

Slowly, I crawled out of bed and adjusted my black sweats on my hips. I went to move the blanket on top of Brooklyn lying on the floor, knowing very well that was what any gentleman would do, but then I stopped myself. I shook my head harshly and put my cold and demeaning armor back on and walked out the door before I did something that I'd regret later.

I don't care if she's cold.

I don't care if she's uncomfortable on the hard floor.

My feelings were officially off.

After doing my business in the bathroom, realizing that we were on the road again, I walked out past Jackson asleep in his bunk with his wild, ginger hair standing up in several different directions. He was snoring so loud it sounded as if he were actually sawing logs. Then I moved quietly into the living area and walked right over to Finn and smacked him on the head. He jolted awake almost instantly, his drool laying on the naked woman's back where they were lying, still as naked as the day they were born.

"What the fuck," he grumbled, looking up at me with half an eyelid peeled open.

"You're a fucking idiot, Finn."

"Huh. Why?" he asked, laying his head back down and wincing.

"Because you brought home a stray, and Brooklyn walked in on you two passed out on her blanket."

Finn turned to look at me again with his bloodshot eyes. I could see the wheels turning in his head as he replayed the night through.

"I thought we were done with the whole 'Let's fuck random girls on the bus' shit. I thought we made a rule to do it in dressing rooms or hotels."

Finn finally pulled himself up and swiped Brooklyn's purple polka-dot blanket over his lap. The woman he'd fucked shifted beside him, and both of our gazes went right to her ass. It was a nice ass, but that was beside the point.

"I didn't mean to," he groaned, rubbing a hand over his face.

"How do you not mean to?" I stood back, slightly amused.

"Well, I just brought her back here to play some songs on my guitar, because there were too many people around, and then I saw that Brooklyn wasn't sleeping here like usual, so I guess one thing led to another and…" He shrugged.

I scoffed. "That's because Brooklyn was with me, you idiot."

"I figured she was asleep in a bunk." Finn ran his hand over his cropped hair but then paused and flicked his gaze up to mine. "Wait. She was with you? What does that mean? Like… with you with you?"

My whole body tensed. "You know better than that."

"So you two were working on songs?"

I couldn't deny hearing the excitement in his voice, which only flicked on that fucking guilt-ridden feeling that I continued to get when I couldn't write a damn song. I was letting all my band members down—everyone, essentially—and I had Angelina to thank for that. Or maybe I just had myself to thank.

"Don't make a big fucking deal out of it, or he'll stop writing," Jackson yelled from the bunks, obviously listening to the conversation.

Finn pulled his hands up in surrender, and I stared down at him. "Deal with this." I pointed at the naked woman. "And then you're on Clorox duty. Brooklyn is pissed that she had to sleep on the floor because you two were spreading chlamydia all over the place."

Finn growled. "You catch chlamydia one fucking time and no one lets you live it down."

Jackson started to howl with laughter from the bunk. Then, the woman who we thought was sleeping peeked her head up and said, "I've had it three times. It's not that big of a deal. They're just being jerks."

I almost laughed when Finn's face turned to disgust. "That's disgusting."

I tuned the two of them out as I walked to the front of the bus and knocked on the closed space that Rod and Kent usually hid out in. Rod opened it up and nodded with his five-o-clock shadow. "Mornin', King."

"Are we staying in a hotel tonight?" I bluntly asked, crossing my arms as I nodded at Kent who was driving.

"Yeah, we'll be there in a few and then rehearsal and sound check tomorrow. Why?"

"Because Asshat One needs to clean up that couch before Brooklyn will sleep on it, because he just spread chlamydia around on it. She doesn't need to be sleeping on that shit."

A crease formed in between Rod's eyes.

"What?" I snapped.

The crease disappeared and smile lines appeared. "Nothing." Then, he peeked around my body and smirked at Finn and Naked Chick who were arguing over the fact that having chlamydia once wasn't nearly as bad as having it three times.

Just then, Brooklyn, with her sleepy face and loose hair, walked out of the bedroom, and all eyes went to her and then to me. I knew what they were all thinking, and if they knew me at all, they'd know that nothing happened between us.

I was ready to lash out, to say something so everyone would fuck off and stop assuming that Brooklyn was actually getting to me or that she'd somehow swooped in and fixed everything after spending one night together talking.

Her fiery gaze landed right on Finn, and her small hands went directly to her hips. "First off, it's gross if you don't use protection during sex with random partners, so regardless if you've had chlamydia once or ten times, it's equally disgusting and downright stupid. Second, if I have to sleep on the floor again tonight while Mr. Selfish over there takes all the damn covers and leaves me the crappiest pillow of them all, I'll never pop a Pop-Tart for you ever again. Or play rummy."

I bit the inside of my cheek to keep from smiling. My teeth clenched in an attempt to keep my face emotionless.

I found Brooklyn humorous as hell, and watching the fire in her eyes blaze, as if she were totally unbothered by being thrown on a tour bus with the world's most popular singer/songwriter and his band, was amazing. I'd admit, at first, I thought Brooklyn was worthless and a complete waste of time. But now? I could see that she was something entirely different. *Fuck, maybe she can get me back on track.*

I had to turn around when I saw Jackson climb out of his bunk and stand behind Brooklyn, bowing down to her and clapping for her speech.

A small grin was creeping along my stone-cold face. It was unfamiliar and almost made me feel as guilty as before. A true smile wasn't something I'd done since before I found Angelina on that hotel floor. I almost didn't feel like I deserved to smile, like I wasn't worthy of it. But goddamnit, that was two times in ten minutes that I had to tell myself to stop raising my cheeks, all because of a timid, yet spitfire woman who I'd learned taught children music for a living.

Before I turned around to walk back into my room, I saw Rod eyeing me. His mouth turned up just slightly before he turned around and acted as if nothing was different. Because *nothing* was different. The guilt was still there, even if I was blinded by Brooklyn for a few sparse moments.

CHAPTER TEN

BROOKLYN

I was impressed, completely engrossed in all the fine details that the penthouse we were staying in had. In all my life, even living in such a popular city like New York, I had never stayed somewhere fancier than the Ramada. We were staying in a suite that literally went by the name The Penthouse—and it was magnificent.

There were several bedrooms—I think four—in our particular suite, one for each band member and then me. They gave me my own room. Kent and Rod, along with Reid's bodyguards traveling on the other tour bus, got a less fancy suite, but they insisted I stay close to Reid so we could work together. Rod apparently told Carissa—who continued to text and ask for updates every other day—that Reid and I were making a little bit of headway; headway meaning nothing, really. So what, he described a spoon, and we had a decent conversation last night. None of that truly meant we were making any headway with actual songwriting, but hopefully, it was just a stepping stone we had to step on to get to the bigger stuff.

Jane had texted, and I gave her a brief update on Reid, leaving out all of the stuff from last night. For some reason, I felt like the conversation that Reid and I had was private. There was something about it that made me want to keep it under lock and key. Maybe it was the fact that he made my body do certain things with just a simple stare, or maybe it was because my heart ached slightly when he'd given a small piece of himself to me. I wasn't sure. But the second I said it aloud, or recognized that I thought Reid wasn't just some complete famous asshole who threw rude remarks my way, and that he was an actual person with real feelings who was struggling with something, it made it real. It meant I was beginning to care or get too invested, and I didn't want to do that.

It was pointless to hide it from her, because we planned to meet up one night after one of the shows, because it just so happened that she'd be in the same city and state as us at the same time, ironically enough. So I knew it was only a matter of time before she'd see right through me. But for now, I was comfortable with denial. Deny, deny, deny. *Reid King does NOT make my body melt.*

I was still disturbed that Finn had slept with a groupie— who he parted ways with halfway to Dallas—on my favorite blanket. The housekeeping was doing the laundry right now, and I'd slipped them a crisp twenty to make sure they washed it twice in the hottest water possible. I still wasn't sure I'd use it again, but it was always good to have a backup blanket on the bus. I rolled my eyes at the thought of sleeping on Reid's floor again without a blanket as I stepped into the suite shower that was big enough to fit my entire apartment into.

Finn was pissed that he had to Clorox the bus when we got to the hotel. Jackson stayed behind to laugh at him the entire time and to take pictures. I guess it was funny that someone so successful and popular had to clean for once. It was like Reid was punishing him, and I found that hysterical, mainly because Finn was throwing a fit. He kept telling me that he was sorry, but I didn't buy it. I could have sworn I heard him saying he was going to drag me into "the war," but I had no idea what he was even talking about. Jackson only smashed his lips when Finn was going on and on about "the war," so I'd have to be on my toes from here on out. Those two were like teenagers, constantly joking with one another and pulling stupid pranks. It was exhausting watching them.

The blissfully warm water from the shower coated my skin as I poured some type of fancy body wash into my hand. I truly couldn't believe how big the shower was compared to my normal-sized shower. My mind instantly went to the gutter, thinking about how easy it would have been to have sex in there. I mean, you could lie down on the floor, in any position possible, without hitting your head or having that awkward this-isn't-comfortable sex position that often happened in showers.

At least, for me it did.

Shower sex wasn't fun when the shower was normal-sized. It was uncomfortable, and the last time I'd had it—with, nonetheless, a bar hook-up that was supposed to be a one-night-stand type of guy who turned into the next morning too—I'd slipped and smacked my head on the shower door while he continued to ram into me from behind. He obviously thought my groans from hitting my head were *moans*, so he only picked up his pace, thinking I was enjoying the sex.

Newsflash: I wasn't.

After rinsing the soap from my face, basking in the rich vanilla scent, I finally peeled my eyes open.

And that was when I saw it.

Something long, black, and slimy was lying on the shower floor, just in the corner near the small bench seat. (That's right, there was a long bench seat in the shower, too.)

"Agghh!" I let out the loudest, piercing scream I'd ever made as my eyes locked onto the snakelike creature in the corner of my shower.

I hurriedly pushed open the shower door, stepping out of the steamy shower as fast as I could. As soon as my foot hit the tiled floor, I ran to the bathroom door, unlocking it with a single thrust of my hand. When I yanked the door open, eager to get out, my foot slipped, and I yelled out again. But before I fell, calloused palms wrapped around my waist and I gasped. My hands wrapped around sturdy wrists as I snapped my head upward, staring directly into a face that made all the fear disappear out of my body. Reid's amber eyes were sparking as his palms tightened on my naked, wet torso. My breath caught in my throat, water droplets cascading over my nose and onto the floor below us.

Reid's strong jaw was tightened as he raked his gaze down my wet body. For a moment, I totally forgot about the snake in the corner of my shower. I only stared at the world's hottest man as he took me in. Each lingering stare left a burning mark on my body, and what couldn't have been more than a few seconds, felt like hours. I was pinned to my spot, not even trying to hide my bare breasts—or anything, for that matter. In fact, Jackson, or Finn, or even Rod, could have walked through the wide-open door of my temporary bedroom and seen me naked in Reid's arms right inside the threshold of the steaming bathroom. Reid moved his gaze up to my face—his now reddened and splotchy. The steam from my shower was enclosing us both, both of our chests rising and falling, desperately trying to get a grasp on reality. I watched in awe as Reid's tongue darted out to lick his lower lip, and I swore I was ready to give him anything and everything in that moment. His dark hair was messy on top, his tight white t-shirt clinging to every toned muscle on his upper body, his scorching eyes drinking me in like I was the richest of whiskies.

Then, his eyes went to my kidney scar, and reality fell on top of my head harder than the water from the shower. I gasped and broke him out of his trance. He quickly blinked his eyes and removed his hands from my slippery skin, remembering who I was and where we were. His distinct Adam's apple bobbed up and down as his eyes roamed over to the shower, looking anywhere but at me. I snatched the white, fluffy towel from the nearby towel rack and quickly covered my body, embarrassment washing over me. *What the hell has gotten into me?*

Reid slowly walked over to the open door of the shower, and his head ticked to the side once he saw the black, unmoving snake in the corner of the shower. I peeked my head inside as he walked farther, the wet floor splashing with each step. He slowly bent down to the devil's creature as I stood back, frazzled and still out of breath.

Reid picked the snake up, my eyes widening at the same time, and then he shook it.

The snake didn't do anything, and I had never been so confused.

Reid glanced up at me, his eyebrows raised, and shook it again in my direction.

I gasped, but then I realized that the snake was totally not moving—or real.

It was a freaking rubber snake.

Now, the whole "I'm bringing Brooklyn into the war" statement from Finn earlier made sense.

I'd bet my kidney that Finn put that snake in here to scare me—and me betting my kidney was a serious matter, considering I only had one.

Reid slowly walked over to the shower door, the snake in his hand, about to step over the slippery tile and onto the dry floor, with his dark gaze set toward me.

Warmth spread through my chest and down every limb. He narrowed his eyes like he was angry with me—or maybe with himself—and then stepped out of the shower and left the bathroom, leaving me alone, all hot and bothered, surrounded by so much sexual tension that I wanted to melt right there.

Reid King, the most talented man I'd ever met and easily

one of the most attractive men I'd ever seen, just saw me naked.

He saw me naked, and the look he gave me had my stomach dropping so low I didn't think I'd ever be able to pick it up.

————

After finally getting the guts to leave the bathroom, I sat in my room with a firmly closed door (FYI, if you leave your bedroom door open in a suite, people can hear you screaming when there's a fake snake in your shower, and they're likely to come investigate) with my legs crossed underneath me. A bottle of Fiji water was clenched in my hand, the silver platter of room service still on my bed, and I only sat there, *still* trying to clear my head from earlier.

Reid King saw me naked, and now I had to be in a room with him, pretending like it didn't happen.

I'd written down a few lesson plans for upcoming sessions, and the next was to work on writing a dummy song. A dummy song meant writing a song about something totally insignificant, something creative, yet something that the world would never see. I figured it was a great start to getting the ball rolling. The sooner Reid and I collaborated and figured out a song, the sooner I could leave and stop feeling so… anxious. Our last session was getting to know one another, to maybe make things a little more comfortable. But now? God. It felt like I had a gorilla squeezing my throat at the same time an elephant was sitting on my chest.

Reid King saw me naked, and I didn't even try to hide the fact that it turned me on. I *liked* it. I liked that he saw me naked. I *liked* the way his hands gripped my torso.

Small beads of sweat were forming on my forehead.

Just go in there and act professional, and tell him you're ready for the next lesson. I blew air out of my mouth and shook out my shaky fingers.

Working with kids was never this stressful or intense. I rolled my eyes as I pulled my legs over the bed. Of course working with Reid would be stressful and intense. Just look at him! He was the broodiest, most stubborn, most talented, attractive-as-sin man in the world.

Grabbing a pen and notebook, eyeing my old, wood-chipped guitar for a brief second, I walked over to my room door and swung it open. *You have maybe ten yards to get your bearings together before you knock on his door. Chill.*

Then all the air evaporated from my lungs.

My face could have been used as an example for the old adage "Looking like a deer in the headlights."

Reid freaking King was standing right outside my door.

The lie detector test determined that having ten yards to get my bearings together was a lie.

I had negative three seconds, and my bearings were most definitely not together.

"Reid," I breathed, instantly wanting to punch myself in the face.

"We have a lesson to finish, right?" he asked, all calm and relaxed.

I coughed, shifting on my feet, averting my eyes elsewhere. "Um…"

Reid shifted on his heels. "We never finished our twenty questions from last night."

Confused, I brought my gaze up to his. "You want to finish our twenty questions? I was going to say we could work on some actual songwriting…"

Reid's lower lip disappeared behind his teeth, causing my mouth to go dry. *Why was I so out of control?*

Reid's eyes from our little shower episode shined brightly in my head like they were on a jumbo screen that I couldn't look away from. He drank me in, every inch of my wet body, and the twinkle in the amber color was nothing less than lustful. That was why I was so out of control; I suddenly had a taste of what it was like to have someone like *him* give me a type of carnal attention, and now I wanted more.

"You know," Reid said, that lip of his jutting out from behind his teeth, "I think I'd rather do the whole twenty questions thing than try to write right now. Remember… baby steps?"

I narrowed my eyes for a brief second. I was certain that I'd give Reid King anything he wanted in that moment, and that was a big, big problem.

"Fine," I answered, acting just as normal as him as I crossed my arms over my small chest. "But the next lesson, we're getting down to work, okay?"

We had to. Otherwise, Carissa and the rest of the record label would fire me on the spot and that couldn't happen. It *wouldn't* happen—I'd make sure of it. Because if I were to get fired or let go for not doing the job I was sent here to do, then that text message I'd gotten from Cara earlier about them thinking about selling their second vehicle would come true.

Reid pushed through the threshold of my door, walking right past me, and plopped down on my bed. "You've got it, Teach. Now, where were we?"

CHAPTER ELEVEN

REID

I couldn't stop staring.

I couldn't stop staring at her, even though she was several feet away from me on a lounge chair in the corner of her room. I may have shut down my heart for good, and I may have been a melodramatic bachelor who had internal scars all over his chest, but my dick still worked, and I hadn't been with a woman for many, many months.

I hadn't had sex since Angelina, and that was a long while ago. I knew the difference between a one-night stand and having somewhat meaningful sex, but after I found her carving out her stomach to get rid of the "baby," it just freaked me the fuck out.

The what-ifs were enough to get my dick out of any pussy that I didn't *truly* know.

Although, I wasn't sure I even truly knew Angelina.

Even the thought of having sex with another woman after the vivid memory of Angelina made me recoil.

But God, the image of Brooklyn, all doe-eyed in the shower, naked with water pouring down her body, her curves glistening under the steam… my body kicked into overdrive.

And what scared me the most?

The guilt didn't come.

Something came… but it wasn't the guilt.

I had to force myself to walk out of the bathroom. I kept reminding myself that (1) she was my music teacher, which I was supposed to be pissed about; (2) sex was off limits with anyone, especially her; and (3) Angelina…Angelina and the not knowing.

The thought of Angelina snapped me out of my trance long enough to walk away, to put some necessary distance between me and Brooklyn. I got myself together and brushed it off my shoulder, and yet, I still found myself at her bedroom door, asking to get back to work.

Work.

That was what I was calling *this*. Me in Brooklyn's room the night before a show, finishing up a game of twenty questions that didn't truly need to be finished. I needed to focus on my writing, collaborating with her to get my shit back in line.

What I didn't need to do was focus on the curve of Brooklyn's hips as she adjusted her jeans on her legs.

"You're wearing jeans," I said aloud, suddenly noticing the difference of her.

"What?" she asked, giving me a strange look.

I glanced at her tight skinny jeans once more before repeating myself.

"You're wearing jeans. You never wear jeans."

"Nice observation, Reid. Would you like me to add another gold star to your chart like I do for my students?"

I almost… *almost* cracked a smile. God, the mouth on her was nothing I'd ever dealt with before—at least, not from someone who wasn't Nana or Carissa.

"Actually, maybe if I had a gold star chart, I'd be better at writing songs. Rewards and all."

Brooklyn's mouth rose before she suddenly wiped it

away, sighing. "Okay, we each have one question left, and then it's time to move on to some serious lessons. You have one show tomorrow night, and then, on the tour bus, we're getting down to the next lesson. It's time to start making headway."

I nodded. "Okay, then shoot. It's your turn." I sat up and scooted against the headboard of her bed, with about fifty pillows, and realized I felt more relaxed here than I did in my own room, alone, either staring at a notebook full of blank paper or lost in my own thoughts.

Brooklyn's pink-tinted mouth opened. "What do your shows make you feel?"

I hastily took my stare away from her mouth and moved it up to her eyes. "What do you mean?"

Brooklyn ran her hand through her auburn locks, the tangled mess looking even more tangled than before. "What do your shows make you feel? When you're up there onstage, with your bandmates behind you, having your back, creating music with you, fans screaming your name, bras being thrown at your feet... what do you feel?"

"Why do we always have to get so intense with these questions? I thought this was an exercise to make me comfortable."

Her eyebrow hitched. "You look pretty comfortable to me, sprawled out on my bed."

I blinked, not moving my indolent posture. "You first."

She pulled back, confused. "Me first?"

I sat up a little taller and stared at her. "What do my shows make you feel?"

Should I have wanted to know the answer to that? No. Because why should I have cared? She was my music teacher, and whether or not my shows had any effect on her shouldn't really cross over to my music-making and our lessons. But I wanted to know. I wanted to know if that look of awe in her eyes was for the song. My words? Or was it my tone? Maybe just the music in general? What was it? What did she feel?

Brooklyn stared back at me, our eyes locking onto one another. It was strange how, just like last night, the air changed between us once things weren't as light or relaxed. It was uncanny. The room grew quiet, and our stares were locked and loaded, so much emotion coming from the pair of us for no reason other than the fact that we may be alike in some ways. Maybe she wore her emotions on her sleeve, too. Maybe she felt passion as deeply as me. Maybe she actually *listened*.

"I'll only answer if you do," she whispered, never once blinking or moving a muscle in her body.

"Why don't you want to tell me?" I asked.

She broke our stare for just a moment before answering. "Because feelings are personal, and what your music makes me feel is personal."

I nodded slowly, understanding exactly what she meant.

Then she perked up, as if a lightbulb went off above her head. "I'll tell you first, as long as you promise to answer me after, *and...* as long as you help me with something."

My eyebrows knitted together as I sat forward. "Help you with what, exactly?"

"Getting Finn back for putting a fake snake in my shower."

Ah, and we were back to the shower fiasco.

I answered quickly. "Deal... but this doesn't mean we're friends now. Got it?"

She smiled. "I wouldn't want to be your friend anyway."

I could feel the muscles along my cheeks moving upward. "Good, as long as we have that out of the way. How do you plan to get Finn back?"

"What good are you if you can't tell me how to prank him? He's like a little mouse. I have no clue what he dislikes, or likes, other than chlamydia."

I chuckled and shook my head. "Oh, I used to prank them all the time back before..." I let my sentence trail off as I hurriedly tried to push the thought of Angelina away. "I know what we can do to piss him off."

Brooklyn jumped up onto her feet, barely making a sound with her small frame. "Okay, lay it on me. What are we gonna do? Because everything I've thought of in the last hour has been stupid."

I shot up from the bed and angled my head to the door. "Follow me, Teach."

As soon as Brooklyn and I made sure that the guys were long gone—probably eating out somewhere before they came back and rested for tomorrow's show—we walked over to the mini-fridge that held all the tiny bottles of liquor—the ones Finn would snag to drink when he got back tonight.

He lived for those tiny bottles, and I had no idea why. It was some sort of ritual or tradition of his. I had messed with them before, and the outcome was hilarious. He threw a hissy fit whenever someone fucked with his sacraments before a show. He thought they were good luck or something ludicrous like that.

I strode over to the kitchen as Brooklyn stood back, probably wondering what the hell I was doing.

Snagging the hot sauce bottle that I knew would be in there, I walked back over to her and asked her to untwist all the lids of the liquor bottles and line them up. She did as she was told, and I took my steady hand and started to drop small drips of hot sauce in every bottle, even the clear ones. Finn never looked; he usually just threw them back and would yell out some stupid, loud noise like he always did.

"Ah, the ol' hot sauce in the liquor bottles. Nice."

I peeked up at her. "You've done this before?"

She shook her head but laughed. "No, but once when I was younger—like way younger than I should have been— my friend Kellie and I wondered what it would be like to get drunk, so we drank all her grandma's vodka, and in an attempt to save ourselves from getting in trouble, we filled the bottle back up with water." I continued twisting the lids to the bottles back on when Brooklyn continued on with her story. "And then... we put it back in the freezer."

I paused and glanced up at her, ready to tell her how stupid of an idea that was, but she smirked. "I know, I know. Water freezes, liquor doesn't. Lesson learned."

"So, did you get in trouble?" *Why do you care? Stop giving a fuck about her stupid, silly stories from her past.*

She shrugged, pulling her light sweater around her body. "Not really. But her grandma did start locking up the alcohol after that."

I chuckled while placing the bottles back in their rightful places. *So, little Miss Goody Two-Shoes, who usually wore girly dresses with a bright smile on her face, wasn't all that good when she was younger. Interesting.*

Brooklyn tiptoed over to me and whispered from behind me. She was so close I could smell her sweet vanilla scent wafting around us. "So, now what?"

I turned my head just slightly. "Now, we wait."

Just then, we heard the guys outside the main door to our suite. Brooklyn sucked in air, and I turned on my heel, pulling her by the hand and back into her room. Her hand was so small and soft in mine, my rough palm rubbing along the smoothness of her skin. As soon as we were in her room, I glanced down at her hand in mine and then instantly pulled mine back.

Have you lost your fucking mind?

Brooklyn's cheeks turned pink, the small freckles on her cheeks almost glowing. I could feel a slight sense of her soft innocence caging me in, so I did the one thing I always did: acted like a dick to push it away. "What? Never held someone's hand before?"

Then I snorted and turned toward the door, listening to see if Finn went to the bottles.

Brooklyn inched closer to me—so close I had to hold my breath so I stopped smelling the vanilla. It smelled edible, if I was being honest. Like the fucking birthday cakes that I'd only started getting when I moved in with Nana.

A loud grunt fell out of my mouth, and I looked down at my black Vans. "Did you seriously just stomp on my foot?"

Brooklyn turned her bright-green eyes toward me, a spark of fire flickering in the golden specks. "Yes."

"Why?" I asked, giving her an intense look.

"For the rude comment."

I bit my lip so hard it was bleeding. I was *not* going to give her the satisfaction of making me grin again. Not tonight.

I'd already given up too many smiles with her around.

There was something about her that unwrinkled a piece of my heart. Like the bent pieces weren't so bent with her around, and that was obviously unacceptable. Completely intolerable. No fucking way was this woman going to piece me back together. There was no way in hell. If anyone was piecing me back together, it was myself. Me, myself and I. The King of Music. Reid King—the only person I'd ever rely on again.

"So?" Brooklyn asked, barely above a whisper.

I turned my head slightly back to hers, both of us close to the door to listen to the guys. I raised my eyebrows. "So what?"

She shifted her gaze back to the door for a slight second before peering up at me. "Are you going to answer the question?"

I played stupid. "What question?"

"What do your shows make you feel? Don't forget we're in the middle of a lesson, *student*."

"A bogus lesson," I mumbled and quickly moved my foot out of the way, just in case she tried to stomp on it again.

"You promised."

"As did you."

"And I'll answer as soon as you do."

I sighed annoyingly, leaning against the wall closest to the door. Brooklyn was still beside me, but I tipped my head back, resting it along the hard surface so I didn't have to be in her space any longer.

A quietness fell upon the room, my heart thumping in my chest with a burning desire to cut the conversation short and retreat back to my own room. It amazed me that, last year, I could sit down and write several songs, but now, I could barely speak about how my music made me feel. It was like my feelings had disappeared. Like I'd somehow shut them off. But I knew this was a step in the right direction. Brooklyn's lesson wasn't bogus, and she knew that. She somehow knew I needed to do something, express myself in some way or another. I sighed again and continued to look up at the ceiling, my chest burning with each beat of my heart.

"They make me feel... *alive*."

I let that linger in the air for a little while, the squeezing around my body lessening as each breath passed my lips. I was afraid to admit the rest. I was afraid to admit that the only time I ever truly felt alive was when I was up onstage, momentarily distracted from the shit show in my life. Because if I said it aloud, then it'd make it more real. That was why I kept everything regarding Angelina inside, buried so deep that no shovel in this world would be able to dig it up. I didn't want it to be real. I didn't want Angelina to be where she was—wherever the fuck that was. I didn't want some version of the truth lingering in the air, causing me to wonder every second of every day what the hell was true and what wasn't.

Did Angelina make everything up? Was this Lori woman she was supposedly with even real? I knew Angelina didn't literally cut a fetus out of her stomach like she'd mumbled, but why did she say that?

The harshest thought popped up and almost made me double over—did she... abort it, in an attempt to hurt me? That one always got me. Every time. I never wanted to think she'd do something like that, but then again, I was certain I never truly knew her in the first place.

Slowly, I dissolved all the thoughts that were scattering in my brain and lowered my head to Brooklyn. She was peeping up at me with a determined look in her eye, almost as if she were proud of me.

I instantly wanted to throw up another wall.

"We're going to get you back to that," she whispered, taking one tiny step toward me. We were so close that our chests almost brushed along one another's. I held my uneven breaths. "We're going to get you back to feeling alive more than just onstage. We're going to bring that life back into your writing. Do you understand me?"

I clenched my jaw tight, wondering how the fuck she knew exactly what I was feeling. How did she know that I felt lifeless the rest of the time? How did she know that the only time I was okay was when I was up onstage?

I continued to stare down at her. "And what do my shows make you feel?"

Brooklyn blinked once, then twice, then parted those soft-looking lips. "Excited."

Something flicked on inside of me. I wasn't sure if it was the fact that I felt vulnerable, or maybe it was the fact that I was inches away from a woman as honest as Brooklyn. The more time I spent around her, the more I realized that I had her all wrong. Brooklyn may have seemed sweet and timid on the outside, covered by those dainty dresses, but she was fiery, too. Passionate. She possessed a quiet beauty but had a crackling to her that screamed dangerous. Her body heat simmered all around us, and I was burning in more than just my chest. A hotness covered my skin.

She spoke quietly, but her words were loud. "It makes me excited to see someone put that much emotion into their music. To know you have *that* much feeling inside of you is mesmerizing."

Brooklyn swallowed, and I darted my eyes down to her lips. Then, involuntarily, I moved my gaze over that same bare shoulder from the other night, the oversized sweater she was wearing dipping just low enough that I could see a tiny strap of fabric from her bra. I could feel the desire pooling in my veins. There was something so *real* about her, something so quiet yet daring. It might have been the way she didn't care that I was who I was, or maybe it was the way she truly resembled an actual fire, silent yet flickering at just the right times, beautiful but threatening.

I quickly snapped my attention to the door as I heard Finn spew a line of cuss words before stomping closer to Brooklyn's room. She hurriedly stepped away from me, shaking her head and smashing her lips together.

The knock was loud from behind my head, so I stepped back and opened her door, meeting Finn's cold stare head on.

He was confused at first, pulling back just slightly. "What are you doing in here?" he demanded.

I raised an eyebrow. "Working on songs with Brooklyn." *Lie. I was getting caught up in Brooklyn, not working.*

He scrutinized me for a few seconds before the glare on his face turned into a shit-eating grin. "Working on songs with Brooklyn? You mean, putting hot sauce in my fucking liquor bottles with Brooklyn?"

I heard a small giggle from behind me, and I couldn't help it. My mouth started to turn upward, and that was when Finn dove onto me, wrapping his arms around my body and holding on tightly.

I mumbled, "What the fuck? Get off me."

He only hugged me tighter as he yelled, "No!" His hot sauce slash rum breath caused me to groan.

Out of nowhere, Jackson came around the corner and slammed into us, also wrapping his long limbs around our embrace.

Brooklyn sounded from behind. "Wow… I mean, Reid did say that you guys have orgies. I just didn't think it was with each other."

I groaned again, trying to push my bandmates' heavy weight off my body. "Why do you guys have a boner for me right now?"

Jackson was the first to let go, and then Finn followed. Finn looked over at me and cheesed. "It's just nice to have the old Reid back, even if it's just to put hot sauce in my little baby bottles."

I rolled my eyes and huffed when both Jackson and Finn ran through the suite yelling, "Rod! We're making Brooklyn a part of the band! She got Reid to fucking smile for once! He pulled the hot sauce trick again. He's back!"

I turned around and looked at Brooklyn once, my eyes as intense as the feeling I had inside of me. I turned on my heel and walked to my own room, leaving her and my fucked-up desire alone.

I wasn't back.

Not all the way, at least.

CHAPTER TWELVE

BROOKLYN

Another show down, and I was thankful to admit, once again, that I did not get yelled at by any crazy women wearing all black with a headset perched on their head. It seemed that Reid telling off the one at the first show I went to spread around like wildfire, and everyone had left me alone.

Reid and I had gotten into a semi-normal routine. We hadn't made a whole lot of headway on songwriting, but I would say that we were moving from acquaintances who gave each other dirty looks and bantered constantly to acquaintances that were *actually* collaborating. I mean, the man had seen me naked, so that definitely meant we were closer than we were before... right?

Each night that he was not doing sound check, or rehearsing, or better yet, actually performing, we kind of went into our own little world—wherever that may have been: a hotel room, the back room on the bus, his dressing room, wherever. The only problem was that we truly went into our own world. We started off talking about music, or verses, or tunes, and then ended up getting totally off topic and acting as if we were old buddies from high school. There were some nights that I could tell he needed a break, like when the angry lines formed on his forehead from frustration. So I would typically leave him alone and end our "lesson" for the night. That was usually when I hung out in the front of the bus with either Rod and Kent or the guys. And by "hung out," I meant whipping their butts at rummy.

Reid groaned from beside me and crumpled up yet another piece of paper and threw it at the wall. "This isn't working. I'm done."

I rolled my eyes. "That's what quitters say."

"Fine, then I'm a quitter."

I laughed out loud. Reid was acting like a child, pouting with his arms crossed over his chest. "You are worse than my youngest student, Reid. My God. I've never seen a grown man pout like you."

He jutted out his lip. My eyes flashed to it for a brief second before I quickly turned my head. "Fine, let's just work on some tuning. How's that? Maybe get a tune going first and worry about the verses later?"

"That's not how I usually do it."

"Well, bucko," I said, standing up and walking over to the corner of the room to snag his acoustic guitar. "My dad always said that if something isn't working, change it and try again. And I hate to break it to you, but you sitting there pouting like a three-year-old—for the millionth night in a row, I might add—because you can't get the words down, isn't working. So…let's go."

Reid angled those dark eyes up to mine, his light lips forming a scowl. "You're so bossy."

I lifted a shoulder. "Only with you."

He eyed me for a few more seconds before smirking. Reid smirking wasn't as unusual as it was a couple weeks ago when I'd first started to collaborate with him. In fact, he'd even laughed a few times over the last couple of days, *and* once, he came out of his dungeon (the room we were currently in) and watched me smoke Finn and Jackson in a game of rummy. But it still sent a jolt of excitement through my body. I told myself that the only reason it made me excited was because it was one step closer to breaking Reid and putting him back together so he'd finally get over the writer's block he was enduring, but it most definitely wasn't the only reason.

My parents and sister still thought I was in Cali on a teacher's retreat. I'd managed to avoid FaceTime calls and only talked on the phone to Cara. That way, I didn't have to pretend I was in some random closet again. And each time we talked, the pit in my stomach grew larger, because no matter how badly I wanted to push away the topic of our family's financial issues, they always came up. Her voice always dropped when she'd start up, as if it were a warning. *"I don't know, Brooklyn. No matter how much I beg Mom and Dad to stop throwing around the idea of selling their house, they keep mentioning it. I threw a fit when I saw a realtor's card on their counter the other day. I know they're trying to help, but I just…"* And then silence would encase us both. The only thing phone calls with my family did was (1) make me homesick, and (2) make me realize that I needed to stop getting caught up in Reid's good looks and our simple, in-our-own-world conversations and get down to work. The sooner Reid and I worked together and he pulled his head out of his ass, the sooner I'd get paid and all our problems would disappear.

Jane had checked in occasionally but only to make our plans for meeting up soon, which I so desperately needed in order to get away from all the testosterone I was currently knee-deep in. Rod had kept Carissa up to date and had pulled me aside only a couple times to tell me that he truly saw a change in Reid, but he wanted us to get working on a verse or two, as the record label was all but salivating at the mouth for something. A verse. A line. Anything, really. And I was right there with him. I knew we needed to throw them a bone; otherwise, they'd be breathing down Reid's neck… again.

Reid's voice startled me out of my thoughts. "I'll only tune if you'll tune, too."

I slowly brought my eyes up from my lap and landed them on him. "Why do you always make this about me?"

"I know you have your own guitar. I've seen it."

I hitched an eyebrow and cocked my head to the side. "Creepin' around my stuff at night or…"

"It's only fair that I hear my music *teacher* play music. You've heard me play music."

I narrowed my eyes and gripped his guitar tighter in my hands. "You play music for a living."

"And you teach music for a living."

I sighed, irritated. "That's right. I teach. Don't you know that saying? *Those who can't, teach.*"

He smashed his lips together to hide a grin, grabbing his guitar from me. "I don't believe that for a second."

"What don't you believe?"

"That you can't play."

Fidgeting on my feet, I intoned, "I'm here to collaborate with you, not to play you my own songs."

Reid's head tilted to the side, that dark hair moving effortlessly on his head. "What? Are you afraid or something?"

I chuckled sarcastically, looking up to the ceiling with my finger on my chin. "Hmm, let's see… am I afraid to play a song in front of Reid King, the King of Music? Um. Yeah."

"Why?" he asked, his tone slightly lower. *Why?* Was he serious?

I spoke truthfully. "Um, probably because you've never really spared my feelings…ever."

He nodded, agreeing with me. "Okay, how about this? I won't say a word. But I only think it's fair that we work together; otherwise, it's just like you're judging me from afar all while trying to *teach* me."

I threw my hands up in the air. "You literally play for millions of people who judge you constantly! Nice try. And I'm not really "teaching" you to write music. I'm here to bounce ideas off of, to collaborate with."

He paused and grinned, that small dip in my stomach turning into a gaping hole. "Do you play for your students?"

Ah, shit. He got me there.

I blew air out of my mouth and stomped away. Fine. Reid King wanted me to hold his freaking hand while he tried to come up with a catchy tune? Then so be it. It wasn't like I needed his approval anyway. I wasn't trying to gain his respect or really cared about his opinion. He was rude and broody most days, so who gave a flying shit?

Not me.

I snagged my guitar after walking down the small hallway past the bunks, my quick and brash movements showing off just how irritated I was. Finn and Jackson looked at me for a second and then to my guitar before smiling. I gave them a pointed look and asked, "Has he always been stubborn?"

Both of them nodded and then threw their heads back and laughed.

I rolled my eyes and stomped back into the room where Reid was sitting all nice and comfortable, with his guitar in his strong arms, leaning back onto the propped pillows. For one second—and I mean one *tiny* second—I pictured him in only his worn jeans, holding his guitar, playing a song.

My mouth went dry.

"You're annoying," I spat, sitting down on the bed, cross-legged, with my old, wood-barren guitar resting in my arms. It was more like I was annoyed with myself for noticing how brazenly attractive he was on the bed with his guitar, but whatever.

He smiled, showing off all his straight teeth, and I was certain, right then, that I'd died.

"Why don't you come out into the crowd for the shows?"

After reviving myself, I peeked up at Reid. I placed my fingers where I wanted them on my trusty, ten-year-old guitar and asked, "Like, out in the actual crowd? With the girls throwing their bras at you? No thanks."

"But it's so much better down there."

I laughed softly, pulling my hair to one side. "How do you know? You're up onstage playing."

He casually lifted a shoulder, putting his attention back on his guitar. He looked so relaxed in that moment, his unruly dark locks naturally falling over his forehead. His shoulders untensed, his arms looking as light as feathers. "You should try it next show. Go down into the crowd. Take the first row or something. I bet you'd like it more."

I thought for a moment, and then a devil-like grin slithered onto my face. "Who said I liked your show to begin with?"

Reid shook his head, but I could see the small smile creep on his face, even if he was trying to hide it.

Before he could say anything equally as snarky, I said, "If you come up with a tune tonight, I'll do it at tomorrow's show."

He flicked his eyes up to mine almost instantly, the deep amber color glittering in the dim light. "Deal."

I nodded my head once before taking a deep breath and gulping. My gulp was loud, like an actual cartoon character gulping as Wile E. Coyote chased them, and then I slowly started to strum my fingers over the strings on my guitar. I could feel Reid watching me, no doubt judging me. The tune I was strumming was nothing special. My fingers moved over familiar strings, fiddling over an E chord, then a G, back to a B, and so on. I wasn't creating an actual line of music, just showing him that I, too, could play a little bit so that maybe he'd shut up and start working on his own tunes.

"There. Now quit being a baby and start working on some stuff. I'll write the notes down as you go."

Reid grimaced at me, and I grimaced right back. We did this often: had stare-offs. We would lock eyes and almost speak to one another without actually saying anything, like we were at an impasse, just staring at each other in our own world, wondering which one of us would break first. He was used to getting his way, and I could see why; his looks demanded attention and appraisal. He was intimidating, to say the least. I knew he wanted me to look away first, but I never did, and I could tell that puzzled him.

"So bossy," he mumbled before running those talented fingers along the guitar.

What would it be like for him to touch me like that? With such grace and passion?

I sucked in air loudly. So loud that Reid's attention was taken away from the task at hand. "What?" he asked.

My face was blazing as hot as a flaming Cheeto. "Um…" I started. "I… I have to pee." *Lie.* "I'll be right back!"

I all but ran into the bathroom, glowering at myself in the mirror. My auburn hair was messy, falling all around my flushed face. My green eyes were shining brighter than I'd ever seen before. I smashed my lips together in disgust. *Stop letting his looks affect you!*

I whispered to myself, "He's just a normal guy playing guitar. Stop being so stupid." Okay, yes, watching Reid's hand glide up and over his guitar gave me actual goosebumps, but I'd been around other guitar players before. *But Reid King makes your stomach drop with one, teeny-tiny lift of his lip, and no one you've ever met can command an entire arena of people with just a single flick of a finger on a string.* My face flamed even warmer as I remembered the way he looked at me in the shower the other night, the way his hands felt around my body. *Holy shit, stop!*

I hurriedly turned the small nozzle on the sink to the right and splashed some water on my face. I took a few deep breaths before drying my cheeks and returning to the bedroom. As soon as I shut the door behind me, I paused, my feet glued to the floor like feathers glued to a boa.

My eyes were on Reid and only Reid. His head was bent down low, his eyes closed as his fingers moved effortlessly over each string on the wooden instrument. His strong jaw looked as if it could actually cut me; the ripples of muscles along his forearm were teetering back and forth. My heart stuttered in my chest. Reid King was attractive, but what I was watching was so much more than just an attractive man playing a guitar. It was like I could see inside him. I could see the beautiful harmony of how his heart beat for his music. I could see all the emotion that he'd been keeping at bay pour out of him and into that piece of equipment.

Reid King was the music, and the music was Reid King—they were one.

And I was totally, one hundred and fifty percent, enthralled by it.

———

My heart was fluttering in my chest, nerves causing me to bounce on my two feet. I was uncomfortable, but I never backed down from a deal, so there I was, standing in the third row of Reid King's show, surrounded by drunk women and rowdy men. I'd promised Reid I would watch his show from down below if he strung a few notes together on his guitar and got a melody going, and that was exactly what he did last night. So, yeah, there I was.

My head flicked upward as the lights dimmed. I watched as Reid's bandmates came onto the stage, Finn holding up his drumsticks as a simple gesture to the crowd. They all went crazy, screaming, jumping up and down on their feet, bumping into me every so often. Anxiety clawed at my very skull. *If they go this crazy over the band, how will it be when Reid walks out onstage?* I could always hear the crowd when I'd been backstage, watching him work his guitar and sing with soulful rasp in his voice from the side. But now that I was down here, I was a little on edge.

I wasn't only anxious, but excited, too. I was feeling all sorts of emotion. The first show I went to, I was excited to hear his music, to hear Reid sing live for the first time. But this time, I was excited because I knew that Reid being onstage meant that he was happy. Maybe even the only time he was truly content was onstage, and for some reason, that made me feel lighter, happier.

I sucked in a breath as the crowd grew silent and the familiar tune of his number one hit, "Loving Her," began playing. The strum of the guitar mixed with the beat of the drum meant that Reid was onstage, but the lights were so dim now that you could only see shadows and dark figures.

It didn't matter, though.

I knew what he looked like when he truly got into a song, the way his body went tense but somehow his arms would appear relaxed as he held onto the guitar. It was almost as if it were an actual limb of his. I knew the exact cut of his locked jaw, the way his brown locks bounced with the nod of his head. He truly got swallowed by the melody of each song, and in turn, it swallowed everyone around him, too.

A tiny smile found its way onto my mouth when the spotlight shined brightly onto Reid's figure at the same time his voice sounded around the arena. It was strange, really—the *entire* arena roared with love for Reid King. It should have been loud and caused me to cover my ears, but it was silent where I was standing. The only thing I could hear was Reid and his voice that seemed to float in every cell of my body. The only thing I could see was *him*. My eyes followed him around the stage, catching his eye and a small sliver of a smile when he'd lock onto me. It was a subtle acknowledgement; no one else would have noticed—definitely not with the alcohol swishing in their systems—but it sent a spark of light into my chest every single time. I was absorbed in all things Reid King. My hips even began swaying at one point. Reid was right; being down below the stage was so much better than being backstage. I was completely engrossed and gripped by the show he put on, by the music that was pouring out of his soul, and that was probably why I didn't notice the commotion going on behind me.

I knew it was Reid's last song, and even though we'd all been standing and watching in awe for hours, I didn't grasp it. It was like Reid King sucked me into his music to the point that I hadn't realized any time had passed.

Something took my attention away from the last chorus of "Knowing You," and I angled my head over my shoulder. I caught the eye of a teenaged girl sporting a tight miniskirt and a crop top, standing very closely to her group of friends—who were all also wearing miniskirts. When she looked at me, her eyes widened beyond belief. It worried me, so I scrunched my brow and yelled, "Are you okay?"

"Watch out!" she shouted, and that was when I felt a push.

I gasped and stumbled forward, hitting my stomach off the metal bars that were blocking the front seats from the back. "What the—"

All the words were stolen from my mouth as I was slammed onto the harsh concrete ground. I couldn't breathe. My chest wheezed for air as I blinked rapidly, watching two grown men from above punch one another brutally.

I wanted to move. I *needed* to move, but I couldn't. I was trapped in a WWE match, pinned to the ground with a man straddling my body to get to his opponent. Then I winced and rolled to my side at the same time he stepped right onto my left side—the side that held my only working kidney.

Oh shit.

My heart sank as I tried to cover my head, afraid that I would get hurt again, but then I unexpectedly felt a strong grip on my arms and was thrust upward. My breathing was labored, my eyes trying so desperately to lock onto something familiar, but everything was blurry. It wasn't until I was safe from the crowd that I realized Reid was carrying me so fast I was likely to have windburn.

I hadn't even realized the music had stopped playing.

The only thing I was focused on was not getting stepped on and getting the hell out of the way.

"Brooklyn, look at me. Are you okay?"

I blinked the moisture away from my eyes as I was carried farther into the darkness behind the stage. My arms were wrapped around Reid's neck, his sweat coating my fingers. I finally focused on his eyes, but their golden color that usually glittered was dark and intense. "Brooklyn, where are you hurt?"

I croaked, barely able to string words together. "I… I'm fine." But I knew I needed to get my side checked. The transplant was over a year ago, and I was in the clear with a clean bill of health, but it was still important for me to protect my only working kidney, considering it was doing the work of two kidneys.

"You're not fine," he blurted. "You were just trampled on. Where are you hurt?"

I shook my head. "Reid, really. I'm okay. It just knocked the wind out of me."

Reid stared down at me with a disapproving scowl on his face. I felt like a baby bird in his strong arms; I was as light as a feather to him. He continued to carry me through the long hallway, my side aching just slightly.

"I've got the doc coming right now," Rod yelled from behind. Reid didn't even look back or acknowledge him. He just kept carrying me down the hall.

"What happened to the show?" I asked, my voice still a little breathy from the fall.

"It ended."

I wanted to roll my eyes and say something like, "No shit, Sherlock," but then I heard footsteps from behind. Reid swung me around gently to his door, and that was when I spotted Jackson, followed by Finn. They looked just as sweaty and red-faced as Reid.

"Holy shit, man! I've never seen you move that fast. Like… ever," Jackson shouted, almost wheezing. I wanted to laugh, because his flushed cheeks literally matched the color of his hair.

"Is she okay?" he asked, looking down at me when he reached us.

At the exact same time, I said yes, and Reid said no.

Finn snorted from behind.

"I'm *fine*," I repeated, still in complete shock that I was in Reid's arms.

"Brooklyn, you should have seen him. He looked like Superman!"

Reid pushed through the door of his dressing room, took me directly over to the couch, and sat down with me still on his lap. I went to crawl off, but his grip tightened on me. "Stop moving," he demanded.

"Reid! I'm fine!" I reiterated for what felt like the tenth time. I quickly unwrapped my arms from around his neck and looked away, unable to meet his eye.

Just then, the door to the room flew open, and Rod, who was completely out of breath, walked in with a woman right behind him. "Let's take a quick look at you," she assured as soon as her eyes found me.

I went to move off Reid's lap again, but just like before, his strong arms grew tense, and I stayed put. I growled, but at the same time, a little piece of my heart softened.

"You're not going anywhere until she checks you," he said, voice rough.

The room grew silent as I peered up at him. *Could it be? Did Reid King really have a heart?*

I smirked. "Careful now, Reid. People might actually start to think we're friends or something."

I heard a chuckle from one of the bandmates, but Rod swooped in and took Reid's attention off me. "Let the doctor check her out, and you come with me."

"I'm not leaving until I know she's fine," Reid snapped before looking at the raven-haired doctor.

"Reid," Rod said, sighing. "Carissa's on the phone. She's been calling every hour. It's...*important.*"

I felt Reid's body twitch underneath mine. His entire body turned to stone—his arms, his legs. In fact, I think even his chest stopped expanding. *What's important?* My mind instantly went back to that first day I heard him in his dressing room, throwing things and talking about lawyers to someone on the phone.

"Reid, I swear I'm okay," I said, grabbing his still sweaty

jaw and angling it toward my face. The second my hand touched his skin, it felt like I'd been electrocuted. I hastily pulled it back and looked down at my lap. Reid let out a loud, annoyed breath, the warmth of it hitting my own skin, and then he finally released his arms.

I swung my legs, hiding a wince from the pain in my side, and moved over so he could get out from underneath me. I watched his lean body as he stormed out of the room, Rod hot on his heels.

Jackson and Finn exited the room shortly after, leaving the doctor and me alone.

The doctor reached over and grabbed her stethoscope, her pinned, black hair glossing under the dressing room lights. "Does it hurt anywhere? You took quite a fall." She reached over, ready to listen to my chest.

"I think the wind got knocked out of me, but I'm pretty sure I'm okay."

The doctor paused, listening intently, and then nodded. "Are you sure? I'd like to check over everything, because if not, Mr. King will probably get angry."

I laughed. "Mr. King? That sounds so... professional to me."

She laughed, too. "We can't all be on a friend basis with him like you, lucky one."

I pulled back, my expression a clear indication of my denial. "I'm not friends with him. We're just... colleagues?" *What were Reid and I?*

"Yeah, well, I've never seen someone dive off a stage to save their colleague. Some of my co-workers would turn the other way and then address my wounds later as some extra practice."

He dove off the stage?

The thought was ripped away as I sucked in air when the doctor pressed on my left side. She slowly lifted my flannel shirt up and then snapped her mascara-laden eyes up to mine. "You've had a nephrectomy."

I nodded curtly. "I'm fine."

"You donated to someone?"

I swallowed before answering. "My sister."

"Does it hurt right here?" She pressed her cool fingers to my side, moving right along where I knew my only kidney rested.

"Not really. It hurts a little lower—probably where the guy accidently stepped on me."

The doctor continued to press along my skin, waiting for a reaction of some sort. Then she ran her cool fingers over to my tiny scars and raised her eyebrows. "Whoever did your surgery, did a great job on the stitching."

I nodded my head and smiled, but worry was eating away at me. "You think it's okay?"

She slowly pulled my shirt down and smiled warmly. "I don't think you have anything to worry about. I think you're right; you're just sore from where he accidently stepped on you, and you'll likely bruise, *but* if you have any unusual symptoms in the next few weeks, you need to get it checked out immediately."

"What kind of symptoms?" I asked, sitting up a little further and adjusting my shirt.

She blew air out of her mouth as she packed up her things. "Any severe pain, lethargy, extreme nausea, or throwing up—anything like that. Are you still on supplements?"

I shook my head no, and she grimaced.

"I have a feeling that Reid is going to want you to get checked out even further at the hospital, just to make sure the injury didn't affect the kidney. To make sure things are still working as they should."

I quickly shouted, "No! I'm fine."

Her face was stern. "He's going to insist."

My body felt hot. "Please... don't tell him."

She furrowed her brow. "Why?" Then she took a step back, eyeing me. "He doesn't know?"

I rolled my eyes as I stood. "I told you, we're not friends, and he doesn't really know much about me, and to be honest, I'd like to keep it that way. Plus, I…" I swallowed, feeling embarrassed. "I really can't afford to go to the hospital to get more tests. I feel fine."

Her azure eyes softened. "I'm sure Reid will pay…"

My eyes grew wide. "Absolutely not!" I'd rather chew my arm off than have him pay for me. "You can't tell him!" I all but yelled. "Doctor's confidentiality and all that."

The doctor's mouth split into two, then she shook her head gently. "Fine, I won't tell him, but please, if you have any issues, any pain… any of the symptoms that I listed…" She reached into her bag and pulled out a small card. "Call me, okay? I can check on you during the next show, but in the future, feel free to call me, okay?"

I smiled. "Thank you, I… I really appreciate it."

"Of course, *not friend* of Reid King."

Then she turned on her heel and walked out the door.

Reid King and me, friends?

No way.

I bit the inside of my cheek.

But why did Reid King caring about me, even just for a millisecond, make my heart skip a beat?

CHAPTER THIRTEEN

REID

Rod was right. As was Carissa.

After last night's stunt, I would be the center of every single entertainment magazine, article, show, etc.

I got it. I jumped off the stage in the middle of my last set and grabbed Brooklyn off the ground for many, many eyes to see. But she was a helpless woman getting stepped on during my concert—what was I supposed to do? Leave her there? Keep singing?

I audibly groaned, rubbing my hand over my face feebly. I knew that if it were anyone else, some random fan, I would have stayed onstage and let security handle it, because that was what I was supposed to do, but it wasn't just some random fan—although some of the articles were saying it was.

They were calling me a knight in shining armor because I "saved" her. The video was on every single social media outlet, every single online blog, *everywhere*. There I was, Reid King, sweaty as hell in my faded flannel and black jeans, swan-diving off the stage and swooping a beautiful woman off the floor as security tackled the two men responsible for the fight, and then rushing her backstage before anyone jumped on my back.

It was reckless.

It was extremely stupid on my part, especially because I knew that there would be some people who thought Brooklyn wasn't just a fan, and that she was *more*.

More, as in my girlfriend or lover—which she was neither. We weren't anything other than two adults collaborating on music together.

Carissa mentioned that me being seen with another woman—even if it was Brooklyn—would help get Angelina out of the press. It would show the press that I'd moved on; therefore, Angelina and all the gossip regarding her would be long gone.

Maybe I should just move on.

I clenched my teeth so hard that Rod probably heard it all the way in the front of the bus. I knew I'd never get over it, not until I knew the truth. Not until I *faced* the truth. I was holding onto something, and yet, I had no clue what that something was.

I stared at my phone, ready to press play on the voicemail that I listened to like clockwork, ready to try and decipher it as if there would be some new clue as to what truly went wrong with Angelina. Maybe there would be something new that I hadn't heard before, giving me even just a slight glimpse of the truth, but then I heard Brooklyn's muffled voice outside my door.

"Oh my God. Will you stop?!"

Then I heard another voice, one that I didn't recognize.

"Please let me see him! I can't believe you hid this from us. Some teacher retreat? You little liar!" I cocked my head as I moved closer to the door. A tinier voice sounded. *"Wittle wire."*

Brooklyn laughed softly. Her laugh was like a slight breeze on a warm summer day, blowing over my skin at just the right time. The muscle caged inside my chest skipped a beat each time I heard it.

Brooklyn's hushed voice sounded again. "Stop teaching

my niece bad words. And I didn't tell you guys because you'd ask a million questions."

"How did this happen? How the heck are you on a tour bus with Reid King?" I had realized by then, after eavesdropping, that Brooklyn was talking to someone on the phone. "THE REID KING!"

My lips tugged upward. "Well…" Brooklyn started. "You know Jane's uncle? He thought I'd be a good fit for Reid, and… the pay is…."

The other woman's voice suddenly turned stern. "No." Then, who I was assuming was Brooklyn's niece repeated in her tiny voice, "No!" The other woman sounded again. "Don't even think about it."

Brooklyn, sounding innocent, asked, "Think about what?"

"I'm not taking the money, Brooklyn."

My brow furrowed.

"You won't have a choice."

"Brooklyn, no. You've given me enough! Can't you see that? Just lift up your shirt and look at those scars!" *What?* My mind instantly revisited the visual of Brooklyn, naked and glistening with water from her steaming shower the other day, my hands tingling as heat coated my body. She did have scars, though. I remembered quite vividly.

"La, la, la. I can't hear you," Brooklyn teased. "Oh! Look! There's Reid. Gotta go work on music stuff!"

"WAIT!" the woman shouted.

"What? Look, I gotta go. Seriously. He's, like, waving me down."

"Let me see him!! Please! Just flip the camera around really quick. You can be nonchalant. Then I'll let you do whatever you want with the money. Come on! I'm your only sister! Jack already knows I think Reid King is the hottest ever. Let me get a sneak peek. AH! I can't even believe you're with REID KING!"

Brooklyn stuttered, caught in her lie. "Uh… um."

I found myself laughing silently before I realized that I

was actually laughing. *When was the last time I actually laughed?*
Like a true laugh? Shaking my head, I pulled open the door
and met Brooklyn's startled look. Her face flushed instantly,
the color of it resembling the auburn color of her hair. She
stared at me, and I stared right back, my cheek lifting just
slightly. I put my hand out and ushered her to come closer
to me. She shook her head, so I leaped over to her and, with
one single snatch, grabbed the phone out of her hand.

"Hey," I said, looking into the phone, realizing that
Brooklyn was video-chatting her sister—who was an exact
replica of Brooklyn, except with darker hair.

Her sister screamed, "OH MY GOD!!" before dropping
the phone. Brooklyn laughed from beside me but quickly
grabbed the phone back.

"Sorry! That's all you get! Love you! Bye!" Then she
hung up.

When Brooklyn finally tore her eyes away from her
phone and looked at me, I raised an eyebrow. "So, who's
the bigger fan? You or your sister?"

Brooklyn scoffed. "You should know the answer to that.
Definitely my sister." I eyed her closely, knowing very well
that the blush creeping along her neck meant she was lying.

I scrutinized her, enjoying the fact that she fidgeted
under my stare. "I don't believe you. I think you're one of
those closet super fans."

She scoffed again, placing her hand over her heart. "I am
not a super fan! Ugh, if anything, I'm a lesser fan."

I leaned back onto the door, still grinning. "A lesser fan?
Please enlighten me."

She crossed her arms over her flowy, cream dress. "A
lesser fan is someone who may have been a super fan at one
point but, after meeting the real you, changed their mind."
A smile was hiding behind her lips. "After meeting the *real*
Reid King—the one who acts like a child most days with
those pouty scowls and temper tantrums—I changed my
mind."

I threw my head back with a loud laugh. "You're full of

shit, Teach."

"Ugh! Am not! You're not the nicest person—even if you did jump off a stage to rescue me."

I turned my head toward her and winked. "I'm a real-life Superman. How could you not be a super fan?"

Her cheeks instantly turned pink, but she quickly recovered and grimaced. "Ugh! Let's just get to work!"

I bit my lip to hide my grin as Brooklyn pushed past me, guitar in tow. I knew I was feeling a little lighter lately, and I also knew that it had nothing to do with me strumming a few tunes together and had everything to do with the person that continued to push me into doing so.

My chest grew tight as I walked through the door, trying to hold on to the thought of Angelina and my last phone call with Carissa. But it was funny how hearing Brooklyn's voice on the other side of my door caused me to break my nightly habit of listening to Angelina's voicemail.

I had to reel myself back in before the need for the truth escaped me all together.

———

"This sounds fucking stupid," I spat, pushing my guitar away.

Brooklyn sighed softly from beside me, her legs crossed at the ankle with a paper and pen in her hand. "Reid, it doesn't sound stupid. Just because you think it sounds stupid doesn't mean other people will."

I tore my eyes from her legs. "If I don't feel it, then it isn't good."

That was how I knew my music was good. I *felt* it. The words that had just tumbled out of my mouth were bogus; they were only words. There was no meaning behind them. None at all.

"Just because *you* don't feel something from what you just sang, doesn't mean *I* didn't."

I paused before pulling my guitar back over, my fingers

plucking over the strings with as much familiarity as a boxer putting on his boxing gloves. I played the same melody I'd been messing with for the past two nights with Brooklyn and closed my eyes, trying to tie in another line of words.

I kept playing the same harmony, but nothing else came. I was too caged up, too uncomfortable, my mind going in ten different directions, none of which were the right one.

I was about to throw my guitar across the room when my ears perked up.

My fingers still moved gracefully over the heart of my guitar as I heard one of the rawest and purest voices sing from beside me.

"We met in chaos, oh, sweet chaos.
I promised I wouldn't give in to you, even if just for a few."

Before I knew what was happening, my heart grew inside my chest. A warm vine started to wrap itself around the thing that beat so deeply inside the contents of my ribs. Something awakened inside of me.

My fingers stopped moving as I stared at Brooklyn, her eyes closed, her mouth opened with beautiful words pouring out. Her cheeks were a light pink with small pieces of her auburn hair framing the roundness of her face. She was beautiful before she sang, but now? Now she was stop-you-in-your-tracks stunning. The innocence that poured off of her, the silent beauty that seemed to surround her essence, the way she laid herself out there—her voice bare and *real*.

"Did that make you feel something?" I was snapped out of my trance when I realized that Brooklyn was talking to me.

I cleared my throat, removing my fingers from my guitar. *Did that make me feel something? Yeah, all the wrong fucking things.*

I shrugged, unable to produce words.

"Do you want to know what it made me feel?"

I slowly nodded, keeping my eyes trained to her eyes and

no place else.

"It made me nervous. That's what I was feeling when I sang. But it didn't make you nervous, did it?"

I swallowed roughly, as if I'd just gobbled down a handful of rusty nails. "It didn't make me nervous. No."

Brooklyn shifted beside me, adjusting her dress. "Exactly my point. Just because you feel something when you sing a certain verse or song, doesn't mean the rest of the world is feeling the exact same way. Words are words. It's all about how you react to them. Everyone is different; everyone feels things differently. The way you feel is justified by you, and you alone. Just like the way I feel is justified by me, and me alone. Stop worrying about what someone else is going to think of your music, and just do it."

Silence passed between us. There was commotion in the front of the bus, but it seemed like the second Brooklyn and I came back to this room and shut the door, it was just her and me. Nothing could penetrate the walls we were building.

Desperate for an escape out of the intimate conversation, I mumbled, "What are you? A Nike commercial?"

The apple of Brooklyn's cheek lifted, then she smacked my arm. I jolted away and couldn't help the smile crawling along my lips. "I hate you," she said through her own grin.

I smiled back at her, my eyes roaming over her raised arm ready to smack me again. Just then, Rod knocked on the door and opened it without hesitation. First, he looked at me, confusion flickering on his face. Then, he trailed his eyes over to Brooklyn who was on her knees with her arm over her head, seconds from hitting me. He cleared his throat as he tore his eyes away from the scene. I could read his expression clear as day. He was curious. He was curious about what we were doing back here and why the hell Brooklyn and I were smiling at each other.

I quickly wiped the happiness off my face.

"So, I have a feeling that you still haven't given Carissa a suggestion for tomorrow night."

I flicked an eyebrow up, confused. "For what?"

Rod shuffled on his feet, placing his hands on his hips. "Jamison's charity birthday? You know, the whole reason that Carissa kept calling you last night."

And just like that, my poor mood was back. I angled my head back and stared at the ceiling. *Fuck. How did I forget that?* Brooklyn—that was how.

"Can you get me out of it?"

Rod gave me a look. *The* look. The look your grandma gave you when you burped during Sunday dinner. "Reid, you haven't shown your face *anywhere* since…"

My jaw tightened as the lightness in the air was sucked out of the room. "You can say it. Since Angelina went off the deep-end. Yeah, I know."

Rod looked surprised when the words flew out of my mouth, and honestly, I was, too. I glanced over at Brooklyn, but she kept her face emotionless, almost appearing bored with the conversation.

"If you want the rumors to stop about Angelina, if you want her out of the press, you need to make an appearance, and you need to have someone on your arm so they'll stop. I don't usually like to agree with Carissa, but I do on this one. It's promo at its finest."

I groaned, knowing very well they were right. There were still some tabloids that continued to dig for information about Angelina. They liked to spread rumors and had tons of speculation, and her parents wanted her out of the spotlight. If I gave them this, if I somehow got the attention off of Angelina and her being tied to the hottest musician of today's time, maybe they'd be more likely to give me something in return, like—oh, I don't know—her location or maybe some fucking information regarding what the hell had happened.

"You're right. I need to go."

Rod made an odd sound with his throat while he stood

in the doorway, fidgeting like a child who needed to pee.

"What?" I asked, clearly annoyed.

"Well, who are you bringing?"

I drew a blank. Who could I take with me that wouldn't make it into more than it actually was? A giant promo stunt. I had no one in mind. I used to have girls on backup for things like this, just like Jackson and Finn, but then I had to go off and actually get a "girlfriend," so all my plus-ones were long gone.

"I have no one," I mumbled.

Brooklyn snickered, and I whipped my head over to her, raising an eyebrow. "Somethin' funny over there?"

She smashed her lips together and looked down at the notebook in her lap, hiding her attempt at smiling.

Rod clapped his hands together excitedly. "Perfect! Bring Brooklyn."

She and I both pulled back instantly.

"What?!" Brooklyn shot to her feet. "I'm not going to an event with him! I'm... I'm his music teacher!"

Rod ignored her and looked at me. "It'll be perfect. You know we can't find someone who isn't nuts over you or that'd draw *too* much attention to being your date in the amount of time we have."

He wasn't wrong, but something made me uneasy about the entire situation.

"So, what am I going to say when I introduce her at the event? That she's my music teacher because I can't write a fucking song?"

Brooklyn huffed. "You can write a song, Reid. Quit being so negative about it."

I glared at her and then turned to Rod. He was looking at me with raised eyebrows and so much hope in his eyes that I wanted to gouge them out.

"Fine," I finally said, my chest burning. I had no clue why the idea of taking Brooklyn as my date made me feel so edgy inside, but it did.

Brooklyn gasped dramatically, placing her hands on her

hips. "I can't go! I have plans."

I laughed out loud at her attempted lie. "You have plans? What plans?"

She pouted, pulling her hair to one side. "My friend Jane is meeting up with me tomorrow night."

Rod asked, "Who's Jane?"

I answered for Brooklyn. "Her friend that works at Teen Entertainment."

Rod looked apologetic, but he didn't budge. "Sorry, Brooklyn. We need you on this one."

Brooklyn looked over at me with a smidge of hopefulness in her eyes, like she wanted me to save her from Rod's suggestion. Part of me wanted to, because her puppy-dog look was enough to bring me to my knees, but then I thought about her with her friend Jane at some club in Atlanta, and my entire body burned with a raging dose of jealousy.

"I think it's a great idea, Rod. I'll bring Brooklyn."

She squealed, "No!"

"Finally, you agree with me on something!" Rod exclaimed, throwing his hands up.

Brooklyn looked like she wanted to either punch me or cry—maybe even both at the same time—so I hurriedly blurted, "If you go with me, I'll write a song. It may be shitty, but I'll put actual pen on paper and write a fucking song. For *you*."

Brooklyn's eyes shifted to me, the fire inside of them still there, but I could see the embers dying down. She bit her lip, hands still placed on her hips. "I have nothing to wear."

I rolled my eyes and looked at Rod. "Have Carissa send a dress to the hotel for Brooklyn."

His cheeks rounded as he nodded. He turned on his heel but not before looking back at Brooklyn and giving her an encouraging nod. "Glad to see you two are working well together. Vinny will be pleased."

As soon as he was gone, Brooklyn reached over and threw the pen and paper at me from beside the bed. "Now write."

"I will…" I said, pulling my guitar lazily back onto my lap. "After tomorrow."

She huffed. "What? Do you think I'm going to back out of this ridiculous thing if you give me a song right now?"

"I can't place all my eggs in one basket, Brooklyn. I have to play my cards right."

Her tiny shoulders tensed by her ears. "Ugh, I really do hate you!"

I cocked a smile. "You wish."

And I really wished I hated her, too.

CHAPTER FOURTEEN

BROOKLYN

Ridiculous. It was absolutely preposterous that I had to go to a freaking birthday party with Reid. And not just any birthday party—an exclusive, invite-only, birthday/charity party. The only good thing was that it was for charity. There were going to be tons of famous people there, and here I was, a total nobody, and I had to go.

I was nervous. Okay? There, I said it. I was a Nervous Nelly. The only thing that kept me going most days was that catchy commercial playing in the back of my head that sang, *"Money, money, moneeeyyy,"* advertising one of those quick-and-easy loans that were like 80,000% interest. I couldn't very well use one of those to help my sister and parents pay off their debt and save them from the never-ending medical bills. So, I took a deep breath, reminded myself of just that, and stared at myself in the mirror.

The dress Carissa had delivered to my extravagant hotel room had to have been equal to three months of my rent payment. It was a short, sleek, black cocktail dress, hitting right about mid-thigh. Tiny straps held up the low-dipping V-neck and crisscrossed in the back, leaving my exposed skin for all to see. Thankfully, you could barely see the nasty, yellowing bruise from my fall the other night. You could really only see it when I turned a certain way and the dress dipped down slightly.

The dress was sexy. I, however, was not. I felt like it looked like I was trying too hard to be someone I wasn't. And then, of course, the thought of Reid kept filtering through my head. *What will Reid think when he sees me in this?* My face burned when I found myself spraying some fancy spray from the hotel into my straightened hair to make it appear sleek and glossy, all because I wanted Reid to think it looked good. I almost rewashed my hair because the thought made me so agitated. I shouldn't have cared what Reid thought of my hair. I was supposed to be angry with him. *Ugh.* I couldn't believe he agreed with Rod that I should attend this stupid party with him instead of hanging out with my very best friend who I hadn't seen since I signed the stupid contract to work with him in the first place. The nerve! I had a ton to tell her, and it was stuff that you couldn't just say over a text message. For example: "Oh, hey, Jane. Reid saw me naked. Ttyl." That would not work.

Just as I was strapping my black heel to my ankle, cursing my side for still hurting, there was a soft knock on my door. My heart stopped when I looked at it, wondering if it was Reid. *Oh my God, stop it!*

I took a hefty breath, cracking my neck a few times, and then walked over to the door and swung it open. I was ready to fix a glare to my face because I was just certain it was Reid, but I was met with Rod's face instead.

"Oh, hi," I said, my voice sounding pathetic. *I wasn't disappointed that it wasn't Reid, no way.*

"Hey, Brooklyn," he said as he walked farther into my room.

I actually liked Rod. Reid seemed annoyed with him nine times out of ten, but he was honestly a nice man, always making sure I had what I needed and making sure I was okay. The only thing that bothered me about him was that he was constantly asking me for an update on Reid, but that was probably because Carissa and the record label were breathing down his neck.

The record label wanted an update—or at least a small snippet of a song—like... yesterday, so I kind of understood.

Shutting the door behind him, but not without glancing down toward Reid's door, I asked, "What's going on?"

"Please tell me you and Reid have *something*."

I ran my fingers down my silky hair, smoothing it out yet again. "Something as in... a song?"

He exhaled tiredly. "Yes."

"Is the record label getting a little antsy?"

"A little?!" he all but shouted. "They won't lay off, and they're concerned you're not doing what you were hired to do."

I went to stand up for myself, but Rod held up a hand.

"Trust me, Brooklyn. I know you're doing everything you can. I like the way you are with him, and I like the way he is with you. I see a huge difference in him. Sure, he might not be back to writing chart toppers yet, but I see a difference in him. He's lighter, smiling, laughing. You're breaking down his walls one by one, and the sooner he pops his head through the debris, the sooner he'll be back on track."

Relief sagged in my shoulders. "So they're not firing me?"

Rod looked at me softly, the tired lines on his forehead evening out. "No... I've definitely talked you up a good bit, but you've gotta give me something to get them off my back. Otherwise, they're gonna be speaking directly to Reid, and you and I both know he doesn't like being told what to do."

I snorted. "Yeah, I know. He's a bit of a brat."

Rod laughed, but his relaxed face turned serious again. His back was as straight as a steel rod. "Do you have anything?"

It only took me half a second to panic. Reid crumpled

up every bit of work he did yesterday. He'd snatch the pen and paper out of my hand, scribble something down, and then play the same chords again, trying his hardest to get into the jive of the words he'd written and the tune he was playing. But then, he'd get frustrated, crumple up the paper, and throw the wad across the room.

Those pieces of paper were long gone now.

I let out a heavy breath, nerves eating away at my stomach, and walked over to my bag. I pulled out my torn and ratty notebook, the one that I'd had for years and years, and I hurriedly wrote down the same words I'd bravely sung in front of Reid yesterday.

We met in chaos, oh, sweet chaos.
I promised I wouldn't give in to you, even if just for a few.

Oh, sweet chaos.
I gave into you, for more than just a few.
Oh, sweet chaos.
I was consumed, and you were too.

"Here," I said, thrusting the piece of paper into Rod's hands. "Tell them this is a work in progress. We're adding more to the beginning verse and working on the melody that goes along with it."

Rod eagerly took the paper and held it to his chest as he looked up to the ceiling as if it were a gift from God. *Nope, just a gift from me.*

I held my breath as his hands wrapped around the torn sheet, his eyes scanning the words I'd written down. Then, his mouth drew upward, and he smiled. "This is perfect. Sounds like a typical Reid King song—raw, unforgiving, a bit depressing."

I laughed, feeling a little relieved that Rod bought it. Rod thought the words I'd come up with in my own head were actually words from Reid King. *Wow.*

I just hoped that Reid would be as thankful as Rod was.

"Thank you, Brooklyn," Rod said before turning on his heel and walking back to the door. He looked over his shoulder with a glimmer in his eye. "I'm glad you're on tour with us. I wasn't certain it was a good idea at first, but it was. You're going to be the one to get him back on track."

"How do you know?" I asked as his hand turned the knob.

He cocked a smile my way. "Because he's starting to care again."

Then he walked out and left me standing there, confused as ever.

Reid was starting to care about what? Writing? Music? Life? *Me?* Certainly not the last one. That was as farfetched as it got—*Mr. Let Me Piss Brooklyn Off And Drag Her To A Stupid Party.*

I wrung my hands out a few times before looking back in the mirror. I was getting jumpy. I grew more nervous as time passed. *Hurry the hell up, Reid!* I wanted this night to be over as soon as possible. I snatched my phone and reread Jane's last text message, which was more of a pump-me-up kind of message, because I may have freaked out about going to the party.

Jane: Relax, Brooklyn. Yes, there will be plenty of famous people there, but just breathe. People love you from the moment they first meet you. Just pretend they're normal people. You should be seasoned at being around famous people by now anyway. I mean, you have been on a bus with Reid King for a few weeks and you seem to be doing okay. Just have a drink when you get there. One drink won't hurt you. Plus, I have a BIG feeling you'll be just fine. ;)

I texted back and asked how on earth she knew I'd be fine, and I wanted to know what was up with the winky-face emoji, but she never responded. I threw my phone into my black clutch and held it with a tight grip.

Just then, another knock sounded on my door. *Finally! He probably took his sweet time because he knew I'd be in here stressing out!*

I hurriedly walked over to the door, my heels clicking on the floor with pure rage. I swung the door open, huffing and puffing. Then my mouth fell open, and I gasped.

"What—what?"

Jane's bright-blue eyes widened, and then she whistled. "Damnnnnn, you look hot!"

I was stunned. My mouth continued to open and close, and then she snapped her fingers in my face. "Breathe, Brooklyn!"

"Ahhh!!!!" I screamed, throwing my arms around her neck right there in the doorway. "What the hell are you doing here?!"

Jane squeezed me tightly, and if it didn't bother my side so badly, I would have hugged her for much longer. When I pulled back, I held her by the shoulders. I ran my eyes down her sparkly emerald cocktail dress and cocked my head to the side. "Are you coming to the charity party?"

She smiled connivingly. "Yep! Surprise!" I smashed my lips together, because if I were to have smiled any wider, my lips would likely fall off.

"How?" I asked, shaking my head in disbelief. "I thought it was an all-exclusive, invite-only, no-press-unless-specifically-invited event.

Jane raised an eyebrow. "I was invited."

"What?" I asked, finally removing my hands from her shoulders. "By who?"

Jane narrowed her eyes at me, the shimmer of her eyeshadow catching the lights above her head. "Reid King called me up personally and asked me to come tonight so I could spend time with you. He mentioned something about being the reason you had to cancel, and he wanted to surprise you."

My brow furrowed. *Wh...what?*

"Yeah, that means you"—Jane pushed through the

threshold and stomped into my room before turning around and giving me a look—"have a lot of explaining to do, little missy."

I swore I started to sweat. I wasn't sure if it was from the twenty questions that Jane was about to throw my way regarding Reid, or if it was because my heart exploded in my chest at the fact that Reid went and invited Jane to surprise me. *Why did that mean so much to me?*

I held my breath and peeked out into the hallway. Before closing the door, I looked down both ends of the hallway, and that was when I found Reid, leaning against the wall in his all-black suit, looking like he'd just stepped out of a fancy photoshoot. My mouth went dry looking at his hands tucked into his pants pockets. He angled that straight jaw my way and captured me in a stare so deep that I was completely lost. His lip tugged upward just a bit, and butterflies flew in my stomach.

"Get in here and spill!" Jane shouted from behind, causing me to jump. I hurriedly stepped back into the room and slammed the door behind me.

I openly gulped for more than one reason.

One, I had to tell Jane that I was completely smothered by all things Reid King.

And two, I had to tell myself that, too.

How the hell was I going to make it out alive?

———

"Okay, so, he's pretty freaking hot in person," Jane whispered from beside me.

We were all in the Escalade, Reid driving, Finn up front, and then Jane and I in the middle seats with a lonely Jackson in the back seat. There was another Escalade behind us which held the security for Reid and the band, but other than that, we were all free tonight.

It felt weird not being cooped up on a tour bus with the guys, beating their asses in rummy or being shunned back into a small room with Reid, working on songs—aka, watching him with a grumpy expression plastered to his face as he tried to work with me.

"Who? Reid?" I whispered back, glancing up in the rearview mirror to see Reid's intimidating gaze and locked jaw as he glared at Atlanta traffic like it was hell itself.

"No!" she hissed. "Well, yes, but I meant my date."

I cocked a grin, but Jackson stuffed his face in between ours. "I heard he has chlamydia, so I'd stay away from him. I hear the guitarist of the band is the hottest."

Throwing my head back onto the headrest, I cracked up.

Finn angled his head over his shoulder and asked what was so funny.

I smashed my lips together as Jackson piped up. "Oh, I just caught these two talking about how hot you are… You might have had a chance with blondie here, but I went ahead and told her your secret."

Looking out the window, I kept my mouth shut, hiding a grin.

"What secret?"

Jane, being the extrovert that she is, blurted, "Oh, just that you have chlamydia."

Finn smacked the dashboard, running his hands through his short hair. "I do not!"

My shoulders were shaking with unshed laughter. Jane was openly laughing out loud with Jackson, and when I brought my attention to the rearview mirror, I caught Reid staring at me. Once he saw that he had my eye, he tilted his head and squinted. I wanted to ask him why he was looking at me like that, but he quickly shuffled his gaze to the traffic.

"So, where's your date?" I asked, turning to look at Jackson who was casually sitting in a dark-blue suit with his one leg looped over his other.

Jackson sighed dramatically, running his hand through his tawny beard. Before he could answer, Finn piped up from the front seat. "He can't get a date."

I giggled and looked at Reid who had a ghost of a smile

playing along his lips. As soon as he made eye contact with me, he jerked his attention elsewhere and replaced that smile with his typical, brooding scowl. My brow furrowed, and I stared at downtown Atlanta out the window as Jane and the guys talked about all things music related.

Before long, we arrived at the venue, and the longer I sat in silence, wondering why Reid kept eyeing me so strangely, the more my nerves spiked like iron spears on a warrior's helmet. Feeling out of place wasn't exactly new to me, but this was taking it to a whole new level, even if my best friend was with me. I was the date of Reid King, kind of. I wasn't really his "date," but more like his occupant. When we'd all gathered to climb into the Escalade, he barely even looked in my direction.

But it was fine; it wasn't like I was hoping for a fairytale entrance where Reid took one look at me with my sexy cocktail dress and had to fan himself. He was only doing this to get his ex out of the spotlight, and I was doing this for a big, fat paycheck. *So take that, feelings!*

"Are ya ready?" Reid asked, cocking his head over his shoulder before he gave the valet his keys.

Jane's brow furrowed. "How are there, like, only three presses here?"

Finn answered, "It's Jamison Bayne's birthday party. *Jamison. Bayne.* Come on. Whatever press he wanted was what he'd get."

Jane seemed pleased with the answer, whereas I had no idea who Jamison Bayne was. She unclicked her seatbelt and smiled. "Alrighty, then. Tonight, I'm off the clock. Tonight, I'll just be the date of Finn, the drummer of the infamous Reid King."

Finn winked at her and I chuckled, turning my head once again.

My head snapped over to the driver's side when I heard Reid ask, "Are you ready, Brooklyn?"

"Does it matter?" I shot back.

Reid narrowed his gaze once again and then shook out

his dark locks as he climbed out of the vehicle. I opened my door and hopped out on my own, annoyed that Reid was treating me so oddly. As soon as my heels clicked on the pavement, I took one step forward and ran straight into Reid's firm chest, banging my face off what I assumed were his pecs. *God, why is this so awkward?* Why were we so comfortable with one another in the privacy of the tour bus, or in a lonely hotel room, working on music, yet the second we were thrust into something like this, we both became different people? I was acting like an idiot and walking on unstable legs, and he was acting like we were nothing more than simple acquaintances—not even that; it was like we were strangers. Was he embarrassed that he actually had a heart for once and did something kind, like surprising me with Jane? Was he regretting being nice?

I puffed air out of my cheeks as I brought my eyes upward, zooming in on Reid's defined Adam's apple and his cut jaw. My heart simmered between my ribcage, and sweat started to break out along my cleavage. I tore my eyes away from him and his sexy, all-black suit which just so happened to bring out the shimmering gold specks of his eyes like the very stars above our heads.

Okay, note to self: Reid King was handsome in a suit—even with that grimace on his face.

"You ready?" he asked again, sounding almost bored. He wouldn't meet my eye for more than a few seconds, which only put a spark in my fire that was slowly burning.

I nodded curtly, my nerves washed away by the irritation I felt being near a *different* Reid.

Glancing above my head quickly before being ushered inside by the group, a few flashes of the press's cameras momentarily blinding me as I gripped onto Reid's arm, I realized we were at a fancy-looking club. The glowing neon lights shone above the entrance as I walked through. It took my eyes a few minutes to adjust, but inside seemed just like any other club I'd been to in New York—lights streaming in every other direction, a lavish bar in the distance. The only difference between the clubs back home and this one was the fact that this one had *a lot* of space and it wasn't crammed like usual.

"Why isn't it busy in here?" I asked Finn who was walking beside me with Jane hanging off his arm.

He smirked. "Because Jamison bought the place out for the night. It's an exclusive birthday party held at one of the finest clubs in the United States."

I whispered, feeling stupid. "And who is Jamison? And how is this a charity? It looks pretty birthday party-ish to me."

Reid snorted from beside me, and I almost took my heel to his shoe.

Jackson grinned. "He's asked everyone who got an invite to donate to the charity, and you ever hear of Jami's Band?"

I snapped my head up. "Jamison is… *that* Jami?!"

He threw his head back and cackled. "You're adorable."

"She's hot, not adorable," Jane said, winking at me.

I rolled my eyes as we continued to walk through the club. Reid found a cozy, secluded spot near the back, and I was thankful because I was too stressed to run into anyone famous. I briefly saw Dax Thatcher, one of the oldest rockers that I could remember, being cool in all his glory, and then I saw Chase Brooks give Reid a nod of his head. That was enough famous people for me.

The second I slid into the booth after the rest of the group, Reid stood up and *finally* looked down into my eyes. They lingered there for a few beats before he sighed and asked, "What do you want to drink?"

"Just a water."

"A water?" Jackson asked, dumbfounded.

"Yeah…"

"Why?"

Reid spoke up for me. "Because that's what she wants."

I ignored him, looking over at Jackson. "I don't drink much."

Jackson chortled. "Oh, God. You two are the perfect

match, then. Reid doesn't drink either."

I couldn't help the next words that flew out of my mouth. "Oh, that's right, and when he does drink, he pukes on all of his fans."

I sucked in all the air I could after I said it. Reid's stare bored into mine, and then I saw the slight flicker of his mouth. Jackson and Finn were both losing it beside me, and Jane's eyes were so wide I could see every inch of white that surrounded her pupil. She mouthed, *Oh my God*, and then silently laughed. I looked back at Reid, waiting for that snarky smile to reappear.

Before he had the chance to smile, though, someone came up from behind him.

"If it isn't my brotha from anotha motha!"

Reid turned around quickly, just in time for Jamison Bayne, last decade's most successful guitar player, to wrap his arms around him. I couldn't believe that Reid was friends with Jamison Bayne. In fact, I couldn't believe that Reid had friends at all.

I saw the slight smile on Reid's face as he pulled back and looked up at Jami's face. Jami was recognizable, even to someone like me who didn't pay too much attention to the previous decade's musicians. But not knowing Jami Bayne was a sin. He was all my parents listened to when I was growing up. He had long, straight, hay-colored hair pushed back behind both of his ears. He was dressed similarly to Reid, in all black, except Jami's shirt was unbuttoned in the front, showing some of his sun-kissed, albeit wrinkly, skin.

"I wasn't sure if you'd make it," Jami said to Reid.

Reid sighed and adjusted the buttons on his cuffs. "Anyone else's birthday? I would have missed. But yours? I couldn't do that to you."

Jami cocked a smile. "How ya been since…"

Reid shifted on his feet, looking uneasy. I thought Jackson and Finn got the hint as they slid out of the booth, pulling Jane with them. She glanced back at me, and I shook my head, letting her know I'd be fine waiting with Reid. I was his date, after all, right?

So I stayed in the booth, with my hands in my lap, feeling as stupid as a turtle participating in a race. *Should I stay or should I go?*

"Who's this?" Jami asked, peeking around Reid's body. "Is this… your date?!"

"No… well…" Reid looked uncomfortable as he moved his gaze back to Jami. I gulped and shifted uncomfortably in my seat with my red-stained lips clamped together.

"She technically is, but just for press. You know how it is."

Jami threw his head back and laughed. "Ah, yes. The dreadful marketing tactics…" Then he peered around Reid once more, his icy-blue eyes landing on mine. "Well, are you going to introduce us, or…?"

I grinned as I slid out of the booth. I was pretending I wasn't as nervous as I really was, because, don't get me wrong, I was practically sweating. But after meeting Reid and being crammed in a bus with him looking all cool and *hot* with his guitar every night, I was happy to say that my stress levels had become more manageable.

"Hi, I'm Brooklyn," I said, sticking my hand out to shake Jami's.

Jami's eyes twinkled with mischief as he took my hand and shook it gently. Then he pulled me in a little closer and brought it up to his mouth, his warm lips kissing it tenderly. I blushed, looking away, but that was when Reid cleared his throat.

Jami, still holding onto my hand, lazily brought his head over to Reid. His lips turned upward, and Reid raised an eyebrow. "Just as I thought."

Jami let go of my hand when Reid asked, "What?"

"Oh, *nothing*." Then he turned and winked at me before whispering something into Reid's ear.

Reid shook his head and gave him a cryptic look.

Then, Jami turned to me once more and said, "It was very nice to meet you, Brooklyn. I'm sure I'll see you again at some point."

I smiled, and then he turned on his heel.

"Happy birthday!" I shouted, and he turned around and nodded with a sly smile on his face.

Reid looked over at me, our eyes locking for far too long. "What?" I finally asked, feeling self-conscious. *Did I make a fool out of myself?*

"Noth— Nothing," he mumbled before scooting back into the booth.

"What about my water?" I asked, placing my hands on my hips. Reid's eyes followed my every move. I growled when he didn't answer. "Fine, I'll go get it myself. I see Jane and the guys over there, anyway. I'd ask what you want, but you're being rude."

As soon as I turned on my heel, Reid's warm palm rounded around my bicep. "Hey!" I yelled as I turned around.

"I'll get it," he rasped out.

I gave him an annoyed looked. "Reid, I can get it. Don't forget, we're not really on a date; you don't have to pretend you're a gentleman. I know the *real* you."

Reid's stare went dark. "I said I'll get it."

"I'm going to get it," I argued, feeling like a child. *Why does he bring out the brat in me?*

"No," he said, his voice gravelly.

"Why can't I get it?" I asked, reaching up slowly and peeling his calloused fingers off my arm. My heart started to flutter under his touch, and I couldn't quite handle it as well as I thought I could.

Reid ran his hand through his dark locks. "Because… you walking up to the bar wearing that dress? You'll never get your damn water. If you want to be stopped by every male in this room, then so be it, but you'll get your water a lot faster if I go and get it."

I paused, looking up into his eyes. My eyes drifted down to his mouth—on accident, of course—before shooting back up to where they were supposed to be looking. "Was that a sideways approach at a compliment?"

Reid's hold on his normal, serious, frowning face wavered. His mouth moved a fraction, but he shook his head before walking toward the bar to get my water.

I yelled as a smile was fixing itself on my face, "Get me a gin and tonic. I need something stronger if I'm going to be stuck with you all night."

I slid back into the booth, feeling pleased with my bold self. I didn't even have time to get myself together before he reappeared with my drink in hand and another small glass sloshing with amber liquid.

He slid in beside me, his body language possessing a booming quiet that heightened all of my senses at once.

I sipped on my drink as he sipped on his. I watched Jane at the bar with Finn and Jackson, obviously winning both of their affection. There were a few other people at the bar, mostly famous people I recognized but wouldn't dare talk to unless I absolutely had to. Jane didn't seem too concerned, though, but then again, she was used to this sort of thing. She glanced at me and waved for me to come over, but something made me stay in the booth with Reid. I could feel the air around us shifting as he placed his glass down on the table in front of us.

"I know what you did."

I froze, my hand still lingering on my glass. "Isn't that what I should be saying?" I saw Reid cock his head to the side out of the corner of my eye. "Surprising me with my best friend—for what? To make up for having me come here as your date when you knew it made me more uncomfortable than you walking in on me naked?"

Reid continued to stare at my profile as I kept my hand clutched to my drink. "This isn't about me right now."

"Okay, fine. What do you mean you know what I did?" My stomach tensed at the same time my shoulders did.

Reid leaned into me as I focused my gaze onto the water droplets falling gracefully from the edge of my cup. He was so close I could feel the heat emitting from his body. I could smell the cologne he'd splashed on before leaving the hotel. The atmosphere surrounding us crackled with electricity. It felt like my heart had stopped beating in my chest. His breath gently caressed my exposed neck as he whispered into my ear, "I know you gave Rod your own lyrics and said they were mine."

My heart *did* stop beating in my chest. My throat closed. It seemed as if all of those senses that were heightened just a few minutes ago actually stopped working all together.

Reid's thigh brushed along mine, the scratchy fabric rubbing on my skin. *Nope, senses are definitely still on.*

"I'm sorry," I whispered, pulling my head down to stare at my bare legs.

"You're sorry?" he asked, still close to my ear. Goosebumps broke out along my thighs as I wiggled in my seat.

"Ye...yes. I..." I began to stutter, and I tried to blame it on my already-there awkwardness, but I knew it was a simple reaction to him being so close. My body was throbbing in places it never had before. It felt like I was on fire, and I hated it. Reid pulled back, his breath no longer fanning out along my skin.

I almost felt relieved, but I also felt a longing so deep within my bones I thought they might split in half.

Anyone from a mile away could see that Reid being that close to me had an effect on my body. I was certain that Jane, all the way over at the bar, could see my nipples standing erect through my dark, shimmery dress. I only prayed that Reid was oblivious.

Reid kept his gaze forward, not looking over at me once when he said, "I just wanted to thank you."

The world stopped moving. "You're not mad?"

He huffed out a small chuckle. "Why would I be mad that you gave up your own talent to save mine?"

I laughed, only loud enough for him to hear me. "My own talent? Let's not get crazy."

That was when he chose to look over at me. Our eyes

collided at the same time, and I was pinned to my very seat. "You *are* talented, Brooklyn—whether you're too afraid to admit that or not. You should always follow your dreams, even if you're afraid."

I paused, getting caught up in Reid's dark, dreamy features. "I'm not afraid to follow my dreams." I shrugged, playing with the water droplets running down the side of my glass again. "My dreams have just changed over the years."

"So what's your new dream then?"

I wavered before answering. "My new dream is to get you back to reaching yours." I could tell Reid was looking at me. I could *feel* it. *Man, these water droplets sure are interesting.*

"But why? Why do you care so much?"

Part of me wanted to tell him that I didn't care. I wanted to blurt out that I was doing it all for me, all for the money to help my family climb out of the dark financial hole we were in. I only wanted to push him to where he was before, writing the beautifully depicted songs that he was famous for, just to get the huge payment that would solve everything. But deep down, I knew it was a lie.

Over the last few weeks, working with Reid, we'd built some sort of strange relationship that was half us bickering and fighting over music and the other half almost an emotional intimacy. I knew we weren't physically intimate, but something about our late night, personal conversations that often went a little deeper than we both wanted, felt intimate, sacred. I had grown to care about him.

I felt a sort of dark sadness at the thought of his dreams diminishing because he was struggling so badly with something—and that something was tied to his ex, Angelina. The curious side of me was all but shaking with the need to know more, but the rational side of me knew that it was none of my business. It was evident that Reid was hurt, and I wanted to pull him out of that hurt more than I wanted anything.

I held Reid's eye when I answered, evening out my shaky voice. "Because I think whatever it was that hurt you so badly…that has caused you to be this version of yourself…the one who is struggling so quietly that most people don't even realize it…is something that you didn't deserve in the first place."

Reid's entire face fell. The crinkle of his eye vanished; the clench of his jaw relaxed as his mouth opened just slightly. For a moment, I felt like I could see right through his armor. I could see right through the carefully constructed walls he'd built, one by one. Reid King was a broken man. I knew that something had caused him to build those sky-high walls, blocking everyone and everything out, but looking into his eyes in that exact moment, I could *feel* it. "I don't know what hurt you, or what happened, but I'm going to pull you out of it, and you're going to come out on top, Reid King, even if it's the last thing I do. You will write again, and your music will be a saving grace to people. I just have to make you believe that."

A strange look washed over Reid's features. Admiration, maybe? Confusion? I couldn't figure it out, but suddenly, I felt his hand on my thigh. The roughness of his palm sent tingles to every single hidden crevice on my body. He gently squeezed my leg when he opened his mouth and all but whispered, "I think…" He sighed. "I think I just may be starting to believe you."

We were so wrapped up in one another, both stuck in another deep conversation that was meant for our ears and our ears only, that we didn't even realize that Jane, Jackson, and Finn were all standing at the end of our table, staring at the pair of us. It wasn't until Jackson had flicked a piece of ice in between our bodies that we both jerked back.

"Well, that was interesting," Jackson mused, a cheesy smile plastered on his face.

"Huh? What?" I blurted, my heart racing a million miles a second.

Jane sucked in her cheeks and gave me a look. I could feel the heat spreading along my skin slowly, making me sweat in the worst of places.

"Let's go dance, Brooklyn," Jane said, staring daggers at my face. If she could have dragged me out of that booth by my arm without causing a scene, she so would have.

"Dancing, yes. That's a great idea," I piped up, sliding out the other end of the booth, eager to get away from Reid. Before I let her sweep me to the dance floor, I grabbed my drink and downed it, hoping to ease the tingling in my limbs.

As Jane and I made it to the dance floor, I glanced back and saw Jackson mumbling something to Reid and pointing his head in our direction, but Jane's small hand wrapped around my wrist as she flipped me around.

"You little liar!" she spat, grabbing onto my other wrist and spinning us around to the music. There was basically no one else dancing, so I was certain we looked like a couple of idiots.

"Liar?! About what?" I took my hands out of her grasp. "We look like idiots out here. No one is even dancing!"

Jane rolled her eyes and grabbed onto my hands. "Then we'll start the dance party. After you spilled your little secret of Reid seeing you naked, you told me nothing serious was going on between you two. But let me just tell you...what I just walked in on over there...that was something serious."

I opened my mouth to deny it, but the birthday boy, Jami, strutted over to us, ceasing our conversation. He stood back and nodded, his long, blond hair falling over his shoulders. "I love that you two have the balls to come out here and dance even though no one else is. Especially considering you two aren't..." The rest of his sentence trailed, and I couldn't help but blurt out, "Famous?"

Jane grinned. "Is that okay, birthday boy?"

Jami tilted his head, a coy smile edging around his mouth. "I don't think we've met." He reached his hand out and shook hers gingerly.

"I'm Jane, Brooklyn's best friend. I think I saw you two talking earlier."

Jami nodded at her and then winked at me. *Is Jamison Bayne really having a conversation with us, like we don't live in totally*

155

different worlds?! My parents would freak at the thought of being in the same room as him! "I did meet Brooklyn, yes. Quite perplexing."

I scrunched my eyebrows. "Perplexing? I'm perplexing?"

Jami shuffled on his feet and glanced over at Reid. I did the same, meeting his eye almost immediately. He was staring at us intently, not backing down one bit. "Very," he mused, taking his eyes off Reid and the guys. "You're not perplexing, but the situation is."

I teetered on my heels. "What situation?"

"That Reid King says he brought you for press reasons, as many other celebrities do from time to time, yet he can't keep his eyes off you. It bothers him when…" Jami took a step closer to me, wrapping his hand around my waist momentarily. I gulped, my heart pounding viciously in my chest. "See?" he asked. "It bothers him beyond belief that my hand is wrapped around your waist right now. He can barely stand it."

"That's not tru—" I began to say, but then I saw how Reid's entire demeanor had changed. His shoulders were pulled back, and his eyes were intense as they glared at Jami and me. His hands were wrapped around his whisky glass so tight I thought it might combust. The cool color of his cheeks was splotched with red.

Jami finally pulled back and whispered, "Don't worry. Your guys' secret is safe with me. Just…" He paused before catching my eye. "Just be careful with him, darlin'. He's like a walking minefield."

Curiosity got the best of me, regardless of the rationality I thought I possessed when digging further into Reid's life. *It's none of your business, Brooklyn!* "What do you mean?"

Jami looked cool and casual as the words poured out of his mouth. "Angelina really fucked him up."

I went to ask for more. I was ready to get down on my knees to beg for more, but Jami hurriedly stepped back and looked at Jane and me. "I'm going to turn the music up a little louder. Keep on dancing, you two. I like it." Then he turned on his heel and sleekly walked over to the DJ.

Jane slithered up beside me and said, "See?! I'm not the only one who has noticed."

I quickly grabbed her hand and pulled us farther onto the dance floor. The music started to get louder, and the lights were dimmed even further. "Let's just dance."

Jane looked worried, but she followed suit anyway. In between twists and twirls, she whispered, "As your best friend, I should tell you to be careful, but I know you won't be." I didn't say anything, so after shimmying her hips in my direction, she reiterated, "But really, be careful, Brooklyn. Something about him screams jaded."

This time I didn't put up a fight. I looked over at Reid, who was, once again, keeping his eyes locked on me, and answered, "I'll try."

CHAPTER FIFTEEN

REID

I looked at two of my five bodyguards. "I want her beside you at all times."

"Who, sir?" Jeffrey asked.

I placed the leather band around my wrist without looking up. "Brooklyn. I don't want her out in the crowd this time. I just want her to be beside you and Frank the entire show. You got it?"

Jeffrey cleared his throat, crossing his beefy arms across his puffed-out chest. "Not a problem."

"Why?" Finn asked, all sprawled out on the couch in my dressing room. Why he wanted to hang out in my dressing room before a show, I had no idea, but he always did.

"Why what?" I asked, still messing with the band on my wrist.

"Why do you want them with Brooklyn?" I could tell by the way he said it that he had a snarky smile on his face.

I glanced over at him. "Because we don't want a repeat of last show, right? I'm not diving off the stage again."

Finn laughed loudly. "Why can't you just admit it?"

"Admit what?" I asked, turning around and crossing my arms over my chest.

"That you're starting to care about her."

I rolled my eyes and scoffed. "I don't care about her. But I'm not going to be held liable again if she gets hurt."

Finn stood up from the couch and walked over to me. He placed his hands on my shoulders, and I could feel the rage setting in. "You're allowed to have feelings for another woman. You know that, right?"

I felt my spine coil like a spring, locked and loaded. "I don't fucking have feelings for Brooklyn. Jesus Christ."

I don't. I don't have feelings for her. I can't.

Fucking no.

But why did I have a slight fear that Brooklyn could get hurt again during this show? Why did it affect me so much that the men last night at Jami's party were staring at her like she was their own personal eye candy? Why couldn't I keep my eyes off her swaying hips as she danced with her best friend? Why couldn't I keep my gaze from lingering on her bare legs the entire night? Why couldn't I stop the image of her naked from assaulting my brain every five seconds?

"Then why are you so butt-hurt right now?" Finn intoned, looking into the mirror to perfect his hair before we took stage.

"This is not the conversation I want to be having before performing," I said, feeling more agitated with each word that passed his lips.

"I'm just saying, the whole thing with Angelina is not your fault, Reid. There's no reason to starve yourself of women." I glared at him through the mirror but looked away as he turned around. "Whatever…say you don't have feelings for Brooklyn; you can still be attracted to her. I know that if I were back in that bedroom with her, working on music, songwriting, whatever it is you two are doing, I'd have a raging hard boner the entire time 'cause she is bangi—"

My head snapped up, and I was three seconds from slamming his head into the glass, but that was when I saw the cocky smile on his face. His eyebrows were raised so high they were almost touching his hairline. "Point proven, my dear friend."

"There is no fucking point proven. Now stop fucking with me."

"Don't you see how you're acting when I talk about her? Your fists are clenched at your side, that adorable little vein is popping out in your forehead, and your face is beet red. You. Care."

I shook my head no after glancing at myself in the mirror. *No, Reid fucking King... just no.* I hated that I knew deep down there was something stirring for Brooklyn. I hated even more what Angelina did to me—or better yet, what I did to her. I didn't even know who to blame anymore. Part of me believed that I destroyed her and that was what caused this entire shit show. But the other part, the one that almost made me ill, was starting to believe that she destroyed me, and that it was intentional.

The negative thoughts swirled around the longer I stared at myself in the mirror. Goosebumps covered my skin, and every muscle in my body clenched tightly at the mere thought of Angelina intentionally fucking with me so she could get back at me for breaking up with her. The guilt I carried around grew heavy, but maybe it wasn't my fault. Maybe Finn was right. Maybe Angelina was fucked up to begin with. Maybe it was her plan all along to fuck me up, too.

The one thing I did know was that I wanted the truth. Or closure. *Something.* And it wasn't so that Angelina and I could be *us* again; it was simply so that I could be *me* again. So I could rid myself of the guilt and buried rage. That way, I might stop feeling so fucking wrong for thinking about Brooklyn.

"And that's a wrap!" Rod exclaimed after we all piled onto the bus, Brooklyn included.

I kept my gaze away from hers, annoyed with myself that I couldn't quite do that during the show. I was too worried that she was going to get hurt again, that my two trusted bodyguards were going to somehow let me down—which they didn't—but I still couldn't peel my eyes away from her.

She was wearing tight jeans that accentuated her curvy hips and a loose, black tank top that showed a delicate, lacy bra underneath. Her auburn hair was straight again, just like last night at Jami's party, and it had this natural shine to it that most women—in LA, at least—would pay huge bucks for. I knew that much from Angelina always getting some strange treatments done on her hair.

I knew that Brooklyn saw me watching her as I played up onstage; I just hoped she didn't read too much into it. I needed to dig this pit out of my stomach and write a fucking song so I could dismiss her like a child being dismissed for recess. The more time I spent with her alone, working on music, the more my hold on my attraction—and whatever else it was that was stirring inside of me—was lessening.

I tried my hardest to keep a scowl on my face when she was around; I tried to keep my walls up. But something about Brooklyn made them crumble just a little bit each time. And if we continued to take things slow with the real task at hand—the songwriting—my walls would turn into dust, and they'd crush both Brooklyn and me.

After Jackson popped a bottle of champagne, spraying most of the contents on Finn, we all had a swig, celebrating yet another tour down. I knew I should have been more excited, but that just meant that I was expected to get my shit together for an upcoming single soon, and I had nothing.

That wasn't true.

I guess we had what Brooklyn wrote the other day, but that wasn't the deal. She wasn't supposed to write the songs... I was. Only, I fucking sucked and couldn't. I told her I'd write a song if she went to Jami's party with me, and so far, I had nothing.

"Brooklyn, swig?" Jackson held out the bottle for Brooklyn to drink, but she shook her head.

"You really don't drink much, huh?" he asked, taking it back.

She gave a soft smile. "No. I really don't." Then her hand subtly moved to her side where she rubbed her torso. Her face barely cringed, but I noticed it. I noticed everything about her. Alarms sounded in my head.

"I thought you said you weren't hurt from the other night," I growled, giving her a stern look.

Her face blanched. "I'm not hurt."

I raised an eyebrow. "Then why do I keep seeing you pulling at your side?"

I knew Brooklyn well enough now to know when she was getting flustered, just like last night when I told her I knew she gave Rod lyrics that weren't mine. Her face grew pink, and her big emerald eyes looked elsewhere.

"Do I need to pull your shirt up and look? Because I will."

She gasped. "You will not!" Then she crossed her arms over her chest.

"Nothing I haven't seen before," I mumbled, taking a step toward her.

"Whoa, what?!" Jackson exclaimed, slamming the champagne bottle down on the table.

Finn cracked up, throwing his sweaty head back. I was certain he mumbled something under his breath like, *"I knew it."*

"Oh my GOD!" Brooklyn yelled, throwing her hands up while giving me a death glare. Then she looked over at Jackson with an exasperated expression on her face. "He saw me naked because someone put a fake snake in my shower and I screamed bloody murder."

Jackson paid no attention to Brooklyn, and he looked over at me. "You saw her naked and didn't think to tell us that? Betrayal."

I chuckled and walked back into my room, ready to strip

off my concert clothes and get into something that wasn't clinging to my sweaty skin. Really, I just needed a breather, because anytime the shower thing was mentioned, I started to picture her, and it would be embarrassing as hell to get a damn hard-on right there in front of everyone. The second I was pulling my black sweats and shirt out of the drawer, erasing all thoughts of Brooklyn naked, my phone vibrated, ricocheting off the table.

My heart dropped, thinking it would be no one other than Angelina—out of habit, of course. After my shows, she'd call me, and we'd talk for a good while. That is, until things slowed way down, and she disappeared off the face of the earth, shutting me and everyone else out.

With a shaky, sore hand, I pulled it up to my ear to answer.

"Hello?" I rasped out, the fear evident in my voice.

"Reid, hello. It's Darcy."

My shoulders instantly relaxed at the sound of my lawyer's voice. "You're calling awfully late, Darcy."

She sighed. "Well, I wanted to wait until after your show to talk to you."

Just like that, my heart started to thump. "What's going on? Tell me you have something good to tell me. Have you found out where she is?"

She paused, and I could hear my heart beating like a drum. "We did."

It felt like the world had stopped moving. I gripped onto the dresser and held my phone with a tight grip. "And?"

"Well, we didn't technically find her, but her parents finally folded. After I tell you where she is, you have to swear you'll stay far away, Reid. You have to let us handle this very delicately. Her parents have already refused to give up any more information, but I'm working with the courts on fixing that due to… everything."

She was talking about the whole baby ordeal because, really, at this point, that was all I had connecting me to Angelina.

"Where is she?" I demanded, sweat droplets forming on my temples.

"Reid, do you understand what I'm telling you? You have to stay out of it. Her parents…"

I groaned. "I know. They fucking hate me and think I'm the reason for Angelina running off and losing her fucking shit. I get it. But—"

She interrupted me. "There are no buts. If you interfere, the courts will side with them. If they don't want to give you any information—even if there is… or *was* a fetus involved—then they won't. Tread lightly, Reid."

I paused, taking several deep breaths. "I get it. Where is she?" I could hear Brooklyn's laugh from the middle of the tour bus, but I pushed it away, turning my back on the door.

"She's at Bloomsdale Psychiatric Institute."

Every nerve in my body died. It felt like all the blood from my body was pooling at my feet. *What the fuck? Bloomsdale Psychiatric Institute?* A dagger went right to my heart. *Of all places, she's there?*

I finally managed to get out the word, "Why?" after what felt like an eternity.

"That's what we're working on. I'm trying to get pull with the courts, stating that you need to know this information even though you're not family. If you were married, this would be a lot easier to navigate, but the only thing I have holding you two together is the fact that she said she had a baby and that it was yours."

I swallowed, and it felt like glass. "You have no confirmation on that yet? And what about this Lori person that Angelina kept mentioning?"

She sighed through the phone. "No, this is all the information I have, Reid. Just try to sit tight, okay? We'll get this figured out. I just wish you were on better terms with her parents so we wouldn't be in this mess."

"Why won't they just tell me? What do they want? How is keeping me in the dark benefiting them?" The hold on my emotions was slipping like sand through my shaky fingers.

She's in a mental institution? Did I really fuck her up that badly? I could feel my heart shattering in my chest.

Her voice dropped. "Honestly, Reid. I don't think they know what they want other than for things to go back to the way they were before."

"Well, it's too late for that," I mumbled, running my hand through my damp hair. Exhaustion and frustration were both wrapping around my entire body, causing me to feel more tired than I ever had before.

I just wanted things to be over with.

I just wanted the truth.

And now that I was getting some of it, knowing that Angelina was in some psych ward, I wasn't sure I wanted it any longer.

My mouth opened at the same time I heard someone outside my door.

"Is she at least okay?" The words flew out of my mouth before I realized that Brooklyn was standing in my doorway. She looked angry at first, no doubt from me saying something about seeing her naked in front of Jackson and Finn, but then her brows furrowed as she saw I was on the phone.

I continued to stare, my eyes driving right into hers, because for some reason, I felt at ease. I was afraid to hear what Darcy was going to say, but looking at Brooklyn, I felt a little more in control, like the hold we had staring at one another was the only thing that was keeping me grounded.

"I don't have any specifics. Her parents' lawyer only gave up the information because of legal purposes, spewing that she was at Bloomsdale, where all medical information would be private unless speaking directly to a family member." Darcy paused for a moment, my hold on Brooklyn staying put. Her face softened, her round eyes almost speaking to me, asking me if I was okay. "Now the million-dollar question is if she was ever pregnant to begin with."

I held onto my phone as Darcy said she'd be updating me as soon as she found out more information but for me to remember that I mustn't interfere in any way whatsoever. I understood that, but it didn't really make it any easier to deal with. On one hand, I was concerned for Angelina and the possibility of us having a child together, and then, on the other hand, I just wanted it to be over with.

Guilt was eating away at me like maggots on rotting roadkill. I felt sick as I tried to brush it away to focus on something other than *it*. It was all too much. I felt like I was seconds from passing out. But then, all I saw was Brooklyn in front of me, looking so innocent and worried—worried for me—and it made me feel like I was an entirely different person.

I'm all over the place.

I couldn't get my shit together, and I desperately needed to.

The phone slowly fell away from my ear after Darcy said goodbye and hung up. Brooklyn stepped another foot inside my door and shut it quietly behind her. I just continued to stand in my room, phone in my shaky hand by my side, staring at her.

Just focus on Brooklyn, only her, just for another second.

Brooklyn inched a few more steps toward me, and I stayed still, trying to think of nothing but her.

She treaded lightly on her way over to me, almost appearing afraid that I'd bark some insult her way. She blinked several times between each step, her guard up, ready to take whatever it was I'd throw her way. I could tell she was afraid to come any closer to me, but she kept coming anyway.

Then something happened.

My eyes started to gloss over as she stood right in front of me and wrapped her arms around my torso. Her warm body was pressed against mine, her head resting gently on my chest, which caused air to finally escape my mouth. I gasped loudly for oxygen and tried to calm down.

But it was all too much.

The guilt. The worry. The wonder. The anger. The

memories.

And then the feeling of Brooklyn's tiny arms wrapped around my large body.

I didn't want to fight the feeling inside of me. I didn't want to push it away. I couldn't, because I needed it. I needed some type of outlet for everything I'd been feeling.

Her arms circled around me made me feel like I wasn't so alone, even though I knew I was.

I'd always be alone until I found out the truth and actually faced it. *Did I do this to Angelina? Did I make her this way? Was it my fault?*

My heart pounded in my chest with each rise of Brooklyn's. Then, she pulled back and raised those wide depths of sparkling green irises up to my face. She still stayed close...so close I could smell her soft scent.

"What was that?" I whispered, my voice breaking.

Brooklyn's face relaxed, the corners of her mouth barely rising. "You just... looked like you needed a hug from a friend." Then, she pulled back a little farther and shook her head. "I mean, I just... sorry. That was uncalled for and really unprofessional." Her face burned bright red. "We, um...we need to figure out how we're going to tackle a song—and where—since the tour is over and we live in different time zones."

Brooklyn ran her fingers through her hair and rocked back on her heels, her cheeks still blazing with a reddish hue.

My nostrils flared as I tried to push down all the feelings that were slithering up along my neck like a sneaky black cat. "Can we just figure it out tomorrow?"

Brooklyn's entire face grew serious. "Of course, Reid. You get your rest, and we can figure out our next move tomorrow." Then, she turned around to walk away, her hair swaying behind her. My entire body spazzed.

"Wait!" I all but shouted, reaching my hand out to hers. She quickly turned around, her hair a swirl of reddish-brown hues. "Stay."

Her eyebrows drew together. "You want to work on a

167

song right now?"

I swallowed, knowing damn well I was crossing the line that I drew for myself. "No. I just don't want you to go."

Brooklyn's shoulders relaxed as surprise flicked across her features. I, for sure, thought she'd shake her head and leave, but instead, she breathed out the word, "Okay." And I couldn't help but feel another piece of my wall come crumbling down.

And by *piece*, I meant the whole thing.

CHAPTER SIXTEEN

BROOKLYN

My eyelids felt like they were glued together. They wanted to open, but I was too comfortable to make myself do it. My breathing was calm, my heart relaxed, and I wasn't feeling crammed on the couch like usual.

Then I sprung my eyes open, staying completely still. My stomach dropped as I realized there was a heavy arm draped over my torso. My head slowly turned to the right, the soft pillow making a scratching noise, and then I trailed my gaze over a rounded bicep, all the way up to the strong shoulder and the rugged jaw that belonged to one person and one person only.

"Hi," Reid rasped out still with his eyes closed and an arm draped over me.

Are we cuddling?!!

I cleared my throat, still staring at his relaxed face. "Um, hi."

Reid didn't say anything; he just lay there with unmoving muscles. *Is he asleep again? Maybe he doesn't realize we're lying with one another.*

I remembered last night very vividly. I hugged Reid because I had never seen such a wretched facial expression than I had when I stormed into his room to yell at him for giving Jackson and Finn the wrong idea about us. Then, he'd asked me to stay in his room with him, and the feeling I had when the words left his mouth were unexplainable. I couldn't say no, even if I wanted to. Reid needed me, and I wanted to be there for him more than anything.

I went to lift Reid's arm up, but his face scrunched. "Stop. I haven't slept this good in months."

My heart pitter-pattered in my chest, and I wanted to squeeze the thing to make it stop. I moved my head back to its rightful spot so I would stop getting absorbed in Reid's features.

"Why don't you sleep?" I rasped, my voice no louder than a whisper.

Reid stirred a little bit, and he raised his arm off my body to roll over onto his back, just like I was.

I couldn't control the speed of my heart. It felt like it was about to race out of my chest, pounding like a little drummer boy, waiting for Reid's response. I shouldn't have asked. I did this to myself often. I would think Reid and I were on the same page—friends, or something similar—and then he would pull back and put up his walls again. He did it all the time while we "worked," too. One second, he was putting himself out there, feeling whatever it was he needed to feel, and then he snapped back into reality like a taut rubber band, vanishing before my eyes.

That was why it surprised me that he actually answered. His voice was low, like gritty sandpaper being rubbed along my skin. "Because I have things going on in my head that just won't stop."

I nodded, because I understood that. There were times that I had trouble sleeping at night because I was so worried about my sister, or even more recently, worried about the debt that our family faced.

I understood that, and I understood Reid, even with as

little as he told me. I felt like I knew exactly what he was feeling, just like I knew he needed a hug last night, and I knew he needed me to stay in his room without probing him for answers.

Reid turned on his side and propped his head of messy yet adorable hair on his hand. "Why don't you ever ask?"

I shifted uncomfortably, moving to a sitting position. "Ask what?"

His mouth formed a slight frown. "You never ask what's keeping me up, or why I'm so stuck in my own head, or why I'm a jerk most of the time."

I smashed my lips together before answering. "Because you don't need someone to ask you. You just need to know someone is there in case you ever want to tell."

When someone was struggling with a burden, they didn't need to talk about it. In fact, that was the complete opposite of what they needed. They already knew of their burden, and usually, they knew how to fix it—if possible. What they needed was comfort and love. They just needed to know someone was there to share the burden with them, if need be.

Reid traced my face with his gaze before bringing it back to my eyes. I swore Reid and I could have a full conversation with only our eyes—which was funny because we were both songwriters and used words in the most explicit ways. Yet, something about the pair of us, in a silent room, alone...it was almost like we could hear each other.

Reid opened his mouth to say something, but someone knocked on the door. My breath caught in my throat, and I panicked, not wanting anyone to see us lying together. I hurriedly swung my legs over the side of the bed, allowing them to dangle below. The door swung open within a few seconds, and Rod appeared.

His eyes shuffled between Reid and me a few times before he completely ignored the fact that I'd spent the night in here—if he even realized. I was fully dressed in last night's outfit anyway. The second I sat on the bed with Reid, after I hugged him, we sat in silence. He truly just didn't want to be alone, and I understood that, so I stayed. And then, I guess we both just nodded off at some point and apparently started to cuddle in the middle of the night.

"Okay, so we're close to our departure spot. Have you figured out where you two are going to be working from here on out? I have to say, it really shouldn't take too much longer, considering V is eating up those lyrics you wrote the other day, but you've gotta give them a little more before they throw you into the recording studio and Brooklyn goes on her way."

I could feel Reid's stare on the back of my head. *Why did I have to lie and say Reid wrote those lyrics?*

Reid's voice sounded from behind me. "Yeah, we're going to my house." A five-star, top-of-the-line alarm that appeared in fancy museums blared in my head. *His house?!*

"Like in L.A.? I can get a jet ready," Rod questioned, still standing in the doorway.

"No," Reid answered. "My house in Bloomsdale."

Rod stayed silent, and that was when I glanced over at him. He was standing in the doorway with his hands perched on his hips, staring at Reid with one eyebrow raised.

"Is this about what Darcy told you last night?"

Who is Darcy?

I could sense Reid's tension from across the bed. It all but vibrated throughout the room. "No. I'm not an idiot, Rod. I've been living on the tour bus and in hotels for months. I just want to go *home*."

Rod narrowed his eyes at Reid and then gave him a curt nod. He turned and looked over at me. "Is that okay with you? I'm sure Carissa assumed you two would have been done working by now, so going to Reid's house isn't in the contract."

I smashed my lips together and nodded. "If that's where he's most comfortable, that'll probably help with the songwriting. Will I stay in a hotel or—"

Reid snorted, so I stood up and turned around to stare

at him lying so effortlessly on the bed—casual as ever. *Attractive as ever.*

"You'll stay at my place," he said, peering up at me.

I could feel the heat spreading around my body. *Why am I acting like this? You've been on a tiny tour bus with him for the past few weeks. Staying in a house shouldn't be a big deal.*

I squeaked, "Okay."

Reid shifted his attention to Rod as he gave the okay. I booked it out of Reid's room, hot on Rod's tail, too afraid that I'd actually turn into a ripened tomato from the blazing redness of my face. Not to mention, I needed to get away as fast as possible from Reid and his simmering stare.

Things between us were shifting into a new territory—at least on my end—and I needed to get myself together before I was fooled into thinking that Reid King actually cared about me, or that there was something more personal blooming between us. It felt like he had a certain pull with me, and I with him, like we were intertwined somehow. But I wasn't going to be a stupid, foolish girl that let someone like Reid King crawl under her skin and nestle right into the spot that laid so helplessly inside her chest.

After taking a few deep breaths and getting my bearings, pushing Reid clear out of my head, I walked over to where my clothes were stored and started to pack up a few of my belongings. That was when Jackson slid into my peripheral vision.

"Yes?" I asked, glancing at him once.

He looked concerned, with his tawny eyebrows furrowed and a frown amongst his lips. His normal, friendly charisma that he carried around was gone.

My hand paused as I was shoving a couple of sweaters into my bag. "What's wrong?"

Jackson shook his head before giving me a serious look. "Be careful, Brooklyn."

I removed my hand from my sweater and placed my bag down. "Be careful with what?"

Jackson's voice lowered. "With Reid. He needs someone

like you. I just don't know if you need someone like him." The look on his face was something I'd never seen before. It was as if he wanted to tell me something but couldn't decide if he should or not. He shook his head a few times before saying, "I just... I don't know if he'll ever truly let you in after what happened with Angelina."

I was seconds from asking for more information. What I actually wanted was a five-page essay on Reid and Angelina, but out of nowhere, Reid's door opened and he walked out. He looked at Jackson and me, confusion flickering along his features. Before anything juicy was shared, Jackson turned around and walked away, leaving me more jumbled than ever. Reid walked past me, his strong scent filling my senses. Before he got out of talking range, he asked, "What was that about?"

I swallowed and lied, "Nothing. He was just telling me how much he was going to miss me." Then I gave a slight smile, and Reid rolled his eyes before strolling to the tiny kitchen area.

Jackson gave me a barely noticeable nod from afar, and I did the same to him.

Being careful with Reid was going to be difficult, considering it seemed I'd already misplaced my trusty hard hat. I'd say it was laying somewhere in Reid's bed after waking up with our limbs tangled together.

CHAPTER SEVETEEN

REID

Walking up to the door of my nana's house truly hit home. It'd been two years since she'd passed, and it still felt like yesterday. I knew that grandparents, and even parents, weren't supposed to be around forever, but I'd lost both of them before I even got to my mid-twenties. I still felt like I needed my nana, but I supposed that was the child inside of me speaking. Even just walking through the door made my stomach clench with grief.

I could feel Brooklyn behind me, taking in the scene with that quietness she always carried around with her. I shouldn't have brought her. I shouldn't have even been alone in the same room with her—not after last night—but here we were. *Alone.* In a private place. After having her stay in my room last night and then us falling asleep in my bed. *God. What was I thinking?* She fell asleep before me, her little head nodding off and on after we'd just sat on my bed, untouching.

We were in our own world.

That was how it felt with Brooklyn—like we were in our own little world, like the rest of the population would have been fine without us. I was using her. I knew it. I knew I was hanging onto her because she, somehow, was able to silence the shitty thoughts that I had rolling around in my head. I had promised I would never use another woman as a muse—not after Angelina—but here I was, hoarding a notebook full of potential songs, and each one was about her.

I couldn't help myself last night. She was sleeping so peacefully in my bed, looking more beautiful than ever, and it was like a floodgate was opened. So many words. So many verses. They were coming at me so fast I couldn't even grip the pencil hard enough to write them all down. I was out of breath by the end. Sweating. Mentally exhausted.

My walls were down last night. Completely demolished.

It may have been the phone call from Darcy that sent me over the edge, learning that Angelina was in a psychiatric unit and her parents were *still* withholding information about her.

Or maybe it was just the fact that, when she walked into my room, I didn't want to push away all the shit I'd been shrugging off since the very beginning. Somehow, my hatred and annoyance for being given a "teacher" did a total 180. She gave me life and inspiration; everything about her lit me up inside like a thousand torches being lit at the exact same time. And last night, I allowed those torches to burn for far longer than I should have.

And it was a mistake.

Using someone like Brooklyn was wrong—for both of us. Using her as a muse meant that she was doing something to me, something on a deeper level, wiggling her way into my life, my mind, everything. And there was no fucking way in hell I was getting wrapped up in another woman like before.

I couldn't. And I needed to face the facts: Brooklyn and I could never work. Even if I did somehow move on from the Angelina shit, Brooklyn and I were in two different worlds. It would never work. She didn't belong in a world like mine; she was too pure, too sweet. The media would eat her alive.

So, after I'd written for a few hours last night, I slammed the notebook shut and tucked it away, ignoring what had just happened.

Then I crashed.

I crashed so hard that I didn't wake until Brooklyn's smooth, warm legs were wrapped around mine. I hadn't slept that good since before Angelina went off the deep end, and it made me feel weak. It made me feel weak because, instead of regretting the fact that we woke up tangled up in one another, instead of pushing her away, I all but pulled her in closer, craving even more.

And I was still being weak having her here with me, alone, at my nana's house, to work on songs. I didn't need help with music. The ability to write songs was still inside of me. It was embedded inside my bones; it ran through my veins. I just wasn't sure I wanted to say the words out loud that I'd written inside my notebook. If I said them aloud, shared them with the world, then the walls I'd constructed so carefully to guard myself would be like a two-way mirror. There'd be no hiding anything, from anyone.

"Is this where you grew up?" Brooklyn's voice shot through my thoughts. I spun around to find her standing in the middle of the darkened entryway with her arms hanging down by her sides. Her small, heart-shaped face looked up, and she gazed around the walls.

I chuckled. "No, definitely not."

Brooklyn's hand ran along the old, antique table sitting near the doorway. "But I thought your nana raised you." Then she paused, eyes wide. "I mean, not that I would know that...I must have heard that somewhere."

A deep chuckle escaped me. *I wonder how much Brooklyn learned from Googling me?* I turned around and started to walk down the hallway and into the kitchen. "She did," I called out. "But we didn't live here. I bought this for her after my first tour."

"Oh," Brooklyn answered from behind, nearly running

into me. My throat caught in my chest at the mere thought of her brushing against my body. I quickly moved to the other side of the kitchen and opened the fridge, making sure it was fully stocked like I'd asked Betty, the woman who looked after the house while I was away, to do.

"This is the house that she always dreamt of having, so I bought it outright from the owner, paying entirely too much." I shrugged, rummaging around for a water. "But it made her happy, and that was my life goal. Plus, money's just money."

Brooklyn's harsh laugh filled the room. "That's easy for you to say."

I spun around after shutting the fridge and handed her a water. "What is?"

"That money's just money. When you don't have money, it's not that simple."

I cocked an eyebrow. "I've been poor before. I'm sure you've heard the story of the poor, orphaned boy who rose to the top."

Brooklyn rolled her light pink lips together. "I have, but you can't say that your outlook on money hasn't changed since then. I mean, you have, like, three huge houses."

I leaned back on the counter and drank my water slowly as I stared at Brooklyn standing so innocently behind the island, messing with the cap on her water bottle. I hated that my life was out there on display for everyone to see. I felt cheated sometimes. Everyone knew so much about me, yet I didn't know much about them—not unless I asked. But to be honest, I didn't really care to ask—until now.

The only thing I knew about Brooklyn was that she was an elementary school music teacher who had a knack for songwriting, and that she somehow knew Vinny, which was impressive for not being a blood relative or in the music industry itself.

All of a sudden, I uttered, "Are you poor?"

Brooklyn's wide eyes narrowed as she clutched her water bottle in her hand, the crunching sound echoing throughout the kitchen. "You know I am, otherwise I wouldn't be stuck working for someone as egotistical and grumpy as you." My mouth twitched as she continued. "I told you I needed the money. I'm sure you haven't forgotten that I said that."

I shot back quickly. "I didn't forget, but I also don't know what you need the money for." I grinned as I lowered my eyes to her chest. "A boob job?" I heard her gasp, so I brought my eyes back up to hers. "A new car?" Her eyes narrowed even further, and nothing made me more excited than seeing a fire in her eye. "Unlimited spray tans?"

Brooklyn was simmering now. In fact, if I stepped closer to her, I would probably be burned from her body heat. She all but growled at me and then turned on her heel to stomp away. To where, I had no idea, because she didn't even know her way around the house. I hurriedly strode over to her, unable to hide my growing smile, and grabbed her hand. I spun her around so that our chests were touching. "I'm just kidding," I said, peering down into her fiery eyes. Brooklyn was huffing, completely out of breath and pissed off. I slowly let go of her hand and backed away.

I angled my head to the side. "Come on, now; I know you better than that." I thought for a moment, leaning back on the counter, putting a necessary amount of distance between us. "It has to be something sensible. School loans? Paying off a mortgage?" I suddenly remembered the conversation I'd overheard between her and her sister a few days back, and it clicked. I flicked my eyes to hers, studying her strict posture as the next words came out of my mouth. "I'm going to guess… that the money isn't even for you. It's for someone you care about who is in financial trouble."

Brooklyn's mouth formed a straight line as she kept her line of sight even with mine. Her small frame straightened even more, and I knew I had it right.

"I hit the nail right on the head, didn't I?"

Brooklyn crossed her arms over her chest, and my eyes went directly to her breasts. I gulped as I moved my gaze away. "That's none of your business, now is it, Mr. King?"

I couldn't help it. A loud laugh escaped my mouth. "Mr. King? *What?* Are we suddenly going to be professional now?"

That's exactly what we should be doing. What the fuck are you doing toying with her?

"Ugh!" Brooklyn cried, turning on her heel. "You're annoying! Just show me to my room so we can get to work. We have one week to get some songs written, and you need all the help you can get."

A devilish grin formed on my face as I followed after her sassy, swaying hips. The cobalt dress she wore swished in her wake, daring my eyes to follow.

Brooklyn was right, I definitely needed all the help I could get—just not in the way she was thinking.

CHAPTER EIGHTEEN

BROOKLYN

My stomach growled loudly as I unpacked a few outfits to get me through being stuck at Reid's house for the next week. *Stuck? As if you aren't enjoying it.* I wasn't enjoying it. I wasn't loving the fact that Reid had smiled more in the last hour of being in his nana's house than the entire time we were on the tour bus together.

Reid's nana's house wasn't at all what I expected. When he'd said we were going to his house to work on songs, I pictured some mansion type of place, something similar to V's house. But it was less like V's house and more like my childhood home. We were out in the country, surrounded by growing trees and the smell of pine. The house was nice—don't get me wrong—but it wasn't flashy by any means. It must have been a house that Reid had bought for his nana and then renovated, because it had all the top-of-the-line appliances and updated crown molding, but the décor was something that I could see an older woman having.

I smiled at the small, glass antiques that sat perched on the crochet-doily-lined dresser and the old, brass table lamp that had a pretty pink rose painted along the glass. I ran my fingers along the crochet, almost feeling like I was at home, too.

I just hoped that Reid truly was comfortable here and that he could write some *decent* songs, not just words on paper that meant nothing. Reid needed to get back to the Reid King that everyone knew. Otherwise, the past few weeks were for nothing.

I clutched an oversized sweater in my hand, after wiggling into my favorite pair of leggings, ready to throw it over my bralette, as a knock sounded on my door.

Before I could pull the sweater over my head, the door opened wide, and there stood Reid with his dazzling smile.

"Reid!" I shrieked, clutching my sweater to my chest.

Reid's eyes widened as he scanned my torso. "Shit, sorr—" Then he paused. "What the hell, Brooklyn?"

I clutched my sweater even tighter. "What?! You're the one that just walked into my room!" Granted, I just did that to him last night, but that was different because I was angry with him! I couldn't control myself when I was angry!

Reid stormed inside the tiny bedroom, wafting his cologne all over the place. "You said you weren't hurt."

I paused, feeling the blood drain from my face. "I'm not."

Reid pulled the sweater out of my clenched fingers before I could even fathom what he was doing. I huffed, feeling one hundred percent exposed standing in my leggings and bra. That was it. I had on a thin, lacy bralette and leggings.

It was almost as bad as when he walked in on me naked. *Almost.*

Reid's fingers brushed along my side where the yellowing bruise was fading. His fingers were rough along my smooth skin. Goosebumps rose along every inch of my body as he caressed my side with the softest of touches. My breath caught in my chest, and suddenly, I was feeling even more exposed than before.

I stayed eerily still as he lingered over my kidney scar, running his thumb along its rough ridges. "What's this?" he whispered, his breath sweeping over my shoulder.

My heart was thumping, and blood was rushing to the deepest places of my body. "Noth... nothing," I stuttered, barely able to form a sentence.

"You said you weren't hurt. This bruise is from the other night, yeah?"

I nodded once, trying to keep my breathing normal. Reid's warm hand was still on my side, his fingers sweeping over the bruise again and again, causing my legs to tremble. I realized I had been holding my breath when Reid stepped back out of my personal space and I let all the air out of my lungs, almost gasping.

He had to have known he just affected me, because the way his eyes lingered on my body had him holding his breath, too. Lust was simmering throughout, the room crackling with electricity as if fireworks were seconds from exploding all around us.

Whew.

"Should I call the doctor again?" he asked abruptly, turning on his heel and walking over to the door.

Thank God. Keep walking away. Give me some space to breathe. My life literally depends on it.

"No, I'm fine. She checked me out again at the last show, just to be sure I was okay. It's just a bad bruise."

"Are you sure?" he asked with his back still turned toward me.

"I'm sure."

Reid nodded. I watched from behind as his back muscles stretched along his tight t-shirt, his broad shoulders rising and falling as he took several deep breaths. I had just quickly thrown the thin sweater over my head, ignoring what had just happened, when he said, "Meet me in the kitchen when you're ready."

I sighed. "Okay." And then I turned around to look at myself in the mirror as he left the room completely. I took one glance at my flushed cheeks and full-of-life eyes and shook my head.

Reid King was doing something to me, and I wasn't okay with it.

Or was I?

———

A few minutes later, I tiptoed down the hallway and into the kitchen as quiet as a mouse and then stopped in my tracks. "Are you... cooking?" I blurted, smelling a delicious mixture of fresh basil and garden vegetables. My mouth filled with drool, and that was totally because of the tasty scent wafting throughout the kitchen, and not at all because of Reid looking as if he belonged in some type of magazine. His dark, chocolatey hair was unruly and out of place, making him appear relaxed. His strong jaw formed a sharp right angle as he peered down into a pot over the stove. My eyes traced the strong muscles on his forearm as they moved languidly back and forth, stirring something over and over again.

"I am," Reid intoned, not looking over at me.

I slid onto the barstool behind the large island. "What a sight," I mused sarcastically. "Should I take a picture and post it online with the caption: *'Not only can Reid King sing like a god, but he can cook, too?'* Girls all around the world will be fainting."

Reid snickered as he flashed a devil-like grin my way. "Maybe you should wait to eat before you post anything." Then he turned back around, stirring more. "But just so we're clear, don't post that. It's the last thing I need."

I laughed. "I don't even have a social media account, so we're good."

Reid turned around with a kitchen utensil in his hand. It looked so small compared to his large palm. "Why?"

I shrugged. "I don't want people in my business."

Reid stood back and nodded, giving me an

understanding look. "I get that. I wish people would stay out of my business."

I kicked my legs underneath the island. "You're one of the most private celebrities I know."

He raised an eyebrow, grinning. "You know a lot, then?"

I thought for a moment, embarrassed. "No, but Jane does, and that's what she said, so..."

Reid had turned back around, but I could tell he was smiling when he spoke next. "Not that you Googled me or anything, right?"

I gasped dramatically. "Of course not!" (I so did. I turned into a freaking overpriced PI before I signed my contract.)

Reid laughed loudly, and I smiled. It was nice to see him like this. It was like getting a glimpse of a different Reid— the one that Finn and Jackson often talked about. I already missed those two, and we just had, like, an hour-long goodbye a few hours ago.

I watched as Reid began cutting up onions and garlic on a wooden cutting board near the sink. My eyes followed his every move. I felt the familiar heat creeping up my neck, along my cheeks, and then traveling to my ears. Reid King made cutting an onion look like a stellar audition for Chippendales. For a brief moment, I pictured Reid in only a tight pair of boxer shorts and a little black bow tie, dancing on a stage. *Could you imagine?*

"Brooklyn?" Reid muttered before I snapped my head up to him.

"Huh? Who?" I stuttered, my face now matching the red sauce that was simmering on the stovetop.

Reid smirked. "Can you help get the garlic bread ready?"

My mouth opened. "Oh, yes. Of course." I jumped down off the barstool and rolled my sweater sleeves up to my elbows. I started to rummage around before Reid told me where things were and what he wanted me to do.

I was slathering on a copious amount of butter when I finally asked, "So where did you learn to cook?"

Reid looked up from stirring the red sauce and beamed a gentle smile. "My nana. She always said that I needed to learn how to cook for myself, because I was too cocky to find a wife of my own one day."

I laughed loudly, throwing my head back. "She was probably right."

Reid rolled his eyes dramatically. "She would have liked you."

I had no clue why, but that made my heart blossom like a flower. A jolt of excitement went through me. *Why does it matter if his nana would have liked you? Shut up and make the garlic bread, Brooklyn.* I lost the battle with myself almost instantly. "Why do you say that?"

He gave me a lazy grin. "Because you don't put up with my shit, and you don't try to spare my feelings."

I started to sprinkle garlic on the giant loaf of buttered bread. "Well, someone has to keep you in line, otherwise your head would be as big as the moon, and..." I looked over at him apprehensively. "I don't spare your feelings because I'm pretty sure you don't have feelings." Then I laughed, going back to sprinkling garlic on the bread.

He pulled back dramatically. "What?! I'm making you dinner. That shows that I have feelings. I don't want you to starve."

I paused. "Did Reid King just admit that he cares about something?"

Reid continued to stir the sauce and noodles on the stovetop as I began washing my hands in the sink. "Well, we have to get right down to business tomorrow. I figured we both needed a home-cooked meal for energy."

I smiled. "So, you're saying that you're only cooking for me so that way I can help you tomorrow. Sounds more like you're making this meal for your benefit, not mine."

Reid's head tilted to the side as he squinted his eyes at me. I held back a smile by smashing my lips together, still allowing the warm water to pour over my hands. Reid inched over to the left, and before I knew what he was doing, he threw a glob of butter at my head.

I squealed, "Reid!!" as he threw his head back and cackled, his brown locks bouncing along his head, pure laughter escaping his mouth. I was stunned for a moment. Reid King was... being playful. *Reid King was having fun!*

Happiness took over my body, and I quickly cupped water in my hands and threw it in his direction as fast as I could. It soaked his heather-gray shirt immediately, outlining the ridges along his chest.

Reid slowly looked down at his shirt and then lazily brought his head back up. A flirty look was all over his sharp features, his pouty mouth cocked up into a sexy grin that made my stomach fill with a giddiness I'd only ever felt on Christmas morning.

"Oh, you're going to get it now."

My eyes widened as laughter escaped my mouth. I turned on my heel and began to run around the island, but Reid was much faster than me. I felt water hitting my back, so I turned around quickly and squealed again when I realized Reid was holding the sink sprayer in my direction. He spritzed me again before I could turn and run some more. Warm water coated my chest and bare shoulder as my sweater began to slip down.

I bolted, making a turn around the island and running at full speed down the hallway. I was laughing so hard I could barely see straight, exhilaration sprouting from every pore on my body. That was probably why I tripped over the runner in the hallway and almost fell on my face.

Reid's strong arm wrapped around my waist at the last minute, and before I hit the floor, he turned our bodies, and I landed right on top of him. I thudded onto his sturdy chest, causing my breast to smash into him. Strands of my damp hair were hanging down past my shoulders, dripping droplets of water onto his soaked shirt.

I was an inch away from his mouth, and my eyes were glued to his light lips. His breath was cool along my face, but everything about the moment was *hot*. Reid's arms were wrapped around my back, my legs intertwined with his, our chests rising and falling in sync from the sudden burst of exertion, my heart coming to a complete halt as I felt heat pooling between my legs. Every limb on my body tingled.

Reid's mouth parted, and my body was begging me to inch just a little closer, to just put my lips on his, to ease the burning that was getting more intense the longer I laid on him. I lazily brought my eyes up to his, and he was staring directly at my mouth, too. My tongue darted out involuntarily, and I ran it over my plump bottom lip.

I heard Reid gulp, and I inhaled a sharp breath before he reached up and placed his mouth on mine. The second our lips touched, it was like I was fully awake for the first time in my entire life. Everything disappeared in the room as he moved his mouth over mine, coaxing the life right out of me. I was in a frenzy, focused on the feeling driving me to reach an end goal that I wasn't even aware of.

My body went into straight sex-kitten mode as I moved my tongue inside Reid's mouth to lure it open even further, and instead of our legs being tangled up in one another's, I moved my body and straddled him right there on the floor. Reid's hands gripped my waist as we continued to move our lips, soft kisses turning into passionate, hungry ones. I felt the pads of Reid's fingers inching underneath my sweater, enticing even more sparks as they touched the bare skin of my stomach. My hips moved of their own accord, and a small growl of Reid's echoed in my mouth before a loud alarm was sounding off throughout the house. The shrill noise broke us out of our trance within seconds. I panted, and Reid's grip tightened on my body as his eyebrows bunched together as if he were trying to remember where we were and what we were doing. It was like a punch to the gut when I saw the look of defeat on his face when he realized that I was on top of him and we were just kissing like… *that*. He quickly released my hips, and I crawled from on top of him, moving to rest my back along the cool wall. Reid jumped to his feet and hurriedly strode into the kitchen to figure out what was burning and why the alarm was going off. I could smell the smoke wafting throughout the house, but I couldn't quite get myself to get up to make sure there wasn't some type of fire from the unoccupied red sauce and noodles on the stovetop.

I was too surprised. Frozen. Too taken aback from the kiss. The kiss that tore right through my chest. The kiss that stripped every single thought from my head. The kiss that swept me away completely and had me forgetting that I was being paid to be there.

I stayed in the same spot, sitting on the hard, wooden floor, when Reid came around the corner minutes later. His head was turned down, his shoulders drooping low. I could feel it coming—the straight disappointment.

Reid regretted kissing me.

But I didn't.

"Brooklyn," he said, standing a few feet away from me. I didn't want to look up at him, but I also knew that I needed to, so I slowly raised my head and peered up at his looming stance. His golden eyes drove into mine, steely and cold as ever. "That can't happen again."

I felt the need to jerk backwards, as if the words were there to strike me, and I had the sudden urge to ask why. Why couldn't it happen again? Because a soul-crushing kiss like that felt like falling in love for the first time. It was an all-consuming, one-of-a-kind, something-that-wasn't-just-lust-and-attraction kind of kiss. But instead of asking him and giving him even more ammunition to throw my way, I nodded my head tersely and hopped up to my feet.

I brushed past him quickly, unable to even look him in the eye, and went directly into my room, shutting the door behind me. I rested my back along the oak door and slid all the way down until my butt hit the floor. My shirt was still clinging to my skin from the dampness, and my hair was stringy and hanging down past my shoulders, but the only thing I could focus on was the kiss. My mouth felt singed, burned, *marked*.

Angry that I couldn't stop thinking about the way Reid looked after he realized we were caught up in one another, I crawled over to the bed and snatched my phone. I was seconds from texting my sister or Jane and spilling the naughty truth in my head that slowly circled the idea of me *wanting* Reid in a way that I simply shouldn't, and then I saw Jane's text. It read, "This is your daily reminder to guard your heart from that cynical man we in the music industry call the King of Music. Tread lightly, my dear friend. Love you."

I chucked my phone back onto the bed and raised my fingers to my mouth.

What have I gotten myself into?

CHAPTER NINETEEN

REID

The kiss between Brooklyn and me was something that was bound to happen. I knew it. She knew it. The whole fucking world knew it. But it was a mistake. One that I couldn't take back. And one that I couldn't stop thinking about.

Even as I cleaned up the mess from burning my nana's legendary, homemade red sauce after it boiled over onto the stove while Brooklyn and I were simply losing control on any bit of reality that was left between us, I couldn't stop the thoughts. The way Brooklyn's auburn hair fell all around her heart-shaped face, the damp tendrils framing her lightly pink-tinted cheeks. The playful glimmer in her green eyes when I sprayed her with water as I chased her around the island. The feeling of her body moving on top of mine, showing that she also felt what I felt: pure desperation and lust.

It was all too much.

I recognized the fact that my body hummed afterwards, and I knew that I couldn't hold on to the guilty conscience that had been weighing down on my shoulders since I first saw Angelina on that cold bathroom floor for much longer. Because everything that I was feeling for Brooklyn completely demolished it.

There was just something about her—the lightness she carried, her pure beauty, the way her laugh made my lips tip upward even when I didn't want to smile, the way she pushed me to be better, and the fact that she hadn't given up on me even though every single verse/song/tune that I produced was complete shit. And the reason it was complete shit was because it was fake and forced.

It wasn't the truth.

Every bit of the truth I had locked inside of me was in that notebook that I'd scribbled in a few nights ago after I let go of the denial for a few moments.

I thought that maybe listening to Angelina's voicemail again would take my mind off Brooklyn. That maybe if I reminded myself that Angelina was in a psych ward—no doubt because of me—that maybe I could push Brooklyn away, that I could shove the kiss clear out of my mind. But this time, instead of falling into a pit of darkness that was full of remorse and rotten guilt, I grabbed my notebook and started to furiously write down even *more* lyrics that dripped of hidden reality.

Each verse I wrote, each song I perfected, revolved around Brooklyn.

"This is good… kind of," Brooklyn said from across the living room, sitting cross-legged in another pair of tight leggings and a loose t-shirt that, once again, showed just a hint of her shoulder. The awkwardness from our last encounter was still lingering in the air. She never came back out of her room after the kiss, not even to eat, and now that it was the next day, she could barely look me in the eye without scowling.

"You think?" *Because I don't.*

I strummed my fingers along my guitar, playing with a few chords that were more comfortable than anything. I glanced upward as Brooklyn pulled her old guitar over to her lap, resting it gently along her legs. Her fingers moved gracefully to their rightful spot, and she began to strum a few tunes while quietly singing the bogus verse I gave to her.

"The sun rises in the east, as the wolf howls in the west.
You're not like all the rest."

What did those words even mean? They were bullshit lyrics. I knew it, and she knew it.

Brooklyn suddenly paused her fingers and looked up at me with an imperceptible look on her face.

"You're not doing it right," I intoned.

Brooklyn cocked an eyebrow with force. "I'm doing it exactly like you did."

"You aren't," I countered, raising an eyebrow right back.

Her lips formed into a pout, and something sparked inside of me that was far too powerful to shut down. "I'll show you. Come here." *Do you have no self-control?*

She all but glared at me. "I know how to play guitar."

I side-eyed her. "You do, but I can teach you how to hold your guitar in a better place, allowing you to *feel* the music reverberate through your chest, through your entire body—so that way, you can truly connect." I shrugged while looking back at my own guitar. "But by all means, suit yourself, but it'll make you better in the long run. You know…if you ever wanted to teach guitar lessons on the side."

"No. I don't need your help," she argued with a bite behind her words.

I couldn't stop the words from flying out of my mouth. "Are you angry with me?"

Her fingers stilled on her guitar. I knew she was mad at me; I'd be mad if someone rejected me after having a heated kiss like we had.

"Why would I be angry?" Brooklyn finally met my eye, the fire flaming deep within.

"I think we both know the answer to that," I responded.

Her cheeks flushed instantly, but she kept her glare on me. "I have no idea what you're referring to. I'm not angry about anything other than you thinking that I can't play guitar correctly."

I shook my head. "I never said that. I just said that I could make you better." I shrugged again, going back to my own guitar. "It's fine if you want to stay average. I was just thinking that you said you needed money—you could start teaching guitar lessons, too."

I could sense that Brooklyn was pondering the idea. Silence filled the room. The only things I could hear were my own naughty thoughts of wanting her to be closer to me. I was a corrupted son of a bitch. I shoved her away after our kiss, promising myself that I'd get my shit together, and now I was trying to pull her back in. I was trying to reach that high I felt last night.

My entire body stilled as I heard her little body shuffling toward me. I looked up at her standing a mere foot away with her guitar outstretched in my direction. I could tell she was annoyed that *I* was teaching *her* something, but I could also tell that she really wanted me to.

I shoved my own guitar away, pushing it further down onto the cushion beside me, and scooted my body back so I was resting along the couch. I spread my legs out and then patted the little bit of cushion in front of me, my heart beating against my ribcage with such force that I thought it might actually snap a few ribs.

Brooklyn's face changed to a light shade of pink as she pulled her guitar tightly to her body and finally sat down on the couch in front of me so far away that her butt almost fell off the cushion.

I ground my teeth as I stretched out my hands and wrapped them around her waist, pulling her in closer to my body. Her breath caught—as did mine—when our bodies touched. *I shouldn't be doing this, but God, I don't think I have it in me to stop.*

"Okay, now hold your guitar like you are about to play,"

I rasped.

Brooklyn did as I said, placing her guitar on her crisscrossed legs. She was tense—her shoulders pulled up to her ears, her spine a perfectly straight line, the points of her elbows sticking out from beside her body.

"Relax," I whispered, angling my face near hers to see her guitar. My veins were full of exhilaration, pumping a need throughout my body that was hard to ignore.

Why does she have to smell so good?

Brooklyn's body changed from firm to soft as my breath hit her exposed skin, her posture relaxing, and her breathing nice and easy. I placed one hand on top of hers and glided it slowly down the slope of the guitar, our hands moving together over the strings. I pulled the guitar closer to her body at the same time I moved closer to her back. My heart was in my throat, causing my voice to come out rough and sultry. "You need to feel the guitar through your torso." I briefly moved my hands to her firm stomach. "Let the sound almost lull through your body, allowing the music to flow throughout, to overtake your senses."

Brooklyn shivered under my touch, and every part of my body erupted in flames. She began to play the same tune that I had played earlier, only this time, I could tell she put more feeling into it. I glanced down to her tranquil face, her eyes closed as her fingers moved swiftly over the strings. "That's better, right?" I asked, my voice no more than a soft whisper along her neck. Her neck was so close to my mouth that if I just bent my head down a little farther, I could place my lips on her skin, feeling the softness of it.

Brooklyn's head jerked a little, and her eyes opened, the swirl of green hitting me in the core. She nodded her head slowly, causing some of her hair to fall in front of her face. I reached my arm up and tenderly moved it out of the way, unknowingly losing any hold on the tiny bit of control I had. My calloused fingers brushed along her high cheekbone, moving the silky piece of hair behind her ear. My eyes fell to her lips, and she licked that bottom lip again. And right then, I let another piece of my wall tumble. I leaned in a fraction, Brooklyn's lips parting with a small puff of breath, and then I took her mouth in mine—*again*. My hand cupped the side of her head, my fingers intertwining between the glossy strands, as I moved my mouth over hers, the softness of her lips feeling like a freedom I'd craved for so long.

Brooklyn opened her mouth further as she pushed her guitar out of the way, moving gracefully up to my body, our chests resting along one another's, aching for more. Then my phone rang, and every alarm in my head went off, signaling my body to get the fuck away before I did any more damage.

I broke the kiss and shuffled backwards, my eyes blazing into hers. Brooklyn's eyes widened at the same time, her fingers going up to her mouth.

I stood up and walked a few steps away, still keeping my heated gaze on hers. *What the fuck did I just do?*

Still locking onto her shocked and somewhat upset face, I reached for my phone and saw that it was Darcy calling, and every bit of freedom I had felt while kissing Brooklyn faded away faster than a ship in the middle of the sea. Before I picked the phone up, Brooklyn stood up and looked me straight in the eye. "You better start writing some songs so this"—she walked toward me and moved her hand in between us—"doesn't happen again. Because I'm not sure I can take much more of you kissing me like *that* and then ending it with that look on your face."

Then, she turned on her heel and stormed off to her room, leaving our heated moment on the couch, right there beside our abandoned guitars.

———

Three days had passed since the second kiss. The kiss that took away my inhibitions—yet again—and threw them into the pits of hell. The kiss that stole away every ounce of guilt I knew I should have been feeling. The kiss that silenced the thoughts in my head even *after* the phone call.

The feeling of Brooklyn's soft, warm lips lingered in the back of my mind as I had stormed off to the other room with my phone clutched in my hand. I had wanted to answer, to find out if Darcy had gotten any more intel on Angelina, but I couldn't speak. My mind was going a thousand different directions, my hormones raging, my heart thumping loudly. The strange twinge I felt inside my chest as I watched Brooklyn storm off felt even worse as I shut my door. But oddly, the kiss almost sobered me. It sobered me into reality. Here I was, hung up on a woman who had shoved me out of her life and then brought me back into a fucking shit show—the same one who apparently found pleasure in clamping the unstable, guilt-ridden pieces of my heart in her hand. And then there was Brooklyn, who I was using to make myself forget about said woman.

Brooklyn silenced the bad.

Angelina blared it.

That was why, when I heard Angelina's voice on my voicemail instead of Darcy's, I doubled over. My stomach dissipated into a pit of grainy sand, the kind full of broken seashells and grit. My heart stopped. Icy cold water was dropped upon my shoulders. In fact, the entire world was on my shoulders.

Her voice broke when she first spoke. "Reid, it's *me*." She paused, and I clenched my jaw in anticipation of what she'd say next. "Your stupid lawyer left her phone in my room when she came to speak to me earlier." Angelina's voice was no more than a whisper. "Why did you do this to us? Why didn't you fight for me? Why did you break up with me?" My chest felt like it was split open when she began to whimper. "I'm scared and alone. They won't let me leave or speak to anyone. They have me on all this medication, and I think they're poisoning me. I very well could be dead by morning." I ran my hand through my hair as I clenched my eyes shut. "I'm not sick, Reid. They're lying when they say that. It's all part of their plan to kill me. I need you to come get me. Save me."

Then the phone shuffled once more before it clicked off.

I assumed that Darcy or a nurse had walked back in, ready to snatch the phone back from her. After hearing Angelina's voice, the way it started off soft and sad and turned into frantic and rushed, it made me want to bang my head against the wall.

The Angelina that I knew was all sorts of things, but she wasn't the type that wanted to be saved. She was strong, set in her own ways. It was her way or the highway. She was independent beyond belief, never needing anyone to do anything for her. She didn't like to be tied down, which was one of the reasons why we didn't work out. She was too flighty, one minute wanting to hang off my arm at a red-carpet event, and the next ignoring me for weeks.

Angelina wanted me to save her, but I didn't even know what I was supposed to be saving her from.

Anger and frustration gripped me so hard that I stormed over to my wall, reached my hand back, and punched it, the bones in my hand stinging as drywall crumbled into pieces all around my outstretched arm. Angelina was toying with me. The second I felt like the guilt from our breakup was lessening and the responsibility that I felt for the fact that she was fucked up was quieting, she'd bring it all back up again, saying I gave up on her, on us.

There was barely even an *us*.

That night, after I'd calmed down and iced my hand, I lay in my bed on top of all my covers and tried to do anything other than think of the wretched voicemail. I didn't tell Darcy; I didn't tell a single soul. I kept it under lock and key. It didn't take long for my mind to wander away from the situation at hand and to the moment I was caught up in before the call.

I'd started to imagine the way Brooklyn's soft lips opened up to mine.

I'd started to picture her with her one shoulder peeking

out from beneath her oversized sweater, and her soft hair and how it felt between my fingers. I could almost hear her cheerful laugh. I could see the small, barely there smile on her face.

Then I got pissed all over again when I realized that I was caught somewhere between a harsh reality with Angelina and a fantasy with Brooklyn.

I was a fucking disaster, and not to mention, I was supposed to be focusing on writing a single that would blow my record label out of their fucking seats.

"Reid," Brooklyn said from across the room. She was resting her back along the far wall, as far away from me as possible, which was exactly the same spot she'd been in for the last three days—far, far away from me.

Three days had passed between the kiss, the phone call, and now. Three entire days. Seventy-two hours. And all I felt when I saw Brooklyn was need... and want, and desire. All I felt when I saw Brooklyn was solitude—just her and me in the room, alone. Thoughts of Angelina disappeared. Thoughts of anything disappeared, if I was being honest.

"What?" I snapped, keeping my eyes on my guitar.

"You're not giving this your all, and I don't know why. It's like we've taken one hundred steps back."

I took a deep breath, knowing very well that, in the past three days, I'd done nothing productive. No mind-blowing songs. No amazing melodies. The only thing we'd done in these three days was stay clear of one another as I tried to fight every urge to run my lips along hers again.

I couldn't focus.

That was a bold-faced lie. I could focus, just not on the right thing.

I ran my hand through my hair, feeling the mess of waves on top. I pushed my guitar off to the side as Brooklyn opened her mouth again. "Was it the kiss? Did that make you close up again? Because there, for a minute, you seemed like you were pushing through, like we were making progress, but now... it's like you've closed off again. Like you don't care. You're back to being the Reid King I met weeks ago where you looked as if you were seconds from bashing your fist into a wall, scowling, muttering under your breath, the light in your eyes long gone." Brooklyn paused, taking a huge gulp of air. "Listen… I know the hallway thing was wrong. I know the kiss a few days ago was wrong. We were just caught up in the moment. I get it, but you're holding back, and it's time for you to put a stop to it."

We weren't just caught up in the moment, Brooklyn. Don't you get that?

I stayed still, but every muscle in my body was coiled so tightly that it physically ached. I slowly brought my eyes up to Brooklyn who was standing with her hands on her hips, staring at me intently with that same fire in her eye that I'd seen the first time I'd met her. Suddenly, she threw her arms up and glared. "Was it the phone call? Was it Angelina? *What* is holding you back?!"

With my hands clenched by my side, I grounded out, "Please don't bring her up." *Jesus, just don't remind me of her. Not now.*

Brooklyn rolled her eyes. "Is it about her? Is that why you act this way? Something is eating at you, and until you face it, you'll never again be the Reid King who can silence an entire stadium full of people with one strum of your guitar." She paused, and I could hear my heart thump, thump, thumping beneath my ribcage. "I don't know what happened, and I said I wouldn't ask, but goddamnit, Reid! If you want us to part ways and to stop fighting the urge to kiss each other again, WRITE A GODDAMN SONG!"

Brooklyn's breathing was erratic, her face flushed, her eyes glaring in my direction. She was seething—like a lion ready to attack.

Her words sounded irate. "Just write from the heart, Reid. Sing the truth. Write about what's bothering you. You and I both know that's the real issue here. You need to face whatever it is that's got you all messed up. The second you face it and let go, the sooner your music will have meaning and you'll be able to write the stellar songs that I know you can write. Find that passion again! Find something—anything—to hold on to so it'll help you, because I'm at a loss."

I growled aloud and snatched my guitar back onto my lap.

Brooklyn wanted to know the truth?

Well, she was going to get it.

CHAPTER TWENTY

BROOKLYN

I had never felt so pissed off in my life. My blood ran cold, but my body was simmering. I was fuming. All the pent-up aggression from the last several days was thrown together and had me acting out in ways I'd never imagined, especially not in front of Reid King.

And then, something happened.

The most beautiful melody floated around the room— so beautiful that I was left speechless. The rage I'd been feeling vanished into thin air. Reid's large fingers moved gracefully over his guitar, and my eyes were trained on every single move he made.

He silenced the room with his talent. His face was relaxed, eyes shut peacefully, jaw loose as he skillfully did what I demanded. He wrote a song. And even from the first verse, I knew it was the song.

"I swore I'd never fall again.
Attraction is all it should've been.
But then you gave me your heart

As if it were a delicate piece of art."

I watched as Reid's mouth opened with each raw but soft word that fell off his lips. He moved his body with the music in ways that only a true musician could understand. He played a few more notes on his guitar, causing goosebumps to rise on my arms, and then he began to sing more of the masterpiece at hand.

"We were one touch away from lust.
So much that your kiss was a must.
Losing track of time, with no direction in sight.
I just might…

"But I swore I'd never fall again.
Because my heart couldn't stand to bend.
But then you gave me your heart
As if it were a delicate piece of art.

"I just might…
We're one touch away from lust.
We're one kiss away from a thrust.

"I just might…
Cause we're one heartbeat away from the fight
The fight that could bring us to the light
I just might…"

Finally, after Reid repeated the last verse a few more times, I was able to breathe again. It felt like I was floating around the room with the music, my feet unable to touch the floor. Every part of my brain was locked onto all things Reid King. *He did it.*

He wrote a song, and it was perfect. It gave me goosebumps. Just hearing him made me *feel.* And watching him? That did something else entirely.

I swiftly ran over to him and stood mere inches away

from his crouched body on the couch. His hands stilled, and they were still stuck on the same spot of the last notes he'd played on the guitar. I swallowed my fear and slowly placed my hand underneath his sturdy jaw and raised his head to look up at me. His golden eyes were showing something I'd never seen before: vulnerability. Reid King was at my mercy, even if for just a mere second, and all I wanted to do was take away his vulnerability and fear and hold it for him.

"Reid, you did it," I whispered, keeping my hand underneath his scratchy chin. "You did it." My eyes started to well up, and I had no idea why. Reid continued to stare at me from down below. Motionless. He didn't move once. All the anger and betrayal I had felt since kissing him for the second time melted away. That was the kind of thing that Reid King did to a person. He made you lose focus on everything other than him.

My grip tightened on his chin as I repeated myself. "Reid. You. Did. It." A timid smile broke along my face. "I felt it. I felt every single word you just sang. I felt it in every part of my body. I could feel that those words were true. I could feel them pouring out of your very soul. *You did it.*"

Reid took his face away from my hand, the sharp angle of his jaw now facing toward me. I backed up quickly as he got to his feet after placing his guitar to the side. He stood in front of me, his chest to my nose.

I watched the slope of his chest rapidly move with each breath he took. With every inhale of air, I could smell his cologne. The room began to spin as he peered down into my face.

"You wanted me to speak the truth, and I did."

I took a step back, needing to get out of his space before I did something I regretted. "And how did it feel?"

For every step I took backwards, Reid stepped forward. His eyes dipped down to my mouth before he answered. "Wrong."

Confused, my eyebrows furrowed. "Wrong?" I looked away for a second, wondering why on earth something that amazing would feel so wrong. "Because it was about someone who hurt you? Someone who doesn't deserve you?"

Reid shook his head roughly, his brown waves moving effortlessly on his head.

"Was it... was it about Angelina?"

His jaw tightened as his eyes bored into mine. "*No.*"

"Then who?" I stammered with a low voice. My heart was climbing to my throat. My nerves were standing straight up. Something down below was simmering so hot it was likely to burn me.

Reid took another step toward me. He was so close I had to angle my head up to keep my stare leveled with his.

"You can't honestly tell me that you don't know who the song is about."

Just then, my eyes dropped to his lips, replaying the verse in my head.

> *"We were one touch away from lust.*
> *So much that your kiss was a must.*
> *Losing track of time, with no direction in sight.*
> *I just might..."*

His voice broke through every ounce of armor I had carefully placed around my body before starting today's lesson. The chains around my heart were clanking to the ground, and the burning image of Reid's disappointed look from our earlier kisses turned to ash.

Reid's hand slowly raised, and he cupped my cheek gently, his fingers getting tangled in my hair. "I'm sick and tired of pretending I don't think of you each morning before I even open my eyes. I'm sick and tired of stealing glances your way, hoping that you don't notice. I'm so tired of pretending I regret pressing my lips to yours—because I don't. I know I should, but I don't, Brooklyn. I want you in every way possible. I can try to deny it all I want, but this"— Reid snatched a rolled-up notebook from his back pocket and pushed it gently to my chest—"this right here proves that every single ounce of denial in my head isn't true. It proves that you have embedded yourself so deep within my body that I can't help but allow it to come out when I'm alone at night, scribbling down words to a song that, in the end, revolves around you. For tonight, I don't want to lie. I don't want to pull you in and then push you away."

I was wrong earlier. Reid King wasn't at my mercy... I was at *his*. For the first time since I had met Reid, he was *finally* telling the truth. He was pushing through his barriers. His walls were down; he was exposed. Every ounce of him was in plain sight.

Before I knew it, I rose up on my tiptoes, placing my shaky hands on his broad shoulders. "Then tonight, don't. Don't pull me in and then push me away. Just pull me in and keep me close."

The notebook in Reid's firm grip fell to the ground below us. His arm wrapped around my back, pulling my body flush with his. His head dipped, and his mouth moved over mine with such elegance that I became lost in it. The way his tongue dipped in and darted past my lips had my toes curling. He slowly walked us back against the wall, his hands moving slowly over my curves as his lips caressed mine, beckoning them to move with his. My palms traveled upward, and I weaved my fingers through his hair, a small moan escaping my mouth.

I felt Reid's knee pushing my legs open. His head dipped past my lips and over to my ear, leaving a trail of small kisses all the way down to my collarbone. His teeth carved a path down and over the strap of my bra as he skillfully moved down my shoulder. Then, his hands moved from behind my back and slowly fiddled with the hem of my light sweater, slowly gliding the soft, cottony fabric over my skin and onto the floor.

I watched with a racing heart as he brought his rough hands up to my hair, pulling the hair tie loose so my hair fell in one single whoosh around my face and shoulders. Reid slowly took my hands from his own body and pinned them up above my head. My legs wanted to clench together to fight the fire that I was feeling in between them, but Reid didn't allow me to. Instead, he began kissing, licking, nipping every inch of my body. He started at my collarbone and moved down to my chest. My breasts were heavy with need, wanting desperately to fall out of my bra. Reid licked the skin, his chin scratching along the lacy fabric before moving down to my stomach.

With each kiss, my stomach tensed and I felt an urge so strong I thought I might cry out.

When Reid was finished kissing my skin, he slowly stood back up, spreading my legs out even further with his jean-clad knee. Our eyes locked so hard that nothing could penetrate our stare.

He released his hands from pinning me and placed them underneath my butt, picking me up. My legs were wrapped around his torso, and I gingerly skimmed my fingers to the hem of his shirt, pulling it up and over his head. His shoulders were round and firm, and the muscles along his neck were taut, moving with skill as he carried us over to the middle of the living room.

Reid slowly lowered me to the living room floor and peered down at me. A small amount of panic shot through me, afraid he might back out, afraid he might throw up his walls again, like he'd been doing since the moment we met. But instead, he stood up and took his pants off, standing only in a tight pair of black boxer briefs. The slopes and curves of his body had me breaking out in a full-on sweat. The ripples of his abs protruded as he bent down to slip off my leggings. A small whimper escaped my mouth as his fingers wisped over the bridge of my panties.

"Fuck," he murmured under his breath, and it sent tingles down my legs.

I could only pray that Reid didn't pull his typical stunt and regret this afterwards, because what we were doing had no room for regrets. Whatever bond Reid and I had formed was something that wasn't even in the realm of normal. It was like we were a part of something that only we understood. When we were alone, everything else melted around us. We both felt so deeply, so profoundly.

Our eyes connected, and I couldn't bear to look away. My stomach dipped low. I ran my tongue over my lips and whispered, "Don't hurt me, Reid." He paused, his fingers stilling on my panties, his eyes searching my face as he bent over me. The golden specks shimmered even below his hooded eyes. My heart suddenly skidded to a stop when he didn't say anything. I could already feel it shrinking in fear that he was going to back away and leave me half-naked on the wooden, living room floor. But instead, he bent down and lowered his lips to mine, scorching me—branding me. Reid's tongue reached inside, and he deepened the kiss into an abyss. My back bucked off the floor as Reid snatched my panties off in one single whoosh. He was finished with taking his time with me. He began to move with speed and agility. He reached behind and quickly unhooked my bra, his fingers grazing over my back, and then he stood up and ripped off his boxers, throwing them behind his body. He snatched his jeans up, fished out a condom, and was back on top of me within seconds. As soon as he sheathed himself, he spread my legs wide, running his finger achingly slow over my most sensitive spot. I whimpered, and as soon as his finger was inside, I was gripping his arms for more. I needed more. I needed *him*. I'd never been so driven for a man to be inside of me before. It was like Reid King had the lost key to my most secretive door. Within a single thrust, he was inside of me, my back arching up off the floor long enough for his arm to come behind me, pinning me to his body.

Our bodies were lined with a sheen of sweat, my hair beginning to stick to my forehead as he thrust in and out of me. His lips grazed mine with a rough tenderness only someone like Reid King could possess. His hands roamed all over my body, touching, gripping, feeling every single bit of my skin. I ran my tongue along his as a familiar buildup began pooling inside my lower belly with each movement of his palm on my body. Reid, sensing that I was close to a release, removed his hand that was wrapped up in my hair and moved it in between our bodies, rubbing the exact spot I needed. He circled his finger as my nipples tightened. I threw my head back, slack-jawed, as a needy moan escaped, and Reid began to move faster on top of me. I spiraled out of control when Reid groaned and stilled his body. We both tumbled into a dreamlike state, forgetting the world and everything else.

For a second, it was just him and me, wrapped up in each other's embrace, panting, clawing, kissing.

There were no words.

It was pure passion. Just Reid and I intertwined and lost in each other.

CHAPTER TWENTY-ONE

REID

I stared down at Brooklyn's half-covered, naked body snuggled beneath a gray, threaded blanket on the couch. I grazed her delicate, exposed skin with my gaze, lingering on the slightly yellow bruise on her side from when she'd fallen at my concert a week ago. I stared at the tiny scars that lined her torso and then moved to the dip of her belly button. I watched her slowly rising chest and her relaxed, sweet face as she slept peacefully.

How did things shift so quickly between us? One second, I was throwing death glares her way, pissed off when she'd shoved a schedule in my face, demanding that we follow a bogus plan to get me back to writing killer songs. And the next, I was wrapped around her finger, sneaking in glances whenever possible, thinking of her every second of every day, wondering how I could spend more time with her.

I kept replaying her words from before I had stripped her out of every ounce of clothing and released every bit of fear and regret that was closing in on me inside of her. *Don't hurt me, Reid.* In that moment, the only thing I could think was, *Never... I'd never hurt you.* Brooklyn changed something inside of me. She switched on some kind of emotion that I was destined to wear on my sleeve for the rest of my life.

She didn't want me to hurt her, but what I was about to do would make it seem like I was.

CHAPTER TWENTY-TWO

BROOKLYN

Small beams of sunlight poured through the far window of the living room, making the room appear as if it were glowing, like I was in some sort of heaven. I smiled gently as I pulled a cozy blanket up and over my body, basking in the warmth before I remembered that I was in a sort of heaven. A heaven that had my body smelling of Reid. A heaven that had my heart growing in my chest. A heaven that I never knew existed. *This is heaven on earth, right here.*

My smile grew even wider as I remembered Reid and me. I gently moved my head to the side to look for him but came up empty-handed. I slowly sat upright, keeping the blanket pulled up to my chest as I scanned the gleaming room with sleepy eyes.

I found him within seconds. Reid was sitting on the far edge of the couch, wearing only a pair of pants. His torso had beams of sunlight streaked across it from the window, and he looked like a fallen angel—dark, ruffled hair, sharp contours of muscle along his back, with small gleams of golden sunlight all around him. I put my thumb up to my mouth and gently bit it, trying to relax the giddy feeling bubbling up inside of me.

Last night was like everything fell into place. The hidden, warped feelings I'd been harboring for him boomed like thunder in the background. They were there in plain sight. I let go and he did too. Reid King and I had something I'd never experienced with anyone before. My heart almost felt attached to his, and that was a scary, yet calming, thought.

I slowly swung my legs over the couch, wrapping the blanket up a little tighter around my body, and began to open my mouth, but Reid inclined his head over his shoulder, and my smile fell within seconds.

Dread hit me head on, and I gripped my blanket tighter. *No. I know that look.*

"Brooklyn..." he muttered, averting his eyes away from mine. I stared at his back, the tense way his shoulders were pulled back. Tears stung the backs of my eyes, but I held my ground. I kept my composure. *There's no way he's about to—*

"I need you to leave."

I was stunned. My face stung like Reid had slapped me. The bottom of my stomach fell out from below as I replayed the night in my head—his body on mine, the way he peered down at me and made me feel like what we had was something more, like what we were doing was almost sacred. *Did I make it all up in my head?*

"What?" I stuttered, pulling the blanket up even tighter, as if the thin cotton was somehow going to protect me.

Reid's back was still facing me. "I need you to leave, Brooklyn." His words weren't rough. In fact, they sounded soft, almost too soft to be his.

Hurt and anger both gripped me so hard it made my stomach ache. I winced and grabbed onto it.

"But—"

"I know," he interrupted. "I know what you're going to say."

Reid quickly turned around and stood up, placing his hands on his hips, right beside that V shape his abs formed.

He was standing there just in pants, his bare torso gleaming but his face drawn tight as if he were pained. "You told me not to hurt you, and this is me not hurting you. I need you to leave."

Fury hit me so hard it felt like I was being whipped. I stood up, too, the blanket even tighter in my hand. "No." Reid's jaw muscles worked back and forth. His nostrils flared; his Adam's apple bobbed up and down. I glared at him. "I'm not leaving. You can't just snap your fingers and demand I leave, not after last night."

Reid swallowed as he looked away. He couldn't even look me in the eye. *How dare he strip me naked and have his way with me and then demand I leave.*

"Brooklyn, please," he begged, still keeping his gaze aloof. "I… I can't do this."

I laughed a cold-hearted laugh. "Too late, Reid. You *did* do this."

He pinched the bridge of his nose. "Brooklyn. Just leave."

"No!" I demanded, stomping my foot. "You can pretend that last night didn't mean anything. You can pretend like there isn't something between us, like I'm just an annoying little gnat that was sent here to collaborate on songs with you, but I'm *not* leaving." I gasped, catching my breath. "I'm not leaving because, at the end of the day, I know the truth. I know that there is something happening between us—last night proved that very clearly."

"None of that matters, Brooklyn."

Another slap to the face. The anger simmering below was quickly morphing into hurt. I was hurt. He was hurting me. *How did I let this happen?*

I pinned him with a desperate stare. "Tell me why."

He took a step back and looked away again, unable to meet my gaze. "Why what?"

"Why are you pushing me away? Again. What did she do to you that has you so afraid to feel?"

Reid snapped his head over to me so fast I jumped. His

narrowed eyes were like slits on his face, but I pointed my gaze right back. He should have known by then that I wasn't one to back down from him.

"You want to know what has me so fucked up?"

"Yes," I ground out through the wall of my clenched teeth.

He laughed sarcastically and then shrugged. "Okay, then maybe you'll see that I'm no good. That I have *nothing* to offer you, other than a whole lot of drama."

"That's not true," I argued.

He huffed, shaking his head, walking a few steps toward me. "It is true, Brooklyn. It is. Have you ever once thought about the prospect of you and me being together? What that would mean? You are so pure and so damn *good.* You're kind, and beautiful, and like a fucking beam of sunshine. You're an elementary school music teacher. You're so far away from the world I live in that you'd be fucking swallowed up whole if you were to even put a pinky finger inside it. My world is full of fame and meaningless gossip. It's disgusting at times. It chews people up and spits them out. My entire life is my music, and the one time I put it in front of someone else, they ended up not coming out on top. I couldn't bear the thought of the same outcome happening to you."

Reid stopped talking for a few seconds. He ran his hands through his hair, pacing back and forth in the living room. I stayed completely still, watching him stroll around. Then, he finally stopped and shot a glance at me. "What would you say if I told you I had a child?"

My mouth fell open. "You have a child?" I asked, completely dumbfounded.

A short, sarcastic laugh escaped his lips. "I have no fucking clue. Do you want to know why I'm so fucked up? Why I'm hot one second and then cold the next? Why I pull you in and then push you away?" He didn't give me time to answer. He strode over to me and stood so close I had to peer up into his face. "The last time I saw Angelina, she was lying in a pool of blood on a hotel bathroom floor with a knife in her hand, saying that she cut our baby out of her stomach. I gave up on her, and it turned her into *that*. Me pushing her away made her *do* that." My mouth gaped, and I felt so incredibly sorrowful that tears truly did brim my eyelids. Not for the fact that he was pushing me away again, but for the fact that he was going through something that didn't even sound possible. It sounded like part of a horror story, or part of a wicked movie that had me pulling back from the screen because it was so absurd. I snapped my jaw shut when he spoke again. "So, when I tell you that I'm not intentionally hurting you, and that I'm only trying to protect you, I need you to take it and deal with it. I know what last night was. I know what you felt. But, Brooklyn, you need to just stay the hell away from me for your own good."

I began to shake my head. No.

"Just go, Brooklyn. Please," he begged, his eyes full of regret.

"I'm not going, Reid."

"You are," he commanded, his voice raising with anger.

"No, I'm not."

Reid's voice cut right through me. "You fucking are. Don't you hear me? Do you want to end up like her? When I first met Angelina, we were casual. She was sweet and focused on her modeling career. The more we were together, the more she became obsessed with my lifestyle, begging to go to red-carpet events, loving when the camera took her picture. But the distance got to her. She went off and did her own thing, so I did that, too. I broke up with her and focused on music. I put music first, and..." He clenched his eyes. "And now look at her. I don't even know what the future has to offer me. I don't know what next week will bring. I know nothing. For all I know, I could have a child out there somewhere. Alone. Because his or her mother went off the deep end."

I grabbed onto Reid's forearm; it felt hot in my grasp.

"It's not your fault, Reid. You breaking up with Angelina isn't an excuse for her to do… that. A breakup isn't code for self-inflicting injuries. You have to understand that."

Did he really think that it was his fault?

Reid's eyes traveled down to my hand on his arm, and he closed his eyes, breathing deeply in and out of his nose. Then, he brought those golden eyes to my face with a tight-lipped frown. "You won't change my mind. I won't bring you down with me. Please." He brought his forehead down to mine. "Please leave."

"I'm not leaving," I said again, still eager to show him that he couldn't just scare me away. Not after last night. Not after we let each other in.

He pulled back abruptly, my hand falling from his forearm. "Goddamnit, Brooklyn!" he yelled. "Don't make me say things I'm going to regret later."

I stood still, defeat slowly seeping in all around me. "Then don't make me leave."

Reid looked angry, tormented almost. He shook his head, the messy chocolate waves going in every other direction. "You and I will *never* be anything. There is no reason for you to stay here."

It felt like my heart was being pinned underneath a seven-ton truck. I could feel the hurt in my bones. I could feel it in the deepest parts of my body. But I was *done* begging. I wasn't going to stand there like a pitiful woman who was begging a man to choose her over everything. I was done begging Reid King to fight for me—or better yet, to fight for himself.

I should have known there would be no true benefit of us becoming close; I didn't listen to Jane. I should have been protecting my heart from the very beginning—from the moment that Reid's wall chipped and he let me in. The push and pull game between us was over.

We were over before we even started.

I angled my chin upward, my heartless, cold gaze never once wavering from him. Instead of letting myself break in front of him, I tried hard to remember the text I'd gotten from my sister yesterday. It was a picture of a giant For Sale sign in front of my parents' house—my childhood home. *Just hang on to that, Brooklyn.* "I'm not leaving, Reid. I need the money, so finish your songwriting on your own, and the second I get a call from Carissa or V, telling me that the job is done, I'll be out of your hair."

Reid's shoulders relaxed, but the look on his face didn't fool me; Reid King looked defeated. But this was what he wanted. He wanted me gone.

Reid King was a jaded man, gutted beyond belief, and I had the sutures in my hand, ready to stitch him up. But the second he knew I was close, he pushed me away again, just out of reach.

I was beginning to think that Reid King didn't want to be stitched up, that he was happy being the dreary man that he was. Now, I was left having to stitch myself up.

"Thank you," he breathed, relieved that I was finished putting up a fight.

I turned on my heel and stormed away, blanket still clutched up to my chin. The second I was safely in the spare room, I slammed the door so hard the old, antique frames rattled along the wall. My side ached, my stomach turned, and I, all of a sudden, felt more exhausted than I'd ever felt before. So, I crawled into bed, leaving my broken heart out there in the living room with the culprit.

CHAPTER TWENTY-THREE

REID

How did two days feel like an eternity? The last few weeks felt like they flew by on a multi-million-dollar jet, soaring through the clouds as fast as possible. But now that Brooklyn and I were at odds again, with her hating my guts, two days had felt like an entire lifetime.

It didn't help that I'd barely slept since the night I'd taken her soul in my hands and crushed it early the next morning. I'd been working nonstop on writing an album. My fingers were numb from using them so much on the strings of my guitar, and my voice was hoarse and poor sounding. But I didn't care. I had to get this shit done before I did any more damage to her.

I was tempted to just tell her to leave now and I'd pay her as much as she wanted to be paid. But if I did that, I was certain she'd refuse and then throw something at my head. She hated me, and I couldn't even blame her.

I had torn her to pieces. I had stripped her out of her clothes, buried myself inside of her, felt *way* too many emotions, and then was met with reality hours later. Maybe

I was wrong for taking the reins into my own hands and ending things between us before they went south. Maybe it was wrong of me to make a decision for her; maybe it was purely selfish. Maybe I wasn't protecting her. Maybe I was just protecting me.

I shook my head, my leg bouncing up and down as I stared at her closed door. I wasn't really sure what I was doing anymore. One minute, I was caught up in lawyers, thinking of all the different ways I could have ended things with Angelina. And then the next, I was submerged in Brooklyn's presence, forgetting the world around me, forgetting that I was Reid King, and pretending that my past wasn't still my present.

No, you're doing the right thing.

I had nothing to offer Brooklyn other than a whole lot of fucked-up shit. I didn't even have my own head on straight.

My eyes traveled down to the—once again—untouched food on a plate that I had laid in front of Brooklyn's door. I hadn't seen her open it once in the past two days. The knot in my stomach got tighter. I slept on the couch, hopeful that I'd at least get one glimpse of her in the middle of the night, sneaking off to the kitchen, because, obviously, she couldn't go two days without food. But she had obviously mastered tiptoeing like a mouse, because the hours that I did submit to sleep, I never woke up to her.

I would be lying if I said I wasn't worried.

I would also be lying if I said I didn't feel relieved that I was about to hit send on the email I'd written to V, enclosing a few of the songs I'd somewhat perfected in the last two days. I told myself I wouldn't use another woman as a muse, but every single song I wrote revolved around Brooklyn.

I scanned the email once more before hitting send, wondering what Brooklyn would say when she heard the songs in the next several months after everything was all said and done. Would she be quick to change the song, annoyed that my voice was the one filtering through the speakers? Or would she listen and torment herself with my words—or better yet, the truth? Would she still hate me for breaking her heart and pushing her away one last time?

Or would she still feel me inside of her, chasing away reality like it was my only duty on this earth? Would she still remember what it was like when I touched her body? Because that was exactly what I would remember every time I listened to these songs. I'd remember how Brooklyn rooted for me more than anyone else. I'd remember how she never gave up on me, and I'd remember how *she* chased away my reality.

My phone rang a few minutes after I sent the email. I answered it quickly, hoping it was from V and that he was happy with what I'd just sent.

But it wasn't V. Instead, it was a female's voice. "Reid?"

I stayed silent, unsure if I should confirm that it was me.

"Reid, it's Jane. Brooklyn's friend."

I sat back on the couch, pushing my laptop away from my lap. "Oh, yeah it's me."

"Where is Brooklyn?"

"What? Why?" I asked, rubbing my hand over the bridge of my nose. *Didn't she know that Brooklyn currently hated me?*

"Is she there?" It sounded as if Jane was pacing around while on the phone.

"Yeah, she should be." *I would have known if she left… unless she left in the middle of the night. I heard some shuffling around her room late last night, so I knew she was still in there, avoiding me.*

Panic started to claw at my skin, and I had no idea why. *You were the one that wanted her gone, King. Now deal with it.*

"When was the last time you saw her then?"

"Why?" I asked, trying to keep my anxiety invisible.

"Reid, go check on her right now. I'm worried."

My blood pressure shot through the roof. I couldn't have climbed off the couch faster if I tried. "Worried about what?" I asked, shuffling toward her door.

"Her past kidney issues. I've been trying to get a hold of

her for a couple days, and she texted saying that she felt like she had the flu and that she'd text me later. But she hasn't texted or called, no matter how many times I try to get a hold of her. I remembered I had your number from when you called in Atlanta. Can you go check on her?"

Her kidney issues? What?

Sweat formed on my forehead as I picked up my pace. I didn't bother knocking on Brooklyn's door. I swung it open and scanned the room quickly, seeing nothing but messy covers and Brooklyn's phone on the bed. *Why didn't I come check on her before now? You fucking selfish bastard.*

"Reid? Is she okay?" Jane asked again, her voice more frantic.

I trudged over to the bathroom and pulled the door open quickly, almost ripping it off its hinges. Then, I felt all the breath leave my body. Every ounce of oxygen was gone. I dropped the phone, and it skittered across the tiles, landing with a thud against the porcelain tub. I hurriedly ran over to Brooklyn lying beside the toilet with her eyes closed. Her face was white—so white that she blended in with the tiled floor. I took her limp body into my arms and shook her by her small shoulders. "Brooklyn?" I yelled, giving her another shake. She didn't even so much as stir. I put my head to her chest, listening for her heartbeat. It was slow—too slow.

Fear clawed at the corners of my brain as it tried to take me back to the moment I found Angelina in a pile of blood. I shook away the thought, focusing on the one woman who made everything in my life seem okay, if even for a short moment, and reached for my phone. I hung up Jane's call before dialing 911 and praying to God that I wasn't too late.

In that moment, I'd have given my own heartbeat to Brooklyn. She could have the entire thing. She deserved it far more than I did.

CHAPTER TWENTY-FOUR

BROOKLYN

My lips felt like they were on actual fire. Or maybe they'd been burnt badly. I wasn't sure of the difference. All I knew was that they were hurting—badly. I peeled them open, hearing the breath that escaped my mouth. My head was throbbing as I tried to open my eyes, and when I finally pulled my sticky eyelashes apart, it took me a while to figure out where I was.

Why was it so bright in here? *Wait, why are there fluorescent lights above my head? Why does it smell so sterile in here?* All of a sudden, I could hear a frantic beeping noise. It kept getting louder and louder and louder.

"Brooklyn, calm down," Cara said, appearing out of nowhere.

I shot up quickly, scooting my sore back against the fluffy pillows that my head was resting on. "Why am I in the hospital?!"

Dread washed over me. Oh my gosh. *It was my kidney!*

I felt the blood drain from my face as Cara took my cheeks in her hands. "Relax. You were dehydrated and passed out. You're okay. You're okay."

A held breath escaped my mouth as relief flooded in. My voice cracked. "So, my kidney is…"

Cara gave a small smile. "Your kidney is fine. You had the flu, and you got so dehydrated that you apparently passed out."

It all came back to me as soon as Cara started to talk. After Reid and I fought and I stomped off to my room, I went back to bed. I crawled under the covers and lay there, angry, hurt, annoyed, irritated—everything.

I felt sick.

I thought I was being dramatic and that I was ill from a throbbing heart that Reid decided to stomp all over after he stripped me bare on his living room floor, but I was truly just sick. I couldn't stop throwing up, and, God forbid, I go out into the kitchen where I might run into my new enemy. So instead, every so often, when I had enough energy, I'd cup my hands under the bathroom faucet and gulp water in hopes that it'd make me feel better. Spoiler alert: it didn't.

It was a stupid thing to do—avoiding the only other human in the house I was at when I was *that* sick, considering part of me thought there might have been something wrong with my only working kidney, that maybe my body was failing, possibly from the swift kick I got from the show a couple weeks back. But after a while, the only thing I could think about was how to keep the contents of my stomach inside and not in the toilet.

My brow furrowed after I sucked some water through a straw that Cara had handed to me. "How did I get here?"

That was the one thing I couldn't remember. I really only remembered being angry with Reid and then being so sick I could barely make it off the bathroom floor.

Cara sat down on the edge of my bed and tucked some hair behind her ear. She fiddled with the threads on the blanket and said, "Well, Jane got worried when you'd texted her, and then when you stopped answering, she called Reid, who then called me."

I averted my eyes, hoping to hide the fact that hearing

his name did something to me, because it wholeheartedly did.

"I guess Reid freaked out when he saw you, and instead of waiting for an ambulance, he threw you in one of his cars and rushed you here. He hasn't left." Cara smiled at the end of her sentence, but the only thing that did was turn that little prick in my heart into a punch.

I crossed my arms over my hospital gown. "Can you tell him thanks, but I don't want to see him."

Cara's eyes almost fell out of her skull. "What? Why?! Reid King, King of Music, hot beyond belief, your saving grace, has been in that waiting room, wearing a freaking baseball hat, trying to blend in like he isn't a freaking rock star, for almost twenty-four hours, waiting to make sure you're okay." Cara ran her hand through her hair excitedly. "In fact, he flew me all the way from New York on a redeye so I could be here. Mom and Dad were going to come too, but instead, they stayed back to watch Callie while Jack worked. They've been texting me, along with Jane, every three seconds, asking how you are. OH! And not only did Reid fly me out here, but he's also paying for all your medical costs."

My face felt hot. No. No. No.

"I don't want him to pay for my medical costs."

Cara huffed and gave me a side-eye. "What is wrong with you?" She paused. "I mean, other than being sick."

I bit the inside of my cheek, my head throbbing even harder now.

Cara's eyes softened, as she must have put two and two together. "Something happened between you two."

I laughed. "Oh, something happened, all right." I gently shook my head. "It doesn't matter. Just... tell him I said thank you, and I'm grateful, but I don't want him paying for the medical costs. Tell him the only thing I want him to do is finish a song so I can be paid and move on."

Cara frowned. "Brooklyn."

"What?" I very grumpily asked.

"He won't take no for an answer, you know that, right?"

My heart began to thump inside my chest at the thought of seeing him again. His deep amber eyes, glittering with golden specks, his perfectly tousled brown hair, the sharp line of his jaw, those perfectly pouty lips. *He told you he wanted you to leave.* I began to shake my head at Cara, seconds from pleading with her, from using anything in my reach to bargain my way out of talking to Reid again, but the light sound of shuffling near the hospital door took my attention.

I melted right there as I peered into Reid's worried expression, dark bags underneath his eyes that were almost completely hidden by the low brim of his black baseball hat. He stood in a plain, dark t-shirt and jeans that were beginning to look worn.

"Brooklyn," he breathed, and my heart shattered in my chest. My eyes grew wet, and I clenched my teeth, even though it hurt my head.

Cara stood up quickly and left the room after giving me a pleading look.

If only she knew that Reid King had fooled me into thinking we had something special and fucked me on his living room floor before telling me to get out of his house. Then, maybe, she wouldn't be siding with him.

I gulped as I sat up a little taller in the uncomfortable bed, staring at the metal rods lining each side.

"How are you feeling?" Reid asked. I could hear his heavy footsteps as he approached closer, but I didn't dare meet his eye.

"I'm fine, considering," I mumbled, my hands twiddling back and forth.

Silence passed between us, and it made me uncomfortable. I wanted this to be over with as quickly as possible. The hurt was still there, along with the betrayal. I felt silly, really. As if Reid King and I would ever be a thing. As if Reid King felt what *I* felt.

"I don't want you paying for my medical costs," I said, finally bringing my attention to his. Reid reached up and took his baseball hat off his head, angling it backward. He looked overwhelmingly attractive, even with the tired lines along his face. "I appreciate you bringing me here, but I can pay for it on my own."

Reid inhaled a deep breath and smashed his lips together. But I stopped him before he could argue.

"Just finish the album, and hopefully V will still pay me, even though I'm now"—I looked around the sterile room as bright lights shone down onto the sparkling floor and a glimmer of the sunset radiated through the far window—"in a hospital, technically unable to collaborate with you."

"I've finished a few songs. You'll get paid. Don't worry about that. I wish you would have told me that you had some medical stuff going on. I would have demanded you get your side checked out further, even if it's not the reason you're in here today."

My head flew over to him as pride hit me square in the chest. *He finished a few songs?* Shaking myself out of my pleased daze, I said, "It never came up, and it's not a big deal to begin with. So what? I have one kidney. There are tons of people with one kidney, but anyway… congrats on finishing some songs. I guess… um, take care?"

He snickered, and the monitor that checked my heart rate began to beep louder and louder until I ripped the thing off my finger and threw it across the room.

"Is this really how you want to end things?" he asked, stepping another inch closer to my bed. I wanted the entire thing to swallow me whole.

I mumbled under my breath, shoving myself into the bed. "You're the one that wanted to end things, so yeah, I guess so."

"Brooklyn," he pleaded, his voice sounding as if I'd just broken him in half. I couldn't help my gaze as it trailed up his torso, landing right on his face. "Just…" He looked away momentarily. "Give me time to make things right. Please."

My brows scrunched. *What?* Days ago, he wanted me to leave—no, he *begged* me to leave—but now he wanted to

227

make things right?

"What changed?" I asked, my eyes bouncing back and forth between his. "You said that you wanted me to leav—"

"I know what I said," he interrupted, taking another step toward my bed. His legs were now touching the silver railings. "And you want to know what's changed?"

I slowly nodded my head, unsure if I really wanted to know.

"Everything." Reid's voice shook as he bent his strong arms down onto the bed, causing my entire body to dip down. "Everything has changed after seeing you on that floor, unconscious."

I didn't say anything. I was too confused, and maybe even a little afraid.

"But…" My voice could barely escape my smashed lips. "But you said… even if there wasn't the drama with your past, that you and I would never work." I breathed out a sarcastic laugh. "I mean, look at us, Reid."

"I am looking at us," he hurriedly said, peering down into my face. His eyes were determined, unwavering from mine.

I rolled my eyes, and then cringed when my head began to throb.

"Lie down, Brooklyn," Reid urged, bringing one hand to my hair. I slowly sunk back into the bed, taking a deep breath.

"I'm a plain-Jane elementary school music teacher…"

"I know what you do for a living, Brooklyn."

I wearily said, "And you're… *you*. Reid King—King of Music. There is no future for us. And that's the truth."

Reid shook his head slowly, bending down even further to my face. I was suddenly thankful that my heart rate monitor was laying on the floor, because I was certain that it would have embarrassed the hell out of me right then.

"That's not the truth, Brooklyn."

"It is," I mumbled, feeling myself become drowsy,

despite my erratic heart rate.

Reid dipped his head so close to mine that I could feel his warm breath on my forehead. His scent enveloped me like a warm blanket, and I almost wanted to reach my arms up and bring him down onto the bed with me. Despite him hurting me, despite the cold words he said to me a few days ago, I still felt weirdly comforted by him. I wanted him to curl up beside me. I wanted his strong arms wrapped around my body so we could go back to our little cocoon of just *us*.

I closed my eyes as Reid's lips brushed over my forehead, warmth spreading throughout me. Before he stood back up and left the room, he whispered, "Don't give up on me now."

I said nothing aloud, but I heard the faint words in the back of my head, even if I didn't want to believe them.

I won't, Reid. I won't.

CHAPTER TWENTY-FIVE

REID

Love was a sneaky son of a bitch. Love snuck up on people. I knew that now. I couldn't believe that I ever thought there was a possibility of me ever loving Angelina. What I had for Angelina was completely different than what I felt for Brooklyn. Love wasn't loving the idea of someone, or the mystery, or the stigma that came with alluring beauty or a flirty laugh—much like Angelina had. Love was something that could destroy you within seconds but put you back together a moment later. Love was feeling hope, and comfort, but fear and worry, too. Angelina dug a dagger into my back so deep that it was all I could feel there for a while. But the second Brooklyn came into my life, that dagger loosened and clanked to the floor. I felt more with Brooklyn.

Brooklyn made me feel again.

And the thought of her leaving this earth, especially without me truly facing what I felt for her, was enough to send me to the grave. Nothing mattered after the doctors took her from my arms and placed her on a gurney, rushing her through the ER doors. Nothing at all.

It suddenly didn't matter that Brooklyn and I were from

completely different worlds.

I'd destroy anything that stood in my way from hearing her laugh again, or seeing her happy smile paired with those bright, girly dresses.

Honestly, I'd do anything for her.

Like walk into the Bloomsdale Psychiatric Institute to finally get shit figured out so I could be an actual man—one that Brooklyn deserved—and not the shell of a person I'd been for the last several months.

———

The Good Samaritan Bloomsdale Psychiatric Institute wasn't anything like I'd imagined in my head. The hallway was lined with carpet. Large frames of different paintings hung along the walls, creating a sense of warmth instead of a sense of dread that every hospital and—what I assumed before today—psychiatric institute brought. There weren't loud beeping noises from machines or people in wheelchairs staring at blank TV screens with drool hanging out of their mouths.

It was quiet.

So quiet I could hear my own heartbeat in my ears.

I knew I shouldn't have been there. Darcy would have a freaking fit if she knew, but it was time to put a stop to it all. I didn't care if the media knew. I didn't care much about anything other than ending this, once and for all.

I had no idea where Angelina was. In fact, she could have been gone already, but as soon as I rounded the last corner of the second floor, I stopped walking. A tall, older man with graying hair, wearing a flannel shirt and worn jeans, was standing near a door, all by himself.

I knew exactly who he was. I'd never met him in person, but I recognized him.

It was the one man on this earth who'd like to see my head on a stake, but instead of letting that worry me, I kept pushing myself toward him instead of retreating backwards.

Hearing my footsteps, he turned his head over to me, and it only took one look before a scowl formed on his face. His cold eyes shot through me as I walked closer, but I didn't retreat. *Show no fear, King. None.*

I was sick with dread, every muscle in my body begging me to turn around, but the spark inside of me kept me going. The thought of knowing the truth, the thought of getting my life back on track, burned profoundly.

"Phil," I intoned as I slid up beside him. He turned his steely glare away and focused it through a small window beside a door. The blinds were only half-opened when I brought my attention to where his was, but if I squinted, I could see who was inside the room.

My gut clenched even harder.

My hands grew sweaty.

A chill iced my entire spine.

"It doesn't even look like her," I muttered, stunned. I watched Angelina sit on a bed, fidgeting her fingers together rapidly as she talked with an older woman who had a notepad in her hand and glasses perched on her round nose.

The radiant Angelina with shiny, coal-black hair was pale with large, dark circles under her eyes. The straight ends of her hair were frayed like a tattered blanket. Her toned arms were skinny and looked like twigs hanging out from beneath a too-large hospital gown.

"That's because it isn't *her*," her father ground out, his voice strained.

I cleared my throat, tearing my eyes away from Angelina. I moved over to the other side of the door in case Angelina happened to look up and see me.

Phil spoke again, still keeping his eyes on the small window. "You shouldn't be here."

"I know...but I am." I crossed my arms over my chest, after taking the baseball cap off my head, and leaned against the cool wall. "And I think it's time this is settled."

Phil's head slowly swiveled over to me, but I didn't give him a chance to speak. "Do you think it's fair what you're doing to me?" I asked, my brow deepening. "I know you think it's my fault. That her being here is my fault, but I think deep down you know it's not. You just want someone to blame."

Phil's wrinkly face twitched, his clear eyes glossing over for a moment before he turned his gaze back to her. Silence passed between us. I briefly heard soft music start to play down the hall, paired with the hum of the air conditioner. Then, Phil's wobbly voice started, and it was the only thing I could focus on. "You know, she always wanted to be someone she wasn't." He paused, crossing his shaky arms over his chest. "Even when she was younger. I can still remember the day she said that she was no longer going by the name of Angelina, but of Lori." My head ticked to the side as the name Lori floated around. Phil let out a raspy, biting laugh. "At first, her mom and I thought it was cute, her always changing her mind about who she wanted to be, what she wanted to be when she grew up. But when she became a teen…things changed."

I listened intently, allowing him to gather his wits. "She started going off and doing erratic things, like spending excessive amounts of money—money that she stole from us. She'd shoplift and get into cars with strangers, spouting off that her name was something different than Angelina. She'd go through stages of depression, have major mood swings." He shook his head as he rubbed his hand feebly over his cheek. "It was torture, watching her go through something neither I nor her mother knew anything about. We finally began to seek help from our town pastor, who recommended seeing a counselor, and that was when she was diagnosed."

My world shifted. I had to hold onto the wall in front of me before I fell over. "Diagnosed?" *Did I hear him right?*

Phil wouldn't look over at me. Instead, he looked down at the carpeted floor covered with yellow and purple swirls. "She has a slight form of dissociative identity disorder, amongst other things."

I stuttered, my voice a slight rasp. *"What?"*

Now, Phil was looking at me. "She has more than one personality, jumping back and forth in between two presences of herself. You know *Angelina*, the one that we've been able to hang on to for quite some time—after therapy and medication, that is. We truly thought she was fighting it, getting better, but sometimes, it just takes a simple word or a person to shove her back into being someone else." He sniffed, turning his attention away from my blank stare. "I wanted to blame you for a long time. I have been blaming you for a long time—Cathy and I both. I wanted to put all the blame on you. I figured you did something to her to make her regress into another *self.* That was why she ran off and disappeared for months."

The words flew out before I could even understand what I was putting together. "Is that why she kept saying Lori?"

Phil raised a bushy eyebrow.

"She kept telling me that she was hanging out with someone named Lori. She blamed Lori for disappearing and said that Lori was the one who made her do it." I shook my head, erasing the image. I kept wondering who Lori was, and now that I knew, it was shocking, mindboggling.

Phil nodded. "She was telling the truth. Lori did tell her to do it." He turned to me. "Except, she *is* Lori."

It felt like a thousand bricks were falling on my head while I was on a fast-spinning merry-go-round. I couldn't wrap my mind around what Phil was telling me. I couldn't understand.

"And the baby?" I finally asked, after more silence encased us. Phil smashed his lips together, and I thought he wasn't going to answer me. I thought he was going to continue to withhold that information—the most important piece to this entire puzzle. My stomach knotted, and my fists clenched so tightly together that they physically ached.

"There was no baby, Reid."

A held breath escaped my mouth, and I thought I was going to pass out. I stared up at the ceiling, evening my breath before I croaked out, "Why? Why couldn't you just tell me that from the beginning? Do you know how long I've been blaming myself, worrying myself to death that I...that Angelina was somehow pregnant and that she'd truly done something to it? Do you know how guilty I've felt, thinking that this was because of me? Because I had broken up with her?"

Phil's eyes glossed over again, and I could see the pity clear as day on his face.

I shook my head harshly. "Why did *you* do that to me? Do you know how fucking long I've been suffering?"

"We blamed you, Reid." He rubbed his wrinkly face. "I knew that when you two started dating she'd never tell you about her diagnosis. We rarely talked about it in fear that it would somehow set her off, and I prayed every night that somehow things would work out—that she'd either tell you or that my dream would come true and she would somehow be over it." Phil locked his gaze back onto the window, leaving me standing there with a gaping mouth. "We didn't trust you not to run to the tabloids. We thought you'd find out the truth and ruin her and her career completely. We knew how angry you'd be when you learned that she lied to you, or kept you in the dark, or better yet, told you that you had a child together when you really didn't."

My nostrils flared as I paced back and forth in the hallway. I threw my cap back on my head and tried to even out my breathing. It was a lot to take in, so much so that I felt a bit suffocated. I half-wanted to ram my fist into the wall, and the other half wanted to run the fuck away.

"Turns out," Phil said, causing me to stop mid-pace and stare at him. "Turns out, we didn't need you to ruin her career—she's done that all for herself. She's..." He shook his head, looking down at his worn shoes. "She's not pulling herself out of this one. She's never done something so... drastic before."

I could still feel the remains of anger flowing through my veins, but it was quickly being replaced by something else. I had a sinking feeling in my stomach. It felt like the world was on my shoulders. "It's because I broke up with her, isn't it?"

He shook his head before very sternly saying, "No."

"Then why? Why is she all of a sudden not snapping out of it? Why is she like *that*?" I angled my head to the small window that Phil kept peering into. I couldn't even bring myself to do it. It made me sick.

"It's not your fault. It's not my fault. It's not her mother's fault. It's not even her fault. It just is." Phil's face grew solemn, withdrawn.

I turned the ball cap forward on my head, pulling the brim down as far as possible, and walked over to stand next to him. After taking a few deep breaths, I brought my head up and stared at the woman I thought I knew, the girl I thought that, maybe, I could love one day, as she rocked back and forth and ran her fingers together rapidly. She looked angry and closed off. She looked nothing like the Angelina that I spent several nights with underneath the covers of some bed. She looked nothing like the woman I took to red-carpet events, or the woman who used to throw her head back and laugh when I'd ruffle her hair with my free hand while driving.

Phil's voice came out hoarse and shaky. "Did you love her?"

I thought long and hard about my answer. I stared at Angelina a little longer before taking my hand and placing it on her father's back. "I don't think I even knew her well enough to love her, but I do care for her."

I knew I cared for her. Otherwise, I wouldn't have been standing there.

Phil's shoulders untensed as he nodded his head and smashed his mouth together. He glanced at me out of the corner of his eye. "Can you let her go then? For her sake?"

I hated to admit it, but I'd already let her go. I let her go the moment Brooklyn entered my life and turned it on its side. I let her go the moment my lips touched Brooklyn's. It was like I saw the real meaning of caring for someone when I was with Brooklyn. She never held back with me, she said what she was thinking and she'd meant it. She was *real*. And what I felt for her was real.

"Yes," I said and turned on my heel and walked away from the one woman who I thought had destroyed me permanently.

But I was wrong. So painfully wrong.

CHAPTER TWENTY-SIX

BROOKLYN

I rolled my eyes as I scanned the radio station in my car. Static, static, more static, a country station playing some horrid version of bluegrass, and then Kiss 90.

"Fine," I muttered as I turned the volume up a bit.

I was on my way to my parents' house for a small celebration—a celebration being held because our debt was officially paid off in full. Cara still argued that I shouldn't have taken the job with Reid to pay off *her* debt, as did my parents, and truly, Jack was the only one who backed me up any time they went on a rant, but they were all happy, nonetheless, and so was I.

When I thought back to a few months ago, when Reid and I spent nearly every night together on the tour bus, it stung a little. I liked to look at that short time in my life like a dandelion—the kind that you blow on to make a wish and watch the little seeds fly into the air like little wisps of dust. Dandelion's had a natural beauty. They brought a smile to your face on a balmy spring day, and then they were gone within a second, never lasting long. All it took was someone making a wish, or a small gust of wind in the middle of summer, for the entire thing to disappear.

That was what Reid and I were—a dandelion. It was nice while it lasted, but all good things had to come to an end, and we surely did. I hadn't seen or heard from him since the hospital.

Sometimes, I thought that he never truly came to the hospital. That I didn't talk to him. That he didn't whisper, *"Don't give up on me now,"* after placing his lips on my forehead. But my heart knew better. It was the last thing I thought about before slumber took me under at night and the first thing I thought of in the morning as beams of sunlight streamed through my little apartment window.

It wasn't just Reid that I hadn't heard from. I hadn't talked to anyone from Reid's world. Jackson and Finn were like small remnants of my memory. The only thing that I had reminding me of the duo was the ridiculous cheerleading outfit they had sent to my hospital room. The little note attached to it said, *"You'll always be our favorite team pet."* I laughed about it at the time, and a warmness coated the coolness of my heart that Reid had left behind when he'd vanished, but that was the last time that I'd heard from anyone. I was back to my usual 7-3, teaching my little rugrats the difference between a verse and a chorus.

So now, the memories spent with Reid and the band were strictly set in a no-think zone. More like a no-talk zone, too. Jane wasn't allowed to bring it up—ever. And Cara and my parents knew better than to say anything about it. Although, I was certain they'd bring it up today.

My finger hovered over the second preset button on my dash, the number two long worn off from years of changing the radio station, when the woman host started to squeal. "Have you heard the newest single from Reid King?!"

My stomach did a tiny flip. The male host said, "I have, and I have to say, it's just like Reid King. The guy is unstoppable. First, he vomits all over his crowd of fans on tour,"—insert a puking sound by said host—"then he swan-dives off the stage at a later show to save some poor, helpless girl,"—that'd be me—"and now… this?! This song is just…"

The woman host interrupted. "Amazing. Do you think it's about a real *Brooklyn*?"

My head snapped as my back grew rigid. I slammed my feet on the brakes, and a car horn sounded from behind. My heart raced in my chest as I jammed my finger onto the off button.

My heart pounded the entire way to my parents' house, and the silence of my car allowed me to actually hear the beats. I ignored every single thought in my head about the fact that they said the name Brooklyn.

I don't know anyone named Brooklyn.

Nope.

Name change, coming right up.

You probably misheard them. I nodded to myself as I began to climb out of my car, an early fall breeze causing my auburn hair to fly all around my face. I grabbed it with one hand and pulled it over my shoulder. I watched as Cara came flying out of the house with wide eyes, and I almost retreated back into my car and headed home. *Oh jeez.*

"OH MY GOD!" she yelled, running full speed at my car. She stopped just a few inches from me and smacked her hands onto my shoulders. "Have you heard Rei—"

"Don't even," I blurted, raising an eyebrow.

"Oh, come on, Brooklyn!" Cara squeezed my arms, her palms sweaty to the touch. "You have to listen. You have to. You helped him with his album. His single dropped at midnight. You can't tell me that you weren't sitting beside your Mac waiting."

I pushed her hands off my shoulders.

"I even got Mom and Dad to listen to it."

I walked right past her, all but running to the door. She caught up quickly. "Brooklyn, seriously. You have to listen to it."

"No," I blurted. "Why are you rubbing it in? I'm over the whole me-and-Reid thing. It was a little fluke thing that we had—fleeting fun while it lasted." I placed my hands on my hips. "I mean, seriously. Let's be real. The entire thought of me even helping him on an album was far-fetched, but I pushed myself beyond my comfort zone because we needed the money. Thinking I meant something more to someone like him is absolute nonsense! And you know it!" *Even if he did tell me not to give up on him. He's ghosted me since.*

Cara grabbed my hand and pinned me down with a soft stare. "It's not nonsense, Brooklyn. The second you enter someone's life, they instantly love you. It would make perfect sense for you to mean something to him. Plus, he told you not to give up on him."

I threw my head back and laughed. "Please tell me that you're not actually saying Reid King, the King of Music, loves me." *Nonsense.*

Cara stomped her foot like a child. "Stop it! You have to listen to it. I'll pin you down and tie you to a chair and blare the song until you listen!"

I stopped laughing and grabbed both of her hands. "Can we please just go in there and celebrate the fact that our childhood home"—I angled my head up at the two-story brick house before looking back at her—"isn't up for sale? Can we celebrate that we're both in good health and that we're not worrying about how we're going to afford another year's worth of medication plus past medical bills?" Cara's face dropped. "Please? Can we please leave the Reid conversation alone?"

Her mouth opened and then shut, only to open up again seconds later. "He told you not to give up on him…"

I looked away, locking my eyes onto the copper- and bronze-colored leaves laying in my parents' yard. *He ghosted me! He hasn't talked to me in months. I have a hazy memory of him at the hospital and that's it. Before that, all I can focus on is that way his face looked when he told me we'd never be anything.*

Cara waited a few moments before saying, "Don't give up on someone who means something to you, Brooklyn. You're not a quitter. We both know that."

I smashed my lips together and gave her a pointed stare. She rolled her eyes and threw her arms up in defense. "That's the last thing I'll say about him." Then, she grabbed my hand and squeezed it. "But you really need to listen to the song, okay? Promise me."

I bleakly smiled. "Sure."

She gave me a soft smile and pulled me inside after her. "Okay, now let's go eat cake before your niece eats it all."

———

I kept the radio on silent as I drove back to my shabby apartment. I could probably afford something else now, maybe buy a cute little house close to the elementary school, but I was almost afraid to spend the leftover money from my summer escapade. I never wanted to be in another position where I didn't have enough money for something. What if I fell at a concert and got trampled on and damaged my only working kidney? What if Cara needed another surgery? You just never knew what could happen, so for now, the money was in a nice little savings account that I didn't touch.

Cara's words were on echo in my brain as I ran up the creaky stairs to get to my paint-chipped door. I nibbled on my lip as I tried to push the thought away. *Maybe you could have one teeny tiny listen?*

"No," I muttered aloud. Hearing Reid's voice would only hurt worse, like getting a splinter in your foot and having to walk on it. I just wasn't ready to hear his soulful voice in my head again, because I knew it would wrap around my heart and squeeze it just a little too tight.

It wasn't like Reid and I were madly in love.

But we were something.

That one thing was for certain: Reid meant something to me, even after several months apart. My heart still warmed at the sight of his face—I usually had to turn my head when I'd see it splattered on some stupid magazine in the grocery store. I always ignored the headlines—always. I was too afraid that Reid would be cozying up to some woman at an exclusive party. I didn't want to know.

I turned the corner of the long hallway to get to my door and paused. My eyes zeroed in on a small brown package that was on my doorstep. I furrowed my brow, trying to remember if I'd bought anything recently, and I knew that I hadn't.

I bent down slowly, picking up the package. I shook it while putting it up to my ear. It was light, but nothing seemed to rattle.

I quickly opened my door and shut it behind me, placing the package on my entryway table as I kicked off my Converse. I gave the package a small stare and then walked away.

My pulse was thumping in my wrist, and my mouth was drying out. I was tormenting myself. First, I was avoiding Reid's newest single, and now I was avoiding a mysterious package.

Looking at it again from the across the room, I had the thought to throw it away. But right after that thought, the next was begging me to open it.

Something inside me told me that it had something to do with Reid. All signs of the day pointed to him, but to be honest, I was afraid to open it and it *not* be from him. For all I knew, it could be a sex toy for my upstairs neighbor.

It wouldn't be the first time I'd been mistakenly delivered her package before.

Slowly, I tiptoed over to the brown package again, my socked toes sliding on my hardwood floor. I picked it up and searched for a name.

Nothing.

I took a deep breath and couldn't fight it any longer.

I tore into that package faster than opening presents on Christmas morning.

My fingers shook as I turned a CD over and over again in my hand. It was a plain silver CD, enclosed in a black felt sleeve. I went to put the CD back inside—because there was NO way I was going to listen to it, because I *knew* what would be on it—but something crinkled inside.

My fingers felt a piece of paper in between the felt, and I slowly pulled it out.

Heat blasted me on the head and went all the way to my toes. My face felt hot, my ears were simmering, and my hands were sweating. The first scratchy line of handwriting had my breath catching in my throat.

I told you not to give up on me, and I really hope you listened— although we both know you're stubborn when it comes to me. I'm ready to give in, Brooklyn.

Then, on the backside of the paper, the scratchy handwriting continued.

Thanks for helping me with this album. I owe it all to you.
-Reid

1.   *Oh, Brooklyn*
2.   *I Was Wrong*
3.   *You Were Right*
4.   *I Just Might*
5.   *Love You*
6.   *After We Met*
7.   *I Gave Into You*
8.   *I Faced My Demons*
9.   *In the End*
10.   *Here's The Dirty Truth*
11.   *I'm Here*
12.   *For You*

I couldn't breathe. My eyes scanned each song title of Reid's album several times before I realized that I needed to take a breath.

Surely…he didn't.

No.

The songs were not in a particular order, giving a subliminal message. Absolutely not.

This was all a lie.

Someone had made all of this up. Someone knew that I had this massive *thing* for Reid King, and that we'd had sex only for him to tell me to leave afterward, mortifying me beyond belief, and they created this sick joke.

His album wasn't even ready yet—he *just* dropped his single at midnight!

So why are you holding this note and a CD in your hand?! Who else would it be from?

There was no way.

The paper crinkled in my hand as I clutched my fist tightly. My eyes wandered over to the shiny CD as it laid so peacefully on top of the black felt casing. I shrugged, knowing the only way to know if Reid had truly sent this to me was to pop the thing right into the CD player and press play.

If his voice filtered throughout my apartment, song for song, then I'd know it was him.

If some voice—say, Jigsaw from the Saw movies—sounded through, then I'd know someone was messing with me.

Who would even know to do this?

I thought for a moment, knowing very well that next to no one knew I was alone with Reid King all summer. But then again, tabloids had a way of finding shit out, so who truly knew?

My fingers tingled as I fiddled with my old CD player. I plopped the CD inside and closed the lid, my pointer finger hovering over the play button.

I stood still, trying to even my breath as I debated on whether I wanted to go down this path.

Reid King and me?

That was a far-fetched dream.

Not real.

Then, I thought of how his body moved over mine on his living room floor with the shadows of our bodies moving together on the wall. I remembered how his soft lips nipped at mine as I came undone under his mercy.

It was real.

The most real thing I'd ever felt in my life.

I smashed my finger onto the play button and stepped back, covering my ears for a moment before I slowly lowered my hands.

His voice sounded throughout my room with such grace that I had to hold on to the table in front of me. My hand flew to my mouth as the words left his.

Didn't anyone tell you that I was a beast?
The beast locked in thousand-pound silver, at the very least.
Yet, here you are, Brooklyn,
Unhinging the cage with your innocence.
How can someone be so broken? How can someone be this jaded?

Oh, Brooklyn... how can you be so sweet?
Oh, Brooklyn... you're pulling me to my feet.
I tried to stop it before it began.
But now, oh, Brooklyn... I can't stop it now.

You crawled under my skin
Scratching, erasing, healing,
I wasn't going to let you in.

Oh, Brooklyn... how can you be so sweet?
Oh, Brooklyn... you've pulled me to my feet.
There's no stopping it now.
Oh, Brooklyn...

Didn't anyone tell you I was a beast?
The beast locked in thousand-pound silver, at the very least.
Yet, there you were, Brooklyn,

246

Unhinging my cage with your innocence.
How could someone be so broken? How could someone be that
jaded?

But now, Brooklyn… it's all faded.
I owe it all to you.
Oh, Brooklyn… I'm ready to face the truth.
And that truth is you.

I stood as still as a statue when the song ended. My eyes locked on the 1990 stereo I had taken from home when I first left for college. Reid King wrote a song about me. Reid King broke my heart, healed it, and was now handing it back to me.

My heart stopped as I slid to the floor to listen to the rest of the songs on the album. Not only did the words do something to me, but Reid's voice crawled through my skin and pooled in my veins.

Reid King faced his truth, but was I ready to make his truth *our* truth?

CHAPTER TWENTY-SEVEN

REID

Although I felt semi-healed compared to the last several months of my life, I still felt like there was a little something missing. I knew what it was. I was feeling the disappointment and sting of Brooklyn never reaching out to me—or anyone.

The thought had crossed my mind that she didn't know how to get ahold of me, but that was a lie. She had my new number; I made sure to attach it to the CD. But then again, maybe she never even listened to it. But surely, she had heard "Oh, Brooklyn." Our newest single was blasting from every single radio station, from Pandora to Spotify, YouTube, even the small-town local stations—everywhere. "Oh, Brooklyn" had been sitting in the number-one spot for a month now, and that was fucking fantastic. I felt like I'd gotten my mojo back, but every day that passed that Brooklyn hadn't reached out, it felt like a slice to my chest.

But I was going to be patient.

God knew she was patient with me, and I really couldn't blame her for never wanting to speak to me again, even after the hospital visit. But I truly thought the song would have at least brought her to me long enough so I could explain how I'd changed, how I'd healed, and how I wasn't that same empty man I was over the summer.

Angelina was still in the psych ward, and I'd kept my word to her father. I hadn't gone back. Darcy had closed the case and left her family alone. I never went to the media or spoke on Angelina's behalf.

It was a freeing feeling—and healing—but the last thing on my list was to explain it all to Brooklyn in hopes that she would understand why it took me so long to pull my head out of my ass. I wanted nothing more than to make her mine. I knew there was something special between us, and I wondered every day what it would be like to take her on a date, or to make her dinner again, or have another mini food fight, without the dark cloud lingering over my head.

Rod poked his head into my dressing room. "You ready? You're on in five."

I nodded my head as I stood up off the couch. "Yeah. I'll be out in a sec."

Rod's mouth turned upward. "I just have to say, it's really nice that you're not yelling at me to get out of your dressing room for once."

I chuckled as I messed with the leather band on my wrist. "There's still time in the night for me to yell at you."

He shook his head. "Nah. The old, brooding, asshole Reid King hasn't been around for months."

A devilish smirk formed on my face. "You never know."

Rod rolled his eyes as he exited my room. I glanced down at my phone, hoping by some miracle I'd gain enough balls to call her, just to hear her voice, to remember what being around her felt like, but I told myself no.

She'll find you when she's ready.

But would she ever truly be ready?

———

I yelled into the microphone as the crowd roared with excitement. The lights along the stage were glistening onto my sweaty skin. The brief thought of looking like Edward Cullen under sunlight made me chuckle for a second before I shook my head and brought myself back to reality. This was the first show since the tour had ended, and I was more than ready to be in front of fans again.

The show was actually a make-up show due to a wicked snowstorm earlier in the tour, but hey, we couldn't control the weather in New York, so a fall show was the best we could do, given the circumstances. And at least New York would be the first to hear the new single.

"Do you wanna hear our latest single?" I yelled before pulling the microphone away and angling it toward the abundance of fans.

They went crazy, squealing and screaming.

I laughed and turned my head to glance at Jackson and Finn. They nodded, and I turned around, placing the microphone back onto the stand before adjusting my guitar strap on my shoulder.

"Before I sing the last and final song, I wanted to remind you all that whatever merchandise you purchase after the show, the proceeds go directly to a charity that I've set up. It helps out those with mental health disorders, and I'd love you all—even more than I do now—if you could help this charity out. It means a great deal to me."

The crowd went crazy again, the girls eagerly turning to their boyfriends or whomever to beg them to take them to buy something. I started the charity as soon as I fully processed everything Phil had told me of Angelina. The money raised for the charity goes to several psychiatric institutes all over the United States, Bloomsdale included. It was the least I could do. It made me feel a little better about Angelina disappearing from my mind and heart.

I began to fiddle with some strings on my guitar, signaling to Jackson and Finn that I was ready to play the last song. The background music started up, and Brooklyn's face was all that I pictured when the words began to move effortlessly out of my mouth.

That was how I knew the song was authentic. That was how I knew the song was *real*. I focused on the feeling I put into writing it. I took all my emotion building and bubbling up inside of me and flung it into the song—so much so that I didn't realize that the background music from Jackson and Finn had stopped all together.

It was only my voice and my guitar, playing alone up on the stage with thousands of people staring at me. They all had their glow sticks waving back and forth, but they weren't squealing or screaming like usual.

The arena was almost at a dead silence.

I continued to sing the last bits of the chorus, eyeing the side of the stage where Rod usually stood. I crinkled my brow as I saw my bandmates standing there with huge, shit-eating grins on their faces.

What the fuck?

Then, my heart went soaring when they moved out of the way.

My fingers stilled on my guitar; my head was still angled down to the microphone, but nothing was coming out. I was left speechless.

There she was.

Brooklyn. *My Brooklyn*. The girl that healed me without even meaning to do so.

Her pretty auburn hair fell around her face in curly waves, her sparkling emerald eyes standing out among her fair skin and high cheekbones. She was wearing one of those silly dresses that somehow always made me smile. Her long, lean legs ended with a pair of white Chucks. She gave me a timid smile as she took a tiny step out onto the stage. The crowd was still hushed, whispering murmurs of what the hell was happening.

I finally released my hands from my guitar and stood up a little straighter. I swallowed loudly as I briskly walked over to Brooklyn, her meeting me halfway. Everything melted away the second I was in front of her. I was no longer standing on a stage in front of thousands of fans. I was no longer Reid King, the King of Music. I was just a man completely enthralled by a woman who I thought I'd lost forever.

Brooklyn went to say something, but I didn't give her a chance. My mouth was on hers instantly, and in that moment, it felt like I was *finally* complete. My lips roamed over her soft ones as I threw my guitar over my back. My hands went directly to her cheeks as I cupped her face, bringing her as close as humanly possible. Her warm mouth parted, and her tongue met mine in sync. She whimpered as my grip tightened.

I couldn't hear a single thing except her.

And I didn't want to hear a single thing except her.

She was all I wanted.

She was all I needed.

Brooklyn finally took her lips off mine, and that was when reality came back to us. The crowd was screaming, hooting and hollering for us to kiss again. I was certain that some people were fainting in the crowd. Brooklyn's face turned bright red as she peeked up to meet my eyes.

I rubbed my thumbs over her flushed cheeks. "I'm so glad you're here."

Brooklyn bit her lip, trying to hide a smile.

I pulled her by the hand farther onto the stage, energetically taking us over to the microphone.

My voice was shaky and unlike the Reid King that everyone knew. "Everyone…I'd like you to meet *Brooklyn*."

Brooklyn gasped and clenched onto my hand even tighter. I gave my fans one single wave before pulling us both offstage, running down the hall past my bandmates and the wide eyes of the staff, and flinging us into my dressing room.

She took a deep breath as soon as the door slammed behind us, and I just stared at her.

It was all I could do.

There were so many things I wanted to say, so many things I wanted to do.

Yet, all I could do was stare at her like she wasn't real. I may have been in shock.

"I'm sorry it took me so long," she finally said after pulling her hands away from mine. She stood close to the door and clasped her arms together before spreading them out again. *She was nervous.* The last time I saw her this nervous was the moment before I took her body and made it mine.

I wiped the sweat from my face with my forearm and laughed.

Brooklyn's brow furrowed as she gave me that famous Brooklyn grimace. "What?"

I walked over to her, peering down at her pouty mouth. "You're sorry for taking too long?" I shook my head as another chuckle tumbled out. "I think I should be the one apologizing."

She went to shake her head, but I gently grabbed her chin with my hand, angling her face to mine. "There's so much I need to tell you. There's so much I need to explain, especially about Angelina. And I know a song,"—I shrugged—"or twelve, isn't enough to tell you how sorry I am, to tell you how stuck in my own head I was." I shook my head, angry at myself. "I'm sorry I made you wait so long. I'm sorry I hurt you. I just needed time to…"

Brooklyn searched my face before whispering, "You needed time to face the truth."

I nodded. "There was a lot I needed to face, but by far, the one I needed to face the most… was you."

Brooklyn brought her hand up to my wrist, wrapping her warm fingers around the spot my pulse was pounding. "Me?"

I brought her mouth a little closer to mine. *"You."*

"What about me?" she asked, her breath hitting my lips and making every single bone in my body quake.

"You're everything, Brooklyn. *Everything.* You're everything I didn't know I needed. You somehow swooped in and saved me from myself. I was drowning, completely suffocating, and knee-deep in shit that I had no way of getting myself out of… until *you*."

"I was just trying to help you write a song," she said, a light laugh floating out of her mouth.

I grabbed her chin a little tighter. "Don't you dare downplay what we had."

"What is it that we had, Reid? Because right now, looking at you, standing this close to you, I can't remember much of anything other than the way my heart beats a little faster when you're close to me. I can't focus on anything other than the way my stomach is fluttering. I can't even focus on the fact that Reid King just kissed me in front of an entire arena full of screaming fans."

I wrapped my free arm around her body, pulling her flush to mine. "What we have is each other."

Brooklyn brought her lips so close to mine that I thought I might pass out. "We'll figure the rest out later, right?" she asked.

I murmured along her lips. "There's nothing else to figure out."

She smiled along mine. "Reid. You're a famous rock star, and I'm… *me*. I teach small children music all day long. Two completely different worlds. In fact, I don't even know how our worlds crossed."

"Eh, that's a minor hiccup," I mused, and then I pressed my lips to hers so firmly she fell against the wall behind her.

She laughed, and I gave her a devil-like smile.

"Minor hiccup, for sure."

EPILOGUE

BROOKLYN

My cheeks lifted as Reid's warm lips trailed over my neck and down to my collarbone. "Reid, stop it! You're not making me any less nervous."

I sighed annoyingly, but he knew I was lying. Reid's lips on any part of my body made me forget about the rest of the world—just like it had always been with him. "I'm sorry, I just missed you."

I threw my head back along the wall and laughed. Reid's large hands cupped my butt as he lifted me up and wrapped my legs around his torso. My body simmered, but if I didn't put a stop to this right now, we'd never make it onstage.

"Reid King," I said sternly, smacking his chest. "Put me down right now, because Rod is probably seconds from coming into this room to get us to go onstage. And plus,"—I took my hand and angled his large chin up to meet my face—"it's only been an hour."

Reid pulled his chin out of my grasp and nestled into the crook of my neck. He mumbled, "It's been an hour since I've seen you, yes. But it has been several since I've had you."

My face flushed as his dirty words hit my ears. Reid King

talking dirty to me had to have been my favorite pastime ever.

A knock sounded on the door, and my heart jumped to my throat. Reid yelled, "Yeah?" and then I heard Jackson. "Quit fucking your girlfriend and come out here to do your guys' song that makes me want to fall in love, too."

I giggled in Reid's arms, and a huge, cheesy smile slid onto his face. The last year had been absolutely insane—so many changes, so many ups and downs. But the one thing that had never wavered was the way Reid King's smile lit up my entire world.

There had been many long nights that I'd spent without Reid, which you wouldn't think would have been such a big deal since I went almost twenty-five years without him, but it mattered. Only hearing his voice through the phone or watching him through a screen was tormenting. I missed him so much that sometimes I felt homesick. Being away from Reid was like I was away from home. The entire school year, we were long distance. After we reconciled—because let's get real, how could we not after he wrote an entire album for me?—we lived through short, private visits and long phone calls. Once he explained everything to me about Angelina, we decided to take things slow and keep our relationship private, which was extremely difficult, considering he was one of the hottest musicians of today's time. Basically, everyone knew that I was the Brooklyn from his album but things calmed after a while. We still hadn't released a ton of information to the press. I wanted us to stay under wraps for a little while, until we decided our next step, which was apparently throwing us onstage together to play our song.

Our song meaning the song we'd literally written together through long video chats and midnight talks after shows and events that he had attended over the past year.

Nothing like diving headfirst into the media, right? Everything about my life was going to be exposed—even my family.

"I don't know about this, Reid," I said as he slowly slid me down his body. I adjusted my little black dress that had been laid out for me and cringed with nerves.

Reid reached his large hand up and cupped my face. "You are talented, Brooklyn. It's time you show your light to the rest of the world."

I must have looked panicked, because he quickly said, "Remember, it's a small venue. This is strictly for charity."

I ground my teeth. He knew that the last part would get me to submit. How could I say no to charity?

"I'm just not sure I want to be in the limelight like this. It's one thing being Reid King's girlfriend, but pairing that with a songwriter who has no business singing? Yikes." I covered my eyes with my hands and let out a shaky breath.

Reid gingerly took my hands and lowered them down, still keeping a hold of them as he asked, "Would I willingly put you onstage if I thought you were going to make a fool of yourself? I'm not mean like that."

I raised an eyebrow as a grin started to creep onto my face. Reid rolled his eyes. "Okay, maybe the old Reid would have done that—the one from over a year ago that acted as if he hated you. But the new Reid? Would I do that to you? Boyfriend or not?"

I held a laugh when I said, "Reid King would never willingly make himself look bad, so no."

Reid narrowed his eyes playfully at me, and I finally let my laugh escape.

"Let's just do this before I throw up."

A sexy grin formed on his face. "Ready to be in the spotlight, then?"

"As Reid King's girlfriend or as a songwriter?"

Reid pulled me in close, pressing his firm body onto mine. "Both."

I nodded and stepped up on my tiptoes to place a chaste kiss on his lips. I pulled back quickly, knowing very well that if I let that kiss linger, we'd have people breaking down the door to drag us onto the stage. Reid pouted as I pulled him by the hand. Before I opened the door, I peered back at his pouty stare and said, "After I go make a fool out of myself, then I'm all yours."

Reid smiled at me, and just like that, I was back to forgetting my own name again.

THE END

AUTHOR'S NOTE

Ah! Where do I begin with this one? This book literally came out of nowhere. I typically like to write lighter books (like my romantic comedies) but Truth was a book I just couldn't get out of my head. It was stalking me. Anytime I had downtime—like driving in the car or showering—this book and these characters would creep into my mind. Reid and Brooklyn were very intimate and personal, and once again, unlike the playful characters I typically write. There was just something about them that I loved so much. Honestly, I probably could have written 20,000 more words in this book, heck maybe even more than that! I didn't want their story to end. I didn't want to rush them. I liked their private moments, the ones where it was just the two of them and their conversation guiding them through their little set up. They felt like a cozy couple, two people who were just deep. And Reid. Gosh! He was probably the most tormented character I've ever written. I felt bad for him 90% of the time I was writing his chapters. The stuff he went through. AH! Once again, I have no clue where he or his story came from but after I read through Truth a few times and tweaked some things, I just fell in love!

I know you guys are used to my romcoms but I hope you enjoyed this contemporary, too! It was a nice change of pace to write something that had a heavy topic. I think I even made myself cry a few times while writing, which is always a weird feeling. LOL. Anyway, I'll stop rambling now!

Thank you so much for reading!! I hope you enjoyed Truth and continue to follow me along this indie author route! It's been refreshing and so incredibly fulfilling but also very challenging! I'm excited to see where my next few books go! :)

Xo-SJ

ABOUT THE AUTHOR

S.J. Sylvis is a lover of reading and writing and just recently graduated with her graduate degree focusing on English and Creative Writing (the only fun parts were the writing classes). Besides writing, S.J. Sylvis loves coffee (specifically caramel iced coffee, but really, any coffee will do), binge-watching Gilmore Girls, going to the beach and spending time with her family! She currently lives in Louisiana but is often moving as her husband is in the United States Marine Corps and they go where the military sends them!

STAY IN TOUCH WITH S.J. SYLVIS:

WWW.SJSYLVIS.COM